THE RECKONING

James H Ward

The Reckoning

Published by Howard J Shedden

Gauteng, South Africa

vumbrimu@gmail.com

ISBN 978-0-620-90902-0

2 4 6 8 10 9 7 5 3 1

Cover illustration by James H Ward, digital editing by Denise Janisch

Acknowledgements to Sheena, Tom and especially the rare species.

Layout and cover design by Boutique Books

Printed in South Africa by Digital Action

THE USUTU PLANTATION IN ESWATINI (previously Swaziland) covers 55 000 Hectares. It makes use of 4.5% of the Kingdom's total agricultural land area. Planting began in 1950, and it remains one of the largest man-made pine forests in the world, growing mainly two species of pine tree. It is large enough to create its own microclimate. It continues to produce thousands of tons of timber, mostly exported, earning significant foreign exchange, and contributing to the Eswatini economy to this day.

Chapter 1

IT WAS JUST A CHILD's shoe. A little girl's sandal, lying abandoned on a bed of pine needles and almost hidden in the thin, soft grass growing alongside a faint footpath, where it passed near the foot of a tall pine tree.

They had always been her favourites, and she loved them most dearly among her few treasured possessions. She would kick off and mislay her other shoes but had never lost these. If one sandal ever went missing, she would not even go to sleep until it had been found and reunited with its partner.

It had a ruched elasticated strap across the back to hold it on and was designed to delight a little girl and fit snugly around a tiny foot. Where the two straps emerged on either side of the soft sole, they were lined with neat rows of tiny, colourful plastic flowers: miniature blossoms of sky blue, sharp red, and bright yellow. At the top of the stalks, between the two front toes, there was a clean white daisy, the size of a ten cent Swazi coin, a yellow-centred blossom surrounded by white petals that fully covered the join and adorned the top of the sandal.

Still clearly visible, indented over time into the soft surface of each sole, was the profile of a tiny foot, its shape captured for ever, in length about the same as the breadth of a man's hand. The sandal was also ingrained with the sweat and the dirt of endless play, long days spent in the hot sun, and frequent wear.

She especially loved the bright colours of the tiny rows of flowers and thought the lurid pink colour of the softly cushioned sole was pretty, like that of a fairy princess. When it fell from her foot, she felt that it took with it the last vestiges of the life she had known until that moment. Its falling seemed to sever the last remaining link to her home, a precious thread still binding her faintly to all the richness of the life she knew, and to everyone and everything she loved; all the warmth, safety and comforting familiarity of a deeply loving home.

She wanted to speak, desperate to try to ask the man carrying her to slow down, because she could feel it moving, could feel it jerking slowly loose, but his rough, calloused hand stayed firmly clamped over her mouth and she was unable to make any sound, her voice stifled by his grip. She could only snuffle and cry, sometimes barely able to breathe.

She felt the shoe gradually slipping off her foot and remembered how she would often have to stop playing her games for a moment to tug the heel strap upwards to keep that one on, but he wouldn't let her pull it up now and didn't care. She struggled desperately to save it. The shoe dangled from her small brown foot for a few moments, and she even tried to hold it on by crunching up her little toes, but it finally slipped off, falling silently onto the forest floor, and there it lay.

In her childish innocence, she suddenly thought that her mum would be cross, because she did sometimes lose her shoes, and she even tried to tug the man's hand off her mouth, crying and snuffling, desperate to plead with him to stop for a minute and wait so that she could recover her beloved shoe. But the hand clamped over her mouth was too strong and he ignored her. So, it fell unseen and, in their haste, neither the bigger man, determined to complete their mission, nor his slightly-built partner running up ahead saw it fall. It finally slid off her foot and came to rest, lying peacefully, deep in the eternal shade of the great Usutu plantation.

If it had stayed there long enough, it would have slowly become invisible, covered in dirt and the thick layer of dry brown pine needles that cover the forest floor. The small plants, lichen, fungi and moss that grow around the base of the trees in the depths of the plantation would have eventually made it one of their own and captured it entirely. But, for now, in the hushed stillness of the growing trees, the artificial flowers stayed exposed, clean, bright and clear as ever. The sandal lay where it fell, its vivid colours contrasting against the thick layer of pine needles, an alien resident of the forest floor, abandoned in the chilly gloom and dappled green light under the pine trees.

There is an immense quietness there among the trees that eventually becomes sound itself, filling the gaps left by noise. A gentle murmur of verdant life. The trees seem to be waiting patiently for some untold event, faithful guards left to stand at attention for evermore. The young foliage is a startlingly bright green, fresh and clean.

They cannot abandon their posts and stand regal and tall, gently swaying in a subtle dance sung by the breeze. They seem to sigh in unison, breathing out secrets whispered to one another in confidence, an almost imperceptible union of tree spirits. Buried in the sound there is a sense of life itself, the almost silent noise made by growth, barely audible above the constant, muted rush of wind and the subtle movement of air, deep in the peaceful forest.

That stillness was broken only by the heavy breathing and steady footfalls of worn shoes, the sound of running, as the men jogged on, deeper and deeper into the stately denseness of trees, the pff, pat, pff, pat of their feet landing heavily on the faint path, crunching on the thick bed of dry pine needles. They occasionally broke stride to kick aside a small branch that had fallen, blocking their way, or to clamber over a line of stumps. Decades of fallen pine needles lay ankle deep, sun bleached grey on the surface, and a dusty brown colour beneath, bone dry and thickly carpeting the forest floor.

It was heavy-going for them, running, walking, panting with tiredness during the climbs as the trail rose and then descended, again and again, twisting through shallow glades and old watercourses, meandering down into shadowy dark coppices where great tangled, dusty spiderwebs stretched between the tree trunks, hidden away from the sun. It grew cooler the further they moved into the plantation. Their footfalls echoed softly and then dissipated without a trace into the thousands of trees, as did the sound of their heavy breathing, but they kept moving, jogging steadily, and when they grew tired and had to walk, they still walked quickly, steadily moving deeper and ever deeper into the forest. She had to be kept alive for the final act.

That little child's sandal lay there, fallen, but not forgotten, a silent witness to their passing; an oddly incongruous intruder disrupting the forest's muted colours and breaking its visual harmony. It lay undisturbed, slowly and silently being absorbed into its surroundings and becoming a new part of the eternally cool floor.

Chapter 2

The Bartons

Matt Barton, Khanyisile and their daughter Pumi Jacqueline had returned from their holiday in Mozambique feeling refreshed and relaxed. Khanyi felt that what had happened to her on the beach had somehow completed a chapter in her life, leaving her heart open for something new to grow in it. They were deeply in love, their biorhythms were back together again, and they felt emotionally close to each other. The sun had warmed their skin and the seaside had left in them a sense of well-being. Even the frustrations and delays of the pointless roadblocks, government officials demanding bribes for imaginary offences, and the stress of the border crossing failed to destroy the sense of freedom and pleasure they brought back with them from the pristine Indian Ocean beaches. Matt was now experiencing all the sensations of fatherhood, and he had a daughter who had taken a piece of his heart, something she had to share with Khanyi.

Since that time, the little family had spent almost four blissful years together. Khanyisile had thought at one time that she was expecting a second child, all the signs seemed to say so, but then her body had deceived her. It was not the time. Nompumelelo Jacqueline Barton had grown into a funny, inquisitive, loving child, deeply aware of all that was around her.

Her life followed a steady pattern that was repeated daily, an unvarying and stable platform on which her young personality was being built. She felt embedded and comforted by it, conscious of being loved by many, confident and secure in herself and her family. Each day began early in the morning, when she'd hear the voices of farm workers and irrigators laughing and talking as they made their way across the fields, walking along the road past their house on their way to work. Then she'd hear the familiar, steady, shuuh, shuuh noise of a grass broom sweeping leaves and twigs off the weathered concrete around their house and out of the patio as Nomsa, her minder, began the new day's cleaning. That sound was a soothing ritual to PJ, as much a part of starting each new day as washing her face and brushing her teeth.

Each day brought familiar scenes, well-known voices, distinctive smells, and the presence of many affectionate dogs, idly traipsing around after her for much of the day to see where she went. The wide, quiet, sunlit views and space of a large garden dominated her playtime. She played endlessly, with or without friends, inventing complicated, wildly imaginative games that involved hosts of fairies, goblins, giants and volcanoes, poor orphans, waifs and occasional large family gatherings of bears, horses, barbie dolls and some poor unfortunate creatures who had been decapitated or had lost limbs. They would all be gathered and set out, seated on miniature chairs around low tables for leisurely garden feasts, usually taken under the shade of the flamboyant and ironwood trees.

It was everything that she knew, her whole childhood life, and she revelled in it. Tea made from mud and leaves, and biscuits made from clay, decorated with small flowers, seed pods and shiny stones. She would chatter away to herself, lost deep in her own world. Sometimes she could persuade Khanyi, Nomsa, Matt, even Musa or anyone visiting, to join in and become a guest at her wondrous tea parties. It was always much better if someone were there to join in.

Sometimes Matt would catch a glimpse of her playing in the garden, lost in her own world and bossily addressing the assembled audience of dollies and teddy bears, or would see the sun playing on her hair and feel his heart breaking, just looking at her. She was the symbol of his new being. He found it hard to relate to the life he had left behind those few years ago – to his compact, modern house in England, the strange transient existence he'd known of constantly travelling, and the cold, lonely returns, unlocking his front door to an empty house and his own company. He would sometimes find his mind wandering to the countries he'd been to, the people he'd met, to Emma, and Brian Pearson, and his mate Salikh, the storeman at his old workplace, but found himself unable to perceive them as clearly as he used to. Their memories had been drenched and washed pale, blurred by time and painted into the background by the sunshine and richness of his new life.

Pumi Jacqueline had wormed her way into his heart and effortlessly pushed almost everything else aside. When he sat down at the end of a long day on his feet in the workshop, or after driving out to site to repair some piece of equipment, she would squirm onto his lap, wriggling like a warm puppy, gripping his face with her two tiny hands, turning his head to face her and demanding that he read to her, or listen, giving his full attention to her breathless account of all that had happened that day. She had seen a lizard laying eggs, the dogs had found and killed a rat, or the old gardener Ndephete had shown her a fat caterpillar, or given her a tomato, still warm from the sun and eaten straight off the plant. All these events were enchanting to her and needed to be shared. Each day brought something new.

He would feel her skin, so incredibly soft and smooth under his hands, and sense the warmth and the subtle scent of her body and marvel at the life he and Khanyi had been able to create. Sometimes, he looked at his daughter and thought he saw something of her mother's face, but at other times he thought he could see in her something of his own mother, but that distant memory was ages old and no longer clear. He wished, above all, that Patrick and Melanie had been able to meet her, although he sometimes wondered how they would have reacted. She chattered away to him, switching unconsciously between SiSwati and English without a pause, and would ask him to read to her from her favourite books, even though she knew all the words off by heart. Some evenings, if he were very tired, he would try to skip a page, but her knowledge was word perfect and she would immediately stop him and make him go back to read out the missing bits.

'No, Daddy, that's not when the dragon comes. First, she has to climb out of the castle.'

Duly corrected, he would have to go back to find and read the missing pages out loud. She loved it when either of her parents read to her but secretly felt that her daddy was better than her mama, and really, he made much better dragon noises. Khanyisile read nicely, but more slowly, with a bit less expression, and she couldn't do dragons.

Matt would sometimes be woken by something unknown, disturbed from his sleep – a strange sound or the sudden sensation of a threat, the feeling of something uneasy lying unsettled somewhere in their midst. The presence he thought he felt around them, real or imaginary, would wake him, and he would look out at the peaceful garden bathed in moonlight, still in disbelief at how different the view was to the rain-soaked streets, streetlamps and concrete pavements surrounding his Preston house.

Then he would quietly get up, so as not to disturb Khanyisile, and tiptoe silently down the corridor to PJ's bedroom, to stand in the doorway listening to her soft breathing and watch her sleep, her golden brown hair spread across the pillow, one hand clutching onto a furry blue rabbit that she always took to bed with her. It was a sight that strangely reassured him, making him feel that all was well in the world. He could not put into words quite what it made him feel, but somehow his love for Khanyisile, as intense and strong as ever, had miraculously divided and allowed him to love someone else equally as much and with the same fierce intensity. He would walk over to the side of her bed and give her a tiny kiss on the cheek, and she would sigh and snuggle into her bedclothes, feeling utterly safe and secure.

Chapter 3

The lattice work

Early on in their married life Matt struggled to understand the sheer number of relatives that his wife apparently had, but he began to understand it more clearly when he realised that his wife saw the country very differently to the way he saw it.

She could somehow see the whole country and its people located in a sort of invisible frame. It was an intricate social latticework that, at first, Matt had found deeply confusing. Her grasp of geography and the physical names and places was a bit hazy, tied more to relationships and people than the mere lines and shapes on Matt's maps. She could perceive and position precisely in her living framework, everyone to whom she was related. It was something she always saw easily and intuitively but found difficult to explain.

This hidden structure extended right across the country, and she was connected to it on many different levels. Connected to her own people in a complicated extended family made up of relatives on her terms as a Swazi woman, not based on his Western understanding of that expression.

It was difficult for him, as a European, to understand or grasp this invisible structure at first. To Matt, fresh out of England when they were first married, words like sister, father or aunt were all definitive and precise. They had specific, biological meanings, and either a person was such a thing, or they were not. But in Khanyisile's case her people and her family members were less easily categorised.

Swazi people, historically, tended to have large families. Her true, blood mother – who had passed away when she was small – had seven sisters, who were her real aunts, but none of these had been living close to the family home, although she knew about them all. All of those sisters became her aunts in the usual way, and their children, when she met them, were relatives, but her aunts' daughters also became her 'sisters'. Then, some of her late mother's closest friends also would become her other aunts and mothers, collectively *bomake*. Not only her mother's friends, but some of her aunts' close friends, were also regarded as Aunts in some families, but of a different kind, and then their offspring might become her sisters and brothers too, like an extra set of siblings or elder brothers, depending on their age.

Her father and her stepmother had been unkind to her, but she liked some of his elder brothers, who became to her *bobabelomkhulu* – the big fathers – and then her father's younger brothers (including those he viewed as brothers, who might also actually have been cousins) became her small fathers. Matt, once it was explained to him, began to see how his wife, unlike him, had different graduations and levels of fathers, not just one. The children of those fathers then further added to her extended family, and the one she was close to became like her additional sisters and brothers, apart from those who were real cousins. She didn't even know them all and had never met most of them.

He found that there was a universal term, *Umalume*, that broadly described all her many uncles, but she had many more uncles than her father and mother had brothers. They sat together one rainy afternoon, and he asked her to try and explain it all to him, while PJ watched cartoons on TV, sketching out in a broad family tree the linkages and lineage of her relatives on a piece of paper. He wanted to understand how her family worked, but they soon ran out of space and names. She could not recall all the aunts. There were also her cousin brothers, various grandchildren, and so many small fathers and different uncles that she could not name them all one by one. There were still many connected families she had never visited, mostly distantly connected from her late father's side.

Small wonder that, while traveling in the rural countryside, they would often encounter hitchhikers, only to discover after some time chatting that they were actually related. Matt learnt that this also meant that courting and proposing love was an activity that had to be undertaken with some care, as Khanyi explained to him that a young man had to be careful not to fall in love with someone that he could not marry, as they might find out that they were already related, or of the same clan, or from families that cannot marry. There were some discreet unwritten lines that could not be crossed.

It took some time to understand, but it gradually clarified for him how she saw the country. Across the small nation, just as a large European family would perhaps have several cousins, she had numerous sisters, brothers, uncles and aunts, but also, confusingly, other couples she spoke of as though they were parents. *Babe* and *Make* (mother and father) were terms of respect afforded to many people, but they carried different meanings at different times. It was this huge extended family that meant that somebody could come by and visit, or phone, or they would encounter someone by chance somewhere, and after a suitable period taken establishing their social and family credentials, she would find that they were relatives, which had a very different meaning to actually being related. Sometimes, a long telephone conversation would include establishing these credentials before the principal message could be conveyed, or real communication could begin. The essential placing of the person in the greater family latticework mattered in ways that she could not easily explain, but it needed to be established before proper conversation could begin.

He loved her deeply and just accepted that she had a great many people she considered to be relatives and that, for as they were comparatively well off, from time to time the Bartons would be expected to help relatives out with food, transport or money. He couldn't understand at first why she would feel a need to provide assistance to one of her late mother's sisters who was ill, or provide for someone at the gate begging for food, but she felt obliged to help anyone who was a genuine family member of some kind or other, whatever the circumstances. When she felt that they were undeserving of this, it would often be Matt who would make the decision not to assist them, and she would use him to explain to them that regrettably they could not be helped. He was often surprised to find that this explanation was accepted without too much fuss, and she found it a convenient filter to weed out the chancers and inevitable scroungers.

Something he learnt when they'd first met, after coming out from England to sort out his late brother's affairs, was that when they gave lifts to select individuals walking along the road, she might not know where the town was where they stayed, but it didn't matter. In some way or other, if it were established that they were related, there was always some connection, a friend who knew where they came from, unless they were really just random strangers they chose to give a lift to on a hot day.

People would arrive at the gate and, if they needed help or food, as they usually did, if she could connect them, provided that they linked somewhere in her family framework, they had cleared the first hurdle and assisting them warranted proper consideration. There were also further layers of complexity involving the types of people who were proper, 'a good somebody' just down on their luck, or others, whose behaviour meant they were not 'proper somebodies' at all, just chancers: skelms, gamblers, drinkers, womanisers, thieves, beggars, dagga smokers, vagrants or drop-outs on the scrounge who might just have heard of a strong family name and adopted it, hiding beneath it and pretending it was theirs.

Khanyi would discern these people with unerring accuracy, and she'd storm back from the gate, trailed by a tide of dogs, muttering and sucking her teeth. She either gave them nothing at all, or would sometimes just send down one cup of cold water, but no encouragement in the form of food or money. If they were drunk, the dogs would bark madly at them and she would simply tell them to go away, no matter who they were.

In Matt's background, these matters were straight forward, easy to untangle and define. In his upbringing there was not the same kind of social latticework. He understood clearly-defined familial groups, and readily differentiated between someone related by family or by marriage, or people that were just his friends, but he had never had an extended family or grown up knowing one. His Englishness was slowly eroding and changing, because he found himself introducing his older friend Gabriel as an uncle to his daughter, and often called him Babe Gabriel himself when they were together, meaning he had also become like a father. He just thought his wife was amazing because she knew everyone in relation to everyone else, even if she could not always explain the connections to them. He could see it made her happy to help them, and that part of her caring heart on display made him love her more deeply.

Chapter 4

The crossing

THE WEATHER WAS CHANGING AND there was the delicious, tempting smell of distant rain carried on the wind from afar. The Ministry of Agriculture had been broadcasting instructions to the Chiefs and farmers over the radio, advising them that it was time to take their cattle off the land and plough the fields, and giving them details about which seed varieties to buy in which areas, and when to plant their crops, according to the different farming regions, soils and rain patterns. They provided detailed long-range weather forecasts for different districts. The traditional farmers of Eswatini await these instructions each year, listening attentively to radios in their rural homes, to the wisdom of their extension officers. Once the word goes out, they generally take the advice. It was an important and trusted service to them.

That time of year, the instructions had been heard on the radio for several weeks. Right across the country, those who could afford it were ploughing with tractors, or ploughing the traditional way with small, ancient disc or mouldboard ploughs and teams of strong oxen. Throughout the Kingdom, on ancient fields of rich, flat lands, cleared of stones and tree stumps, the fertile red Swazi soil was being turned over and exposed to the elements. The sound of working tractors strained at full throttle in the distance, and the crack of long *sjamboks* echoed through the valleys, snapping sharply above the broad red backs of oxen. The ploughing left a rich verdant smell of newly turned soil to hang in the air, redolent of growth and fertility.

Whenever they were travelling, if ever they saw cattle ploughing they would slow down and stop on the side of the road and Matt would climb through the fence, if there was one, and simply walk across the furrows to the ploughing team to watch in awed appreciation. The ploughmen would be surprised that someone was showing interest in a task as every day to them as seasonal ploughing, but for Matt, coming from Northern England, the sight of this time-old tradition was a revelation.

He loved to watch the farmers walking behind the beasts, talking to them and guiding them with their long whips. They would stride along surprisingly quickly, not whipping the oxen, but cracking a light whip in the air, on the end of a stick, or occasionally touching a shoulder or their haunches to guide them. He found that he would have to walk fast, almost jogging across the uneven ground to keep up.

The oxen would breathe in heavily through their mouths with the deep effort, pulling in unison as they strode along, walking steadily forward, their mighty lungs drawing in great buckets of air, as they put their brown and tan, grey and dark brindled bodies, enormous shoulders and powerful haunches to the wooden yokes and the plough traces. The chains would jingle gently in time with the steady pacing of the animals, and they would snort at a troublesome fly from time to time, or sneeze at the dust.

It is not easy to keep an ox-drawn implement cutting through the soil, moving and ploughing in a straight line. It takes considerable physical strength, and the ploughman must constantly correct and steer the implement, using the previous furrow wall as a guide. The animals instinctively knew when they should walk on and pull hard. They could feel the resistance of the plough biting into the soil behind them, and they felt it as soon as it had been lifted and knew when and where to turn.

A well-trained team would haul steadily to the end of the fields, and then turn at the headlands with minimal instruction, in well-rehearsed precision. Sometimes, one animal would shake its head at the irritation of flies, the wide horns swinging from side to side. Matt would watch in absolute astonishment, amazed by the ancient skills of the ploughmen and wishing he knew how they trained the animals.

He would hear them calling the creatures by name, giving them instructions. There seemed to be favourite names for lead oxen like Bantom or Jamluti and, if they stopped for a break, the ploughmen would point out to him their strongest oxen with pride. When he encountered them ploughing on lands close to the South African borders and spoke to the handlers, he found that the animals would often have Afrikaans names like Spielman or Renkaas.

It was a gradually disappearing spectacle from a bygone era, different to anything he had experienced, and it always fascinated him. He would walk into the field to get closer to them, trying to avoid catching the animals' eyes, and then wait quietly until he could feel their hooves impacting on the soil beneath them as they went past. He could sense the effort that went into pulling the plough, breaking open the rich red soil, hardened by the dry winter. He would clearly hear their heavy grunting and breathing. Mighty animals swinging their big heads from side to side, putting their shoulders to the yoke. He found it compelling to watch and could not ignore the sight of a team of oxen ploughing.

Matt felt deep within him the need many Englishmen have, to establish and understand their geographical surroundings. He had seen so many different Swazi place names on the map but hadn't ever been to visit them, and Khanyi would mention these places from time to time. Whereas Khanyisile could place many of her relatives clearly in her mind in terms of their family connection, he wanted to see for himself some of the lesser known parts of the tiny Kingdom and have a feeling for how it all fitted together.

He knew the places they had visited as a couple, or the areas he had travelled to for work, like Padraic O'Connor's Shamrock Farms near Sigceni, but that wasn't very frequent and, although he travelled occasionally to carry out specialised repair work, when he went on those trips Khanyi seldom accompanied him. Usually, he was too busy to spend time with her while he was on site, so it was boring for her, and it was too tiring for their child, so he would either travel with Musa or alone. But he still wanted to know where things were, and what they looked like, to get a sense of his surroundings as he became more deeply rooted in Eswatini. He wanted to understand the places Khanyi was talking about when she mentioned that one of her small fathers lived in Hlatikulu, in Balekane, or Siphofaneni. He found that the four main regions of the country were clearly defined and quite different in nature, climate, and scenery but felt that he didn't know enough about them.

It became their habit, usually at weekends or when the welding business was in a quiet spell, to just take a day trip to somewhere that neither of them had been to, or pack a simple picnic and drive out along a road somewhere and see what was there. To go for a drive to there and back to see how far it was. Matt had travelled much of the world by air when he was working for Brian Pearson in the years before his brother died, but that had always been for international welding jobs, never for sight-seeing, and that was a very different kind of travelling. It was this innate desire to explore and better understand the land that surrounded their home that caused them to journey deep into the hinterland, using back roads they had never driven on before. They would drive unhurriedly along quiet gravel roads, pursuing them until they ended, turning into narrow, bumpy tracks, routes that cars seldom travelled along. Or they would simply reached a point where the road became a path, and they could drive no further. They were gentle adventures, mild explorations of the safe kind that suited them both.

Matt loved these little outings – they revealed to him parts of the country he would otherwise have never seen – and Khanyi liked them because it expanded her understanding of the physical country that was her home. She had been forced to leave school young, and could only remember a basic knowledge of geography from those years, but these trips cemented towns and villages into place, filling in the gaps in her knowledge of where different settlements were and what they were like. Best of all, it meant time spent alone with Matt, away from the phone and their work, talking and laughing together, pointing out rural scenes and telling each other about the conversations and tiny details that were so important to them and that were unfolding through their young lives. Each of them tended to look at the rural landmarks and scenery differently, and would point out the things they had noticed to one another, often mentioning tiny details that the other might have otherwise missed. They would drink in the sights eagerly, each absorbing the scenic countryside piece by piece, understanding it in their own way.

They would sometimes decide to go out on the spur of the moment, choose an unknown destination on the map, pack a small picnic and plenty of snacks for their daughter, and set off into the wide unknown. After a long day in the sun and the dust, when they finally drove home with the sun setting behind them, they would have filled in another piece in the jigsaw that helped them to understand each other better, and seen another facet of the rich, diverse country where they had made a home.

That morning, in late September, it had dawned bright and clear, with high white clouds scattered across the sky, all sailing majestically eastwards, with a fresh, cool breeze. It was too good a day to spend at home. Standing close together after breakfast, Matt's arm curled around Khanyi's waist, they pored over the map, discussing different options, and then loaded up the bakkie and headed for Madlangempisi, hoping to drive up into the Malandzela Hills for a view of the scenery up there. It was meant to be a short trip. It was with a sense of excitement that they set off on a route in their hastily packed vehicle, initially heading north west, then turning south, driving into an area where the small unnamed back roads through the bush are crisscrossed by many small tributaries of the Komati river.

They stopped to buy some ice cold bottles of Coke and biscuits at a roadside store, and greeted the shop owner, who played for a while with PJ, then they carried on through the tiny village looking for an unmarked left turn heading off into the hills. This started off masquerading as a road, but it flattered to deceive, soon becoming more of a track than a road. Although it was narrow, it was still just passable and so they made their way slowly along the rough route, occasionally stopping to tend to PJ and her needs. There were fields on either side of them, mostly under cultivation.

PJ liked seeing the cattle, and would drowse a bit or point out birds, huts and bright flowers, chattering away happily to herself and singing.

The small track ran along following its own random path, meandering steadily through the bush. After a time, they came to a ford, a low-level crossing where a strong-running stream ran across the track. There were tyre tracks on the opposite bank showing that vehicles had been through it before, but they looked old. Matt got out and waded into the water, gingerly probing with a stick to see how deep it was. It seemed to be quite shallow and reasonably firm underfoot, and felt like a mixture of small rocks and sand, perhaps the covered remains of a culvert of sorts. He felt his way warily, almost to the other side, and the route seemed okay. He made his way back and climbed back in and they carefully began, the vehicle lurching unsteadily down the bank and sliding into the brown stream. At first, everything went well, and as they drove slowly through the water the river crossing seemed to be easy going, the big bakkie idling along slowly, lurching from rock to rock.

They were almost two thirds across when suddenly one front wheel dropped into a deep trough, wholly unseen, a hole well hidden beneath the swirling brown water. Matt tried to reverse out, but the back wheels began to spin. He engaged four-wheel drive and tried to go forward again, but the van just settled more deeply into the stream, with all the wheels now spinning. He was not very experienced driving on dirt roads, and Khanyi was only beginning to learn to drive. They looked at each other as the water gurgled past, chuckling quietly at them. They were on their own.

'Khanyi love, if I get out and push can you try to drive it out?'

She looked at him uncertainly, but said she would try, although she was a bit nervous. She could barely drive under the best of circumstances.

He showed her how to engage first gear, left the bakkie in low ratio and four-wheel drive, then asked her to keep the window down so she could hear him. He took off his socks, but put his takkies back on so that he could push, rolled up his pants like a sailor and waded round to the back of the van, standing almost knee deep in the cool brown water. He found a good purchase point on one side of the bakkie where he had secure footing and could get his shoulder to the tailgate.

She started the engine, but eager to help, when he shouted, 'Okay, go!' she put it in gear and floored the accelerator, giving it rather more revs than he had meant her to. As the engine roared, the back wheels threw up a mighty fountain of mud and brown water, covering Matt with several buckets full of what rightfully belonged to the Komati River.

'Whoa, stop, Khanyi, stop!' he yelled. The bakkie was still stationary, spinning its wheels and only settling in deeper. She stopped, pressing the brake pedal and stalling the engine. She tried not to laugh as he walked up to her side of the car, but he was soaked and covered in muddy water from his knees upwards. PJ, who had been watching the entertaining scene play out through the rear window, gazed at him solemnly and asked pointedly, 'Why did you spray Daddy with dirty water, Mama?'

Matt crouched down and washed the worst of the mud off himself, lifting handfuls of water from the stream, splashing the mud and grit out of his face and mouth. The brown water seemed now to be laughing at him, as it ran gleefully past the vehicle's wheels. It was a high, heavy vehicle and he hadn't moved it at all. If anything, it had settled even deeper into the riverbed.

They decided to go for help and knew they would have to walk their way out, but there was plenty of daylight left and it was all part of the adventure. They got PJ out of the car and Matt lifted her onto his shoulders. Khanyi tucked up her skirt, exposing her light brown calves and thighs to the muddy water and to her appreciative husband, and waded fearlessly across to the bank, quite unfazed. She had often crossed streams and small rivers barefoot when she was a child, walking to school.

Matt, carrying Pumi Jacqueline on his shoulders, had to be more careful, and slowly made his way over to her, wary of what else might be lurking underfoot beneath the strong current. They clambered with difficulty up the slippery opposite bank, helping to pull each other up, and then, after Khanyi had wiped off her long legs, dried her feet and put her takkies back on, they set off, steadily walking further along the track to find the nearest village, unsure how far away it was.

Matt's feet were squelching in his wet shoes, but his clothes dried quickly in the sun and the warm breeze. He still looked like a man who had spent the morning dipping cattle. He carried Pumi Jacqueline on his shoulders once she became tired of walking, and she kept up a running commentary about everything she could see, and how Daddy had gone swimming in the river, even though it was dirty. Khanyi looked across to her and laughed. After a time, they changed over, and her mum carried her on her back, where eventually she became sleepy and stopped chattering. She was becoming a bit heavy to carry over any real distance.

After walking for about half an hour, with a few short breaks, they arrived at a rough clearing on the right-hand side. A line of heavy, old, weather-beaten grey logs was set deep in the ground to mark the edge of a kraal, creating a rudimentary fence line. They stopped at the home-made gate and Khanyi called out, '*Siyakhuleka ekhaya*', politely making the household aware that they had visitors, almost on their doorstep, or otherwise intruding into a homestead's privacy. After a short time, an elderly woman peered out suspiciously from behind a darkened doorway, blinking into the sunlight and trying to discern who these people were, standing next to the road at her rickety gate.

Khanyi looked warily over the fence for bush dogs, then rattled the gate slightly, and instantly three emaciated mongrels, two light tan and one brindle, scrawny animals built like medium sized greyhounds, leapt out of their sleep in the shade and rushed towards them, all barking furiously but cringing, grimacing and wagging their tails at the same time. Their vertebrae were visible along their skinny backs, and the female was clearly suckling a litter of puppies. None of them had collars. It was at best a half-hearted challenge and they soon tired of it and sauntered back to curl up in their shady depressions dug in the sand. The woman tied a blanket around her waist and came out into the sunlight, then walked up to the gate. She had been washing something and her hands were wet. As she wiped off each hand, flicking away the water, she extended a damp wrist in greeting.

Khanyisile first introduced herself, then her husband, and their child and then told the woman what had happened, explaining, '*Makewam*, we have encountered a problem. We were trying to cross the stream back there, thinking it was hard underfoot, but there was a deep hole, and the vehicle became stuck. Now we need help to get it out of the river.'

She explained where they were headed to and indicated where they were from. The old lady seemed surprised that they were so far from home and enquired what they had hoped to find along the road. There were no further shops or trading stores, and it made little sense to her to travel just to see the mountains and hills that surrounded them. They would always be there.

As Khanyi answered, she drew closer and looked at her intently with a puzzled expression, as though she thought she knew them slightly. Something further passed between them, and Matt could hear by the cadence in her voice and the lilt in her language that she was making a series of delicate enquiries – 'Where was the place you have come from? Who did you say you were again?' And then – 'Who was your father? Where is your real home?'

Although the questioning was gentle and polite, each tentative step along the way triggered a further response, and each answer seemed to bring her closer to some unseen locating point she was seeking. As each reply was received, it was thoughtfully digested and somehow appeared to give her greater comfort. Finally, with the proper context well established, she homed in unerringly on the truth and triumphantly asked them.

'Are you that Khanyisile Dlamini from Vuvulane, kaMhlume?'

Then, having confirmed that, she delved even further.

'Are you not the last-born daughter to the late Samariah Dlamini from Shiselweni?'

She explored slightly further into Khanyi's lineage, while they stood chatting in the sun outside the rudimentary fence line and then, feeling at ease, their status established and confirmed, she invited them all into the homestead.

It transpired that she had heard of this Khanyisile and her European husband before, and had once seen pictures of them in the newspaper, when it carried an article about their wedding. This woman's elder brother was a cousin brother to one of those men who married one of Khanyi's mother's many sisters… This made them almost family.

Their credentials established, her demeanour and expression changed, and suspicion gave way to a warm welcome and a smile. She provided her own name and family details and greeted Matt, firmly shaking his hand, and welcomed them warmly into the clearing and her hut, shooing away the fowls and an inquisitive goat, and chatting happily about the unexpected visit. She summoned a small boy who was solemnly gazing at them from the yard, clutching onto his ragged trousers with one hand.

'Thembinkosi, go and call your brothers from the field. Go quickly and call them. They are ploughing in the bottom fields. Tell them to come with the oxen.' He ran off, excited.

'Hau, I see you properly now', she exclaimed. 'This is the one from England who is very good in joining metal, who has been repairing things for farmers, and you, Khanyisile, you are that girl whose employers were all taken at once. They were lost some time back, together with their children, and then you were marrying with the white one, and this young child is your first born.'

Matt listened and watched, following the rapid conversation with only a measure of understanding, but realising that they were in some way, family, part of the complicated latticework that Khanyi could never fully explain, but aware that the people in the homestead somehow also fitted within her structure in a way that placed them absolutely. These were not just kindly strangers. To Matt, the intrusion of walking up to a stranger's house, talking to them so easily and going into their home, and then asking them for help was unheard of, but here in the rural area it seemed to feel relaxed and normal.

In the cool shade inside the thatched hut there was a distinct and pleasant smell of old wood smoke, the residue of years of cooking fires embedded forever in the timbers and mud walls, and in the grass roofing of the thatch itself. It was a homely smell, and reminded him of the builders the Sibandzes, who had created the shelter over his workshops at home.

A much younger woman appeared, bashful and barely showing her face. She greeted the visitors shyly and offered them strong black tea, a refreshing drink although both brackish and metallic, tasting a bit like the shining and scoured aluminium teapot it was made in. She brought out a worn plastic container with hard little scones that had been baked on a steel plate and were slightly burnt on one side. They drank out of enamel mugs, and the crumbly scones were pleasant enough, but they too tasted faintly of woodsmoke. The older woman explained, 'My sons are coming; they will bring the oxen and they are going to help you.'

PJ had been sleeping on Khanyi's lap through most of this, but suddenly awoke, sat up on the mat in front of them, gnawed on one of the scones and made conversation, explaining in English and SiSwati to the old lady how her mum had covered her dad in muddy water when their van got stuck. The old woman was delighted by her and answered her in a kind of SiSwati baby talk that Matt had not heard before. She mentioned many times how PJ was so healthy. She hugged her and gently squeezed at her limbs, commenting on her body and how well she was growing for her age, and kissed her cheeks repeatedly. PJ giggled because it tickled.

They sat together in the cool shade of the hut and chatted, watching the gleaming fowls as they strutted around, scratching for insects in the bright sun outside, keeping a wary eye on the dogs. The odd bolder chicken would jerk its way into the doorway, peering in at them with beady eyes and clucking contentedly. Several small children had gathered outside, gazing in at the visitors in wonderment and, after a time, two of them came in and sat down, looking at PJ's golden hair and light brown skin with fascination. A little girl sat next to her and began stroking it.

After a time of acute observation, her younger brother, dried snot encrusted on his upper lip, solemnly reached across and made a present of what he had been playing with, handing over to the intriguing new visitor the bleached white shell of a big snail. It had been a precious possession.

Matt was relaxing, leaning back on one elbow, taking in the view outside, the home-made maize tank built from a circle of natural weathered branch poles, supported above the ground by sticks, a round wire mesh cage full of mealie cobs, and hearing all about their ongoing problem with rats, the snakes killing their chickens and the cost of seed and fertiliser.

They began to hear male voices, laughing and chatting and drawing closer as the men walked back to the house. The youngest of them was leading a span of four large oxen with wide, swinging horns. All of them were tame and quiet and breathing heavily. Two slightly older men arrived, one in his late teens with short stubby dreadlocks, and his more distinguished looking elder brother, a muscular man who looked to be in his late twenties.

The younger son stayed outside the kraal, standing at the head of the team of oxen, and the old woman introduced them as her sons, Simon, Absalom and Joshua. She explained the problem to them. Joshua guided the oxen, individually calling their names to catch their attention.

'Khasbedi, come round. Manyamane, turn!'

He began to lead them in a tight turn back on themselves in the narrow road outside. The men each introduced themselves, formally shaking hands with Matt and explained that they had been ploughing, but had been summoned by their small brother, and they were coming to help. They apologised that it took time to unhitch the animals. The men spoke some English and the older one said to him, 'Our mother said you are having a problem with your vehicle?'

'Yes,' Matt replied, 'we got stuck along the way. We thought we could drive through the river, but it was deeper than it looked.'

'Oh, okay, there by the small river?' said Simon, the eldest brother. 'I remember that place, many times the trucks are getting stuck there. Even last week, the lorry carrying bread got stuck there. We know that stream, Aah, it's no problem; we can help you.'

'That's most kind of you. It would be very helpful,' answered Matt. 'It's getting late and we didn't want to drive home in the dark.'

After a little polite conversation, Absolom could no longer contain his curiosity. 'Where are you coming from?' he asked Matt, looking at him closely.

‘We are from near Mhlume’.

‘Okay, you are staying by Mhlume’, a sudden look of recognition swept across his handsome features as he placed them. ‘Okay, so now I think we can go.’

They had heard of these people, a certain Swazi lady with a young child, married to a white man who was running a small business in the lowveld among the sugar cane farms. The young couple took their leave of the old lady and thanked her for her kindness, and they made their way back across the yard through the gate and back onto the dusty road, to the team of oxen standing patiently awaiting instructions.

‘Let’s go,’ said Simon.

So, with the accompaniment of a cracking whip, clicks, shouts, barking dogs and piercing short whistling from the men, they began to move back along the narrow lane to where the bakkie was stuck in the mud. The oxen moved at their own pace, a steady long-legged gait, travelling along the road rather faster than they appeared to be moving. Matt and Khanyi had to take lengthy strides to keep up. The young men were more used to it. The youngest one led the animals ahead and the other two walked along behind, coaxing the animals onwards and keeping them in line.

They both knew the river crossing well, explaining again that a bakery van had got stuck there, almost in the same place a few weeks back. Pumi Jacqueline thought this was a carnival arranged specially for her and was babbling happily to herself. Matt was surprised at how swiftly the heavy animals walked. He watched their broad backs swaying above their shoulders and could hear their breathing, the scent coming off their hot brown shiny skins and their warm breath wafting over them, sweet and wholesome, smelling like fermenting silage. Pumi had to be carried when she became tired and couldn’t keep up. Before long, they reached the van, but the water level had risen while they were away and was now lapping at the centre of the wheel rims.

Joshua skilfully led the beasts down into the stream, and the animals walked noisily through it, their hooves crunching loudly over the submerged stones and gravel, stooping to swallow long, quenching drafts of water, then tossing their heads, long shining strands of spittle hanging from their wide mouths, the shiny drool swinging from side to side. After allowing them all to lower their heads and drink, they crossed to the other side, splashing their way strongly through the muddy water. The animals had done this before.

The young men knew exactly what to do. They quickly pulled the trek chain running between the yokes down to the back of the team of oxen, then shackled a second chain to this and dragged that down into the stream to the bakkie's tow bar, wrapping it securely around the tow hitch and shackling it back onto itself. They asked Matt to walk through the water, climb into the van and help reverse it out of the stream. He climbed back into the bakkie and started the engine, relieved that it hadn't flooded.

With a few terse words, one crack of the long whip above their heads, and an instruction to the lead oxen to pull… 'Donsa Skwatland!, donsa Mahlangeni,' the heavy draught animals put their shoulders and immense weight to the wooden yokes over their necks, and, seemingly with little effort, powerfully pulled the bakkie backwards and upwards, tugging it out of the river bed, dragging it easily right up the bank and back onto level ground. Water came gushing out of the vehicle, running out of the doors and the engine bay, and pouring from underneath, joining the darkened rivulets on the muddy riverbank, already thoroughly soaked by the water dripping off the team of oxen. The strong animals slipped a few times as they lost their footing climbing up and away from the stream, but with sixteen heavy hooves on the ground they pulled it out with energy to spare.

The young men at the head of the team had to bring them forcibly to a halt or they would have dragged the bakkie onwards down the road. Matt tried to reverse the vehicle as best he could, but the animals effortlessly dictated the direction. Back on level ground they stopped on the road, their chests lightly heaving, stamping their hooves as the steam rose off their haunches.

The ploughing team stood patiently, as though wondering what all the fuss was about, with their ears twitching and tails swishing. The rear pair of younger animals tossed their heads and nudged each other, their horns clacking together and swinging dramatically as they jostled heavily against the wooden yoke. They looked around as if to say, 'Is there anything else that needs to be done here?'

Matt was amazed. He had never before experienced the immense strength of four oxen working in harness. He also understood very acutely that between him and Khanyi they would have never got the vehicle out. Khanyi and PJ had safely watched the whole exercise from the bank and clapped and cheered as the van backed out and away from the river. Khanyi had some cash on her and offered it to the men, but they raised their hands and refused, saying they were just helping them.

Matt strongly felt that he should pay the ploughmen and family for their help. At first, they politely refused any payment, but he insisted. He explained that he wanted to thank them because he knew they were busy ploughing and he had taken them away from their work and disrupted their day. After some persuasion, the eldest brother respectfully accepted one hundred and fifty Emalangeni, but only did this very reluctantly. Then they detached their chain from the bakkie, pulled the chains through to the head of the animals and ran them along the ground between their broad backs, so they wouldn't trip on them. Then, with a click and a few words, the huge docile creatures turned and headed off, sloshing their way noisily back through the river and walking away into the dusk towards the homestead and their kraal. Two of them bellowed to each other as they crossed to the other side and sensed they were heading for home.

The Bartons turned the van around on the narrow track and, as the light faded they drove back along the route they had taken earlier that day. Matt had a sudden sense of becoming a part of Khanyisile's extended family, of the invisible latticework of people she knew. Of having become, through marriage, a small part of this widely-spread family that would render help to strangers, drop what they were doing and assist someone just because there was some tenuous relationship tying them together. He began to see how Khanyi herself was a part of so many different families, woven into the fabric of lives that gave poor people strength across the Kingdom.

He thought what would have happened if he had got stuck along some remote country lane in Britain and had gone off walking, to knock on doors and ask for help from total strangers. Perhaps, if they were farmers, they might have helped, but the first hurdle would be approaching people he did not know. They probably would have let him use the phone. Out in the country, in most farming areas he guessed that a farmer might have been willing to come out with a tractor, to give him a tow, but the fact that they were unknown strangers would have created a barrier, and they probably would have wanted payment, or been annoyed about being disturbed.

Here, the humanity of the problem, the shared experience, and Khanyisile's link to her people, her family of small mothers and small fathers, other brothers and sisters meant that help was almost automatic. She had greeted each of the men in turn '*Sawubona buti*,' as though they were her brothers. They had looked at her not lustfully, but tenderly, as if to say, this one we must help her, she has a problem, she has a child. He smiled, remembering at one stage when they were both getting tired, how one of them had calmly taken PJ from Khanyi's arms and carried her as they were walking along, jigging her up and down and chatting to her about the oxen and the maize and the trees. It all seemed very natural and relaxed.

They had been absorbed into the warm embrace of humble people, strangers, simply because they were in trouble, and their homestead was the nearest, and they believed it was their duty to provide help.

Matt grew increasingly quiet driving home, staring deeply into the road ahead, lit up by the powerful headlights.

Khanyi asked, 'Matt, is there something wrong?'

'No, love. I'm just amazed at how you reached out to those people. How did you know them?'

Khanyi thought for a moment then replied, 'No Matt, I never knew them until now, but now I know them.'

He looked across at her admiringly as they drove along. 'You didn't even know those people at all before, so how did you know you could ask them to help you?'

She thought for a while and answered, 'It's true, I didn't know them before, but now they are my family. She is my small mother.'

'But you had never met them!' exclaimed Matt.

'Yes, I never met her until now, but now I know them; next time if I see her, we can greet.' Her answer was unequivocal. They were another thread now identified and woven into her widespread extended family.

PJ had been singing a song about the big cows pulling the car, but had eventually fallen asleep again, lulled by the noise of the vehicle. Matt drove on in thoughtful silence, watching out for stray goats and black cows roaming across the road, or lying asleep on it for warmth. As he drove, the stars began to come out, and he realised again, in a feeling that he would experience alarmingly often, that there were still many things he didn't know and would always struggle to understand about his wife's country. But becoming part of her life meant that he had also somehow become a small part of her unseen family, with all the benefits and demands that brought. He could never be part of this invisible social jigsaw puzzle if it weren't for her, and it brought home to him vividly that he had, through marriage, suddenly acquired an enormous family spread across the country, most of whom they both barely knew. Khanyi was nodding off and soon drifted off to sleep, warmed by the sun and tired from the fresh air and their adventure. Pumi Jacqueline, wholly exhausted by all the excitement and her singing, slept peacefully all the way home.

It had been a grand day out. They hadn't got to where they wanted to go – they had never reached and hadn't even seen the mountains – but they had seen another piece of the country in detail, and put their feet down into the cold mud and felt the water rushing past their ankles. He felt as though he had been christened by the land. They had been helped by four strangers who were now family, and it all began to fall into place. That was why, when people came to the gate, she almost always needed to help them or offer sustenance. He began to see differently what lay behind the many times she would say to him 'No, I don't know that person, but we must help them'.

Chapter 5

Nkomati Farmers Cooperative

THEY HEARD THE ELDERLY VEHICLE rattling along in the distance long before it appeared in sight. It emerged slowly out of the bush, having taken the back roads following the canal to avoid the police, all the while accompanied by a loud clattering and banging noise, and it suddenly lurched around the corner at the end of the block of sugar cane and sailed into view, the young driver wrestling with the steering wheel to keep it on course. It floated and swayed like an old ship under sail.

The left side front fender had rusted through below the mudguard, and the pieces of baling wire holding it in place had worn away and fallen off, leaving it flapping randomly alongside the front wheel, like a guinea fowl scuttling along with a broken wing. A passenger on the left-hand side had one arm out of the window, firmly clamped against the body work to hold the dented door closed. It tended to come open when they went over speed bumps or potholes.

The old engine sputtered and popped, but somehow stuttered along, sounding exactly like what it was: an ancient Toyota Hilux coming to the end of an honourable life, already on its second engine and gearbox. As the old van drew closer, Matt thought that he recognised one of the passengers, the elderly Mr. Ngomezulu from Nkomati Farmers Co-op. They had been among his very first customers in the area. The battered white van skidded to a halt, rocking on its suspension, with one front wheel braking and locking up on its bald tyre. Then the passenger fought with the door until he could force it open, slowly climbed out and moved to open the gate.

The Barton homestead's assortment of dogs flew down the drive in a grand show of barking and threat, but the old man calmly carried on undoing the chain and pushed open the gate at the bottom of the drive. Then he climbed back into the van, banging the door repeatedly until it finally closed, to the accompaniment of the screech of tortured body panels. He secured it again with his hand.

The old van rattled its way up the drive, leaving a blue trail of burning oil exhaust. The bakkie looked in even a worse state than it had been the first time they had visited, and it had been in pretty bad shape then. The driver shut it down and it died with a shudder, like a big dog shaking off a bath.

Khanyisile came gliding out of her office at the sound of the commotion, slim and gracious, and Matt walked across from the workshops to greet them. They exchanged pleasantries and Khanyi offered them tea, which they gladly accepted. The elderly gentleman who had been holding the door closed adjusted his coat, and introduced himself.

'Mr Barton, we are visiting again from Nkomati Farmers' Cooperative. I am Timothy Ngomezulu, as for now I am the chairperson. Last time we visited you and you helped us with our tractor axle, now we are coming to you with another problem. This problem is even more worse. We are facing a critical problem, and we believe you are the one who is more talented and skilful in repairing.'

Matt took him in, watching as he rubbed the sparse grey curls of hair on his balding scalp and wrung his threadbare cap in his hands. He was fond of the old man and was happy to see him again. Khanyi remembered meeting the old chairman previously and he greeted her very politely.

'This other one is my grandson. He is Milton. The other one is my associate, he is Chapter. He is Mr. Chapter Maseko, our Financial Officer. We are together all coming from Nkomati.'

Khanyi came back out with a tray and Matt stayed with them while the tea ritual began, watching as the grandson spooned four heaped spoons of sugar into his cup. He glanced across at Khanyi, thinking the discrete look was just between them, but Chapter noticed the glance and made some comment about the sugar, and the two older men chuckled. Milton shook his head gently admonishing his ancient grandfather, '*Hhayikona Mkhulu, aah No Mkhulu, Haibo*!'

The grandson ruefully explained the teasing to Matt and Khanyi.

'My Grandfather is reminding me, I used to like sugar too much before, I used to take a lot, but now I am married and my wife, she is a sister at the clinic. She is very harsh. She has been blaming me each and every day. She told me I must reduce, or I will get BP, so now I take only four spoons for reasons of health. Before I was used to take seven. Even salt! She is also refusing with salt! She also claims I take too much salt.'

He carried on, shaking his head in amazement. 'But my grandfather, although he is now very old, he likes the tea to taste bitter, he only uses two spoons! Two spoons only!' He shook his head in disbelief.

Matt joined them as they began to relax in the sunlight and stretch out their legs on the warm grass, clutching one knee and leaning back against nothing in that miraculous way. He took a mug of tea for himself, adding no sugar at all. This act caused some polite astonishment and murmured comment. The young driver felt it necessary to explain further and seemed to be quoting verbatim from something he had been taught.

'Sugar is essential to our bodies to create energy for them to survive,' he announced, and added with greater importance, 'since because I am working myself driving tractors and trucks each and every day, my body needs fuel, same like petrol, and we are providing employment to the Kingdom in the agricultural sector, and also producing, so we must support the industry that sustains our livelihood and so we like to eat sugar.'

With this impressive statement of intent completed, he sat back, and his elders nodded sagely at the comment. Ndepethe had been hoeing a new plot for potatoes nearby, creating ridges, and he came across at the sound of the visitors, to greet and contribute his depth of wisdom to the situation. He took a seat to one side after making his greetings and, after shaking everyone's hands, began to roll himself a large cigarette, pulling wisps of raw dark tobacco leaf from a worn Boxer packet, and crushing them carefully in his palm. After a short time, the conversation dwindled. The weather, the families, cattle and the current crop had been covered, and Matt felt it was time to move things along towards the reason for their visit.

'So, Babe Ngomezulu, you mentioned a problem, a bad problem?'

'Very bad, Mr. Button. It is very much bad,' he explained, holding his head in one hand. He let out a low whistle.

'As a collective, we elect to buy a water pump to irrigate our fields, those which are above and cannot be irrigated by furrows. They are far above the canal. We find the exactly right pump, which is very heavy. It is going to power by an engine from a tractor which met with an accident. The engine was still alright, still strong, so we keep it after that accident.

'Already now, the engine is ready, the radiator and water and fuel tank, all are ready. Then we have decided to order that pump, which is very much heavy, and they transport it from Middelburg in Mpumalanga on a truck. Then, after some time it reaches us at Nkomati, and we decide to put it inside using a cane crane. The roof of the pumping station it was still off, we never put the roof tiles up to so far because we still must put the pump inside. Then together we tie the *liketane* around the pump.'

Matt looked puzzled and Milton chipped in, explaining, 'The 'ketane is a cane chain used to lift the bundles of sugar cane'.

Mr Ngomezulu continued. 'So eh Button, we lift the pump slowly, nicely off the truck, then we lift it up over the wall, and it begins to go down to the concrete we have made for that pump to sit. Simeon he is driving the crane.'

At this point the audience, all watching attentively joined in, better to illustrate the scale of the disaster that happened next. Even Ndepethe moved and sat slightly closer to the party to hear the news, smoke pouring out of his nostrils.

Timothy continued with a mournful expression, 'Then, Mr Matt, the chain holding on one side, it was tie by a knot, but I hear that chain just say Kwaa! Somehow that knot which have been tied by the workers it loosen, it loosen quickly, then it just slips through, then I see that very heavy pump is falling to the floor from above the roof, and I shout to Milton, mind Milton, *shesha!* and then we just hear Bwaa! and it hit the ground.'

He swung his arms across his chest and snapped his left forefinger loudly against the top of his right hand to emphasise the scale of the impact. There was a stunned silence.

With a deeply pained expression he continued. 'Mr Button, when it hits the concrete then the ground even shakes, because it's too heavy, this pump. Then we inspect carefully because this is our first pump, still new. It never even worked. We check all sides and seems like it's okay, looks like we are having a good luck. Only the whatyoucall'… portraying a flange with his hands, 'that part has got some damages.'

Matt listened intently, quite enjoying the dramatic telling of the story. Ndepethe let out a low whistle and coughed deeply, listening respectfully and very much still following the narration.

'So, then we discuss, and after some time we decide we must try it. So, we connect the pump to the water pipe, many bolts, and we connect to the engine. After two days tighting all the bolts and the round part and making it to be level and straight, we are ready to try and we start.'

By now, the tension in the small group had risen to such an extent that it was no longer possible for the other two to stop themselves adding to the story. Chapter had to stand up to demonstrate the drama with his hands, arms outspread and reaching to the sky. Milton imitated the noise and action of the water jetting out.

'So, *Mnumzane* Button, the tractor engine it starts and is running nice, no problem, then they open the valve and the pump starts to make pressure and at first it's working nice, then we see a very bad thing … Ffffffwaaaa, the water begins coming out like a river! It even makes a sound of itself,' and he imitated water screaming out of a hair line crack under pressure. 'It says tsweeeeee! It make a sound like that, very loud. The water is spraying all over, even above the roof. It even makes like a mist.'

Chapter came in at this point, as his aged chairman was tiring a little. 'The pressure was over strong. The pressure was plenty. It's when we realise that time when the pump fell down, although it looks okay, now it's got a problem. It's now having a crack somewhere.'

They all sat down. It had been a sad day. Ndepethe who had listened patiently coughed, hawked and spat, neatly covering the resulting phlegm with sand, inhaled deeply and then spoke with emphasis as smoke streamed from his mouth and nostrils. He was scratching out certain patterns in the sand as he considered the matter, then he joined the discussion.

'It's fortunate you came here, because Mr Matt he can easily repair this, he knows such things very well although he is still young. He can repair it without any problem. In welding he is a doctor. He is known to even work in other countries.'

Matt didn't entirely follow this but had heard his name, and something about welding. Khanyi explained for him. Chapter shook his head tragically.

Milton gave a low whistle. 'Aish, it's a big problem. We need to irrigate now, there are many fields already ridged and planted, but we cannot use the sprinklers. The pump cost a lot of money.'

Timothy continued, 'We bring the mechanic there and we ask him to look very carefully, very slow with a torch, then he notice under the pump, near to where it hit the concrete it's having a small, small crack, almost like a line underneath. The crack is about this long (he held his fingers twenty centimetres apart), but it's very much difficult to see, very small in size. The metal is still close together.'

'It was underneath, it's why we never see it at first, it was dark', interjected Chapter, 'and because it was hidden underneath by the whatyoucall, the round flange. So now, we come to you about this pump because it's still new, but we cannot use it. We ask you if you can repair it, but it's too heavy to bring on the bakkie. We want to ask you first to come and see this our new pump, then you are going to tell us what we can do.'

Matt looked at the three men, nodding slowly and thinking to himself. 'Do you know what the pump housing is made of?'

Chapter began stripping the green bark of a small branch with his thumbnail, pondering over this. They shook their heads. Timothy said that it was blue in colour. Milton thought it was a type of iron. Chapter suggested contacting the suppliers to ask them.

Matt asked them to roughly show him the size, and Chapter stood up and demonstrated. The pump housing came up to just below his waist, and he guessed that the outlet flange was about the diameter of a beach ball, perhaps feeding a 12-inch pipe. Matt understood why they had not been able to bring it to him. It was a big irrigation pump.

He spoke. 'Mr. Ngomezulu, you have explained very well. I am clear about the problem now. I think the pump body is made from cast iron. Cast iron is difficult to weld. Usually I can fix it, but I need to see your pump first. Let me come there and see it, then I can decide what we can do. In any case, I would have to bring it here to repair it, because I will need electricity.'

Ndepethe had finished his thick hand-rolled cheroot and illicit cup of tea, and stood up, pronouncing the last word on the matter. He wasn't entirely sure what the irrigation pump or its flange really looked like, but he had absolute confidence in Mr Matt. 'Aaiy, this is not a big matter, Ngomezulu, Mr Matt is going to fix it, you will see. He knows this thing very well, he is fluent, for him it's easy'.

Matt was accustomed to his personal praise singer by now, and just looked at the old man fondly, but rather wished he would be quiet and return to his potato patch. There was some discussion between the members about the costs of hiring a truck, or whether the pump could be carried on a tractor and trailer and towed to Matt's workshop. The consensus was that this was possible, and they agreed to his terms. Arrangements were made on the understanding that if Matt agreed to repair the pump, having inspected it, the cooperative would arrange to transport it to his workshops. Matt thought he could lift it off with an overhead gantry but explained that he needed power and gas to repair it, and had to turn it right over to gouge out the crack, and could not do it in the field. It would be a difficult weld.

The delegation was clearly pleased by the outcome. They stood up, dusting off their trousers. The old chairman thanked Matt and said they were happy he had agreed to visit them, and that they had a strong belief that he could repair it. He explained that they could not afford to buy another pump housing. They had been quoted R37,500 for the new housing alone, and it would still have to be transported back to the factory for repairs.

Ndepethe wandered off, muttering to himself about those who delay or take time when asking help from experts, and how unwise this was. The men shook hands and climbed back into the old van. Having turned on the ignition, Milton, the young driver, leapt out again and wrestled the bonnet open. As he forced it up, it made a loud squawking noise, then he reached in and started the engine with a short piece of yellow wire he carried in his pocket. He had clearly done this many times before. Looking up and smiling he apologised, 'The solenoid is complete buggerup, Mr Button'.

The men slammed the doors several times to try and get them to stay closed, then set off, waving goodbye out of the window. The dogs escorted them to the gate, snapping at the wheels and barking at the noise, then sat down wagging their tails, satisfied they had seen it off the premises, and watched the old van drive away, its rattling noise receding into the distance.

Matt saw Khanyi coming out of the house, smiling. The mere sight of her in jeans was always able to lift his mood. She said, 'Do you remember the chicken they gave you last time? As a thanks for repairing the tractor?'

Matt nodded.

'It is still alive, but old now. It stays there with Ndephete's other fowls. He says it is strong because it came from Nkomati.'

He put his arm around her waist, and they walked inside, laughing. The old man had named the chicken Nkomati.

Days later, Matt drove out to the co-operative offices, following careful directions, and was surprised to see Timothy, the chairman, drive up in a brand new, spotless white 4x4 double cab, gleaming expensively in the sun. He explained that it was his own car, but he was keeping it for when he became old, and very seldom used it, storing it at home in a garage. It still had plastic covers on the seats. He was willing to show Matt the way to the pump, if he could follow. After finding their way to the pumphouse and testing the material to be sure of what it was, Matt decided he could repair it, and on his way back home stopped off and ordered special cast iron welding rods from Mr. Gule, along with some gouging rods, Argon gas, a special TIG gun and several other tools and special materials.

When the heavy, cracked pump housing arrived, securely strapped onto a pallet on the load bed of a farm trailer, safely wrapped in sacking, they slowly offloaded it using an overhead hoist and lowered it onto a pile of pallets, bolstered with other bits of heavy timber. Between him and Musa, they turned it over very carefully, not allowing it to fall at any time but slowly manoeuvring the heavy casting round until he could get to the hairline crack. He began by drilling a small hole at each end to prevent the crack spreading, being careful not to drill so deep as to touch the impeller, and then he began gouging out and grinding a deep, vee shaped channel wide enough to work in, and get enough weld penetration into the thickness of the housing wall.

It was a slow, patient process. Preparing the work area took the best part of a day, gouging out molten cast iron in short stages, grinding away material until there was a clean even surface to work on, and then lightly smoothing the adjoining weld faces with a flapper disc to create a smooth base for a clean, very strong, pressure bearing repair. The following day, unable to preheat such a massive casting, he started a root weld at the base of the crack, using an arc welder. He could only make short weld runs, allowing the casting to cool and normalise between each run. Then he made several filler passes, still joining the two sides of the crack, but gradually, in short stages. After letting the casting naturally cool off, he began to slowly fill the crack with the special cast iron rods, feeding them in small lengths into the gas shielded arc to make the cap welds.

He could sense beneath the pool of white hot metal that the new metal was blending with the old, becoming a part of it, melting into both sides, and he carefully worked his way along, slightly weaving the molten pool left and right, covering short weld sections at a time, and throwing a thermal blanket over the work whenever he stopped, to allow the material to normalise slowly as it cooled. He was very wary of causing new cracks as it cooled and contracted. It was slow, careful, high current welding, taking care not to let the big pump housing get too hot, in case the brittle material cracked. He gradually built up the weld bit by bit along the full length of the crack, and progressively laid down layer upon layer, but it took most of the day, as he had to keep stopping to allow it to cool down naturally without stressing it, and the power supply kept tripping. It was a process that could not be hurried, and he thought of times he'd had to make similar repairs but could only gain access with his 'wrong' hand, or had to complete mirror welds, working in positions where he could not see any of the repair directly, only images reflected in a mirror.

He watched the iron melting in the white-hot molten pool, thinking dreamily about how his life had merged with Khanyisile's, and had turned into something stronger together than either of them had been individually. He felt as though what he used to be was no more, like the deep channel he had been filling on the underside and shoulder of the pump housing. His life had been joined up and filled, turned into something else.

When he had finished, he allowed everything to cool slowly, trapping the warmth to avoid sudden temperature changes using a thick layer of thermal blankets and his leather apron. The following morning, after it had cooled overnight, he began to grind it down, but left some of the cap weld slightly proud of the surrounding casting for strength, then roughly sanded it all off to check that there were no weak points. It was never going to be an invisible, seamless repair – one could easily see there had been welding carried out – but no one could tell where the original crack had been, where the old metal ended and the new section began. It was all one. He was confident that it would be strong enough. After another cooling off period from the heat of grinding, he primed and painted it over in matching blue enamel to neaten everything, feeling the satisfaction of knowing that he had completed the repair as well as anyone could.

Once the paint had dried, Khanyi phoned the Cooperative offices and told them it was ready, and the old Ford tractor and trailer arrived the following day, with Milton at the wheel. They lifted the repaired irrigation pump, again using the chain block, and the young man reversed the farm trailer skilfully underneath it. Then they gently lowered it down onto a pallet, lying it carefully down on three old tyres they had tied down to provide a soft bed for it to travel back to the farm. Matt knew the customers well enough to trust them by then, and Khanyisile gave the driver an envelope with the invoice, addressed to Chapter Maseko and Timothy the Chairman.

Before they loaded it up, Milton inspected the repairs and was greatly impressed, exclaiming that it looked strong, with no sign of the old crack at all. No one could see what had been done to it under the finishing weld or the many layers of strength built into it. He thanked Matt profusely, warmly shaking his hand. Before he left, he climbed to the front of the trailer and handed down a fertiliser bag half filled with clean, sweet-smelling mealies, still in their fresh green leafy wrapping, and six enormous cabbages. He apologised that he had only brought some vegetables to thank them, but it was a long drive on the tractor, and he had left early that morning. Musa took the bag from him and solemnly presented it to Khanyisile.

They lashed down the big pump, securing it and the tyres beneath it onto the trailer bed. Then he started up the tractor and drove away, easing his tractor and trailer through the back gate and onto the road. They could hear its loud exhaust growing fainter as he went up through the gears, and Matt hoped Mr. Ngomezulu would be pleased. The payment (and it was a substantial invoice), came though the following evening, already paid into the bank in full.

Khanyi received a phone call a few days later from the Nkomati Cooperative, telling her that they had reinstalled the pump successfully, lifting it over the walls using D shackles, not tying knots in the chains, and wrapping it in many layers of sacking to cushion the sling. It had all gone well, and it was now working and pumping perfectly, with no leaks at all. They wanted her to greet and thank Mr Button for his repairs and she was immensely proud of her husband.

Witnessing the big pump come in broken, and go out properly fixed gave Ndepethe an abundance of new material for conversations for many months to come, with both the pump itself and the cracked flange growing in size each time he told anyone about it. Matt's renown was spreading.

Chapter 6

The ascending believer

ONE WARM SUNDAY AFTERNOON, THE Barton family were all resting after a traditional roast lunch. Matt's left hand was draped over Khanyi's waist to one side, feeling the warm swell of her hip beneath his touch, but his right hand had gone to sleep, trapped underneath their sleeping daughter PJ, slumbering deeply, quiet and immobile on their bed.

He became aware of a commotion outside: a big disturbance of some kind, raised voices and people shouting some distance away. He eased his hand slowly from underneath his sleeping daughter, shaking it back into life, and gently slid down to the foot of the bed, before standing up, wanting to find the source of the noise. He wandered sleepily into the kitchen, slowly becoming fully awake. He looked about outside. Then, seeing nothing, he walked through to the front of the old farmhouse and went outside, where the source was, and the noise grew louder.

There was a small gathering of people standing around the foot of a very tall eucalyptus tree, near the gate down by the corner of the garden. They all appeared to be looking up at something. Some of them were laughing loudly, and others were shouting upwards, pointing at something, seeming to direct their comments up into the branches of the tree.

He slipped on shoes and walked down to the gate to see what was going on. Both Knox and the gardener were there, unusually for a Sunday afternoon. Looking around, he recognised several other people he knew by sight, as they mostly lived in nearby compounds and estate houses. He asked Knox what the problem was, and Knox shrugged his shoulders and gestured upwards. Matt expected to see a snake.

There, perched near the very top of the tree, clinging precariously to the slender central trunk with one hand and balancing only on one leg, his other limb dangling above the void was what seemed to be a young man in a khaki uniform of some kind. His outfit looked strangely familiar, and the boy seemed to be dancing about, swaying and moving, shaking his legs and hanging one out over the air above their heads. He was howling at the sky, shouting at things unseen, chanting what sounded like Bible verses and emitting strange hoarse cries and phrases that were mostly incoherent. He seemed unaware of the crowd that had gathered beneath him. Matt took a few steps back, moving a short way from the foot of the tree so that he could get a better look at him between the sparse branches.

He appeared to be a schoolboy, probably in his late teens, but he had been chanting and shouting for so long that saliva had dried around his mouth, making a crusty white marking around his lips. He looked deranged, his movements erratic and uncoordinated and his head bobbing around as though he was drunk.

'What's he doing up there?' asked Matt.

'He is very confused, this boy,' said Knox. 'He is a Zionist, and he has climbed up there to become nearer to God. Now he is shouting to God asking him to take him up to Heaven.'

'But he might fall! The branches are weak, and he keeps dancing and letting one hand go!'

'Yes, it may happen,' replied Knox nodding calmly, 'and when he falls down, he will die.'

'Well, can't we stop him? Can't we persuade him to come down?'

'Aah, no Boss. For now he is still mad. After some time, he may return and find himself, but as for now he is mad. He thinks he is talking to God because he is more close to heaven up there, so God can hear him more clearly.'

Khanyi joined them, coming up to Matt's side and taking his hand. She spoke quickly to the people standing around, and then explained a little further to Matt. 'Matt there is nothing we can do for now, until he becomes more tired. He is very much confused. He has probably been at a prayer meeting since Friday. They have been singing and drinking tea and vomiting, and all the time singing and praying, and he thinks he is among the angels now. If we go near to him, he may jump off and try to fly. It's better we leave him there for some time.'

Matt was very unhappy with this response and replied, 'Shouldn't we send someone up there to try and talk to him?'

By now, the boy was screaming aloud, claiming he could see the devils trying to climb the tree, and other winged demons floating around him in the air. Sometimes he would release both hands and lean precariously against the thin trunk, swatting at them, shooing them away, then swaying dangerously as his centre of gravity shifted. Then, suddenly some deep instinctive urge for self-preservation would emerge and save him, and he'd reach back and grab onto the tree trunk again. From time to time, he would turn around to change his footing, giving his single supporting foot a break, but he was constantly unbalanced, shrieking and swaying, his eyes turned upwards, shouting '*Phuma dimon, phuma! Kungafa*!' striking at his own body and gesticulating at the unseen demons that were tormenting him. He seemed to be trying to break off a small switch to lash at them and drive them away.

'Oh, okay, which means there are demons there,' commented one of onlookers pensively, as though she had missed them at first glance, her matter of fact observation belying the drama playing out above them.

Matt was shocked by all this and a bit overwhelmed. Khanyi went on explaining, looking up at the youngster. 'Matt, he has been without food for some days and nights. They have been chanting and using laxatives and vomiting, and as for now he is full of the spirit and still confused. Maybe he will get tired. Then he will become frightened and come down.' She seemed quite matter of fact about this, as though it was an everyday occurrence.

'But shouldn't we call for someone with ladders to try to catch him and bring him down?'

'No, Matt we can't. We must not. If people get close to him now, he is still full of holy water or the elders may have marked him with ashes. He will think they are demons and he will try to jump to Heaven, then he will fall.'

'But he might fall anyway!' exclaimed Matt.

'Yes, he may fall.' She shrugged regretfully. 'At times it happens that they fall, but usually they come down.'

This troubled Matt a great deal. He felt that there must be a better course of action but could not think what it was. The assembled people all seemed to be quite calm about the situation, and were relaxed and cheerful, finding it all quite entertaining. Reluctantly, he decided to be guided by local wisdom in these matters.

Khanyi explained that he was from a sect of red gown Zionists, and still young, and a devout follower of that independent church. She could not explain exactly what had happened, but Matt understood he was in some state of religious rapture and could not feel the danger because he was closer to God up there in the tree. Matt reckoned he was about eighty feet up, but he seemed completely oblivious to the height or the danger. Knox shouted up at him a few times, but he ignored the voice.

Then, during a lull in the demon baiting, Ndepethe bellowed up at him, '*Yay umfana*, wake up, *vuka lapho*, what are you doing there!'

The boy looked down at the sound briefly, then flailed away at the words as though he were swatting a swarm of imaginary flies buzzing around his head.

'It's good,' said Khanyi. 'He notices us now. Talk to him again, Ndepethe.'

The old man took a long pull on his hand-rolled cigarette, coughed deeply, spat and then bellowed up again, '*Yay wena umfaana*, when you fall we are going to leave you here. Your body will be broken and ants will eat your private parts. It may happen we never find your parents to tell them that you are here because you are not supposed to be here. You are climbing the Mnumzane's tree and he is very angry about that. He may decide to shoot you.'

Khanyi explained what he had said and Matt, horrified, hotly denied ever saying anything like that. 'Yes, it's not true, but the old man knows,' said Khanyi.

Ndephete went on, lavishly embroidering and improvising as he went further. 'Yay *Wena Umfaan'wam*, we have nice food here, and even Coke, and white bread. Maybe, if I speak nicely to the Mnumzane, he won't beat you but will give you food if you come down. Maybe, he can give you KFC. You won't reach heaven there in that tree. This is not the right kind of tree.'

Khanyi once again translated, and Matt looked across at the old man, now almost speechless, wondering – what difference did the tree make?'

Something about Coke, KFC and the wrong tree seemed to strike home, and the boy brought his leg in, from where it had been dangling in the air, and carefully seemed to place it on the branch as though the position suddenly mattered. He was still shouting and chanting, but with less intensity, as though he was suddenly aware of where he was. He gazed up at the sky beseechingly, as though searching among the clouds for a sign, then shouted down to Ndephete in a slightly calmer voice, 'Demon, is this the wrong tree? How can I know you are telling a true, not a lie?'

Ndephete was in his element and enjoying being centre of attention. He gave a long explanation that he was not a demon, that he was an Ndlangamandla from Lubombo, and that he knew these trees before, as he was the one who had planted them when he was young. The kind of tree suitable for getting close to Heaven was found only in Hhohho region, not here. It would be better to come down, get refreshed, then he could find those trees on another day.

He asked the boy's name, and the answer came down, '*Thuthuka,*' he was called Thuthuka.

The old man was being very clever. Once he had the name, he called up again, more calmly. 'Thuthuka, *yay wena* Thuthuka, it's better if you can climb down now because soon it will get dark, then many snakes will come into this tree. They like this place. I usually see them sleeping here at night.'

Knox nodded, as though in agreement, shot a sly, approving glance at Ndephete and added, 'Many times, many times, I see the big snakes in this tree at night. They usually live here. Now you are disturbing them and they may become angry and attack you.'

The youngster looked down for the first time and asked in a more normal voice if there really was white bread. There was a hush on the ground.

Khanyi answered him in her sweetest voice.

'We have white bread and tea here on the ground, even sugar. I can prepare it and give you some Thuthuka. We will not beat you if you come down.'

There was a long pause. The boy looked around, as though hoping he would spot the missing flight of golden stairs leading up to Heaven, swatted away a few more imaginary flying devils with the switch he had broken off the tree and then, with a last call out to God that he felt this was not yet his time to enter the Holy city, he began to find his way down. This meant looking down and suddenly realising how high he was.

'I fear this place, it is too high, how can I find my way down? Where is the way?'

The men beneath began guiding his feet, all shouting conflicting instructions to him as he dangled dangerously from one branch and lowered his foot to the next, stretching out on tip toes to reach the lower limbs. It was slow, precarious, and rather frightening to watch. There would be a collective sharp intake of breath when he released his hands to flap at passing demons, or leaned out over the void to swish at them with his small branch, but he gradually climbed down, lower and lower, and the wildness inside slowly went out of his eyes.

The dogs had gathered around in a loose circle below and began barking excitedly at this crazed intruder, clambering about and shouting at unseen spirits high up above them in the trees. It was very exciting for them. He feared the dogs, and wanted assurance that they would not bite him, and to be reassured again that there was still white bread.

With this given, he clambered down, eventually hanging by his hands from the lowest branch, then falling the last few metres onto the ground. Knox grabbed him and asked, 'Shall I beat him now Boss? He is confused in his mind, this one. It will be better if I beat him.'

'No, don't hurt him, let's take him to the house and give him some food.'

Thuthuka, now firmly on the ground, was handed his plain wooden staff, gown and spotless white takkies and seemed to lose much of his mania. He suddenly became very sad and apologetic.

He did not know how he had got into the tree but thought it was because he was having a vision. He was seventeen years of age and was feeling very tired. Their priest had told them they must live closer to God every day, and he had been praying and fasting from Friday after school, without sleeping for the whole weekend. He announced proudly that he had vomited eleven times, also through his nose, to cleanse himself thoroughly of any evil spirits. There had been many healings at the meeting and many demons had been beaten out of people who were sick, and three women who failed to conceive had become pregnant. He had himself seen several demons leaving the bodies of the possessed and dying in the air, left without a host. He'd heard them squealing like pigs as they left. They were drinking only the special tea made in a big tin on the fire. He did not want to have any Coke. He would like to drink water and tea. He wanted only to become a priest and one day would go to Morija at Easter and dance with the elders.

He wished that he had not made any trouble for the Bartons and apologised many times for climbing in their tree. It was not his aim to disturb them, but he was having a vision. He thanked Matt several times, fervently, for not shooting him.

Matt had no firearm and had never had one. He just shook his head, watching and learning with some disbelief. Khanyi came out of the house with a tray, and the young boy thanked her shyly, looking at her with doe eyes, then sat and ate slice after slice of white bread and margarine, sprinkling each slice liberally with sugar, folded and dunked in milky tea. He seemed much calmer now and had stopped flicking away the demons floating about in the air or even denouncing them, shouting at them to leave. They seemed to be much scarcer on the ground than they were in the sky, which was fortunate.

The dogs, sensing some inexplicable illness in him, lay at a distance, but all watched him doubtfully, eyeing him with great suspicion as though unsure of this particular species that looked like a human but didn't behave like one.

Khanyisile gave her name, and Matt's, then asked him where he had come from, and who he was, and when he told her, rather bashfully, she nodded. She had an idea that she knew the place and knew the family name. He said he would like to go there now, as he needed to bathe and get ready for school tomorrow. He needed to complete some homework concerning the geography of the Nile. He mentioned this several times, and its tributaries.

They let him go, much to Knox's disapproval. 'Aah, but Boss, it was going to be better for me to just punish him lightly, just a small beating so that he can remember not to come and climb here again, disturbing us when looking for Heaven next time,' the massive security guard grumbled, but Matt refused. Knox shook his head at the wasted opportunity to instil some semblance of proper discipline into the lunatic.

They watched Thuthuka walk away through the back gate, singing quietly to himself, and Khanyi told her husband, 'Shame, his mother is also mad, this boy. We know her. She is named Eliza something. She is not okay in her head. She often collects papers and plastics and ties them in her clothes, and drinks water from the puddles. At times she barks and chases the chickens. He is almost like his mother, but he is a red gown Apostolic Zionist. His father drinks too much so he is alone there at home. I think his mind has become confused from facing so many problems.'

Matt collected the tea things and they walked back into the house in the darkness, close together. He felt her hand on his shoulder and was thinking deeply. He was marvelling again at the differences between his previous life in England, the one he'd known so well before, and the life he knew now among these people.

The social services would have had to be alerted in his hometown, and the fire brigade called out. Specially trained men wearing all sorts of safety equipment would have appeared, strapping themselves safely to the tree before attempting to climb it. The local police would have arrived, and promptly cordoned off the whole road, stopping traffic. There would have been at least one specially trained social worker, perhaps a child psychologist, and maybe a trained police negotiator, and he thought about the way the event would have been covered by local media. 'Ethnic minority youth trapped following three-day cult ritual' – with comments like 'Previous psychotic episodes', 'Parents partly responsible', 'youth almost falls to his death,' and invariably, 'Social welfare failure!' It would have been on the evening TV news.

Here in the Swazi lowveld, with no one around to help, they had undoubtedly saved his life. The poor delusional boy had been talked down from the tree by an old gardener who understood his fears and motives better than anyone else. He was fearful of snakes, tired and hungry, and his hallucinations had gradually stopped.

He thought back to the way Knox Mkhize had unexpectedly come into their lives, informing them that day that they needed a security guard to stop the workshop equipment being stolen. How he had then saved his life, and Khanyi's when they had that home invasion. How Khanyi had carefully interviewed many different young women before employing Nomsa from a very rural area as a nanny to help her with little PJ and the housework while she worked at their business.

He smiled, thinking of how delighted grumpy old Ndephete had been when Matt had repaired his ancient lawnmower. He was the elderly gardener who had always been part of the house and had just continued working, unpaid, after Patrick and Melanie had been killed. The old man had then become his unofficial publicist, promoting and advertising Matt's welding skills far and wide and wildly exaggerating his accomplishments.

He thought he would never understand the country he was living in and wondered if Thuthuka would ever get to eat his KFC or get to see the place called Morija and dance with the elders. He put down the tray in the kitchen and suddenly took Khanyisile in his arms and kissed her deeply, holding her tight. She was puzzled at first but after a short, delicious moment she relaxed, closed her eyes, went limp and kissed him back. She somehow seemed to make sense of everything.

Chapter 7

The Dreaming

THERE HAD BEEN A FEW days marked by strange, cloudy, unsettled, gusty weather. Distant thunder rumbled ominously out of the north west of the Kingdom, but no rain came from it, just noise. Occasionally, strong winds would sweep across the cane fields and surrounding area without warning, rattling the heavy cane stalks and raising dust off the roads as they passed. But, after blowing for a short time, snapping off the small branches in the flat-topped trees around the garden and blowing down thousands of tiny leaves, they would subside equally suddenly, leaving cooler air behind them for a short time. It were as if the world surrounding them was unsure about what season to choose, and was trying different ones on like items of clothing, unable to find weather that would fit its mood. The change of season affected people differently, but the sudden dusty gusts of dirty wind were unpleasant, leaving grit in eyes and mouth.

An unusual air of irritability had settled over the Barton homestead, leaving a vague sense of unease and disquiet. Khanyisile, usually endlessly patient with her daughter, would uncharacteristically suddenly grow tired of PJ's endless questions, even though she often asked them in a way that was cute, then, highly irritated, would tell her to be quiet, or send her outside to play, and then feel bad about it afterwards.

Matt would come in from the workshop and unexpectedly question some work she had done for them in their office, finding fault with an incorrect invoice, or annoyed that they had run out of something she had forgotten to order that should have been replaced. It made her question herself and her abilities.

There was always love between them, always strength in their little family unit, but it was pushed into corners and set aside by an unseemly urgency of events. Matt sensed something was a tiny bit different between them but could not bring it properly into focus. It went on for a few days, culminating in Khanyisile suddenly going off by herself for a walk, a proper walk, not a stroll – something that she never normally did alone. That act was almost unheard of, the couple usually loving each other's company too much to do anything like that apart. She tried to explain to Matt that she just wanted to clear her mind. To herself, she felt as though someone was trying to send her a message of some kind, but they would not come out into the open and she could not hear it clearly. It was unclear and shifting, and she could not explain it to Matt, because she feared she would sound like a mad person.

Late one night, Matt was woken by her talking loudly and urgently in her sleep. She sounded distressed and worried but was speaking in SiSwati, sounding like she was asking about something. He turned over and placed his hand softly on her shoulder, feeling the warmth of her body through her nightie. He gently woke her up, then put his arm around her to comfort her, thinking it was just a strange dream. Khanyi suddenly sat up, opened her eyes wide and exclaimed, 'I have seen a shoe Matt. It is somebody's shoe, but it's just lost. It's lying down. Matt, the shoe has become lost, it's not supposed to be there. Why is it there by itself?'

She was not making any sense. He sat up beside her, switched on the bedside light and looked at her closely. She was awake now but looked confused. He held her until her breathing slowed and she calmed down, but she was still taking deep breaths and seemed to be muddled, as one sometimes is after waking from a very deep dream. He spoke to her gently. 'Khanyi love, I think you were having a bad dream. I heard you talking in SiSwati and asking someone about something, but it wasn't clear. Are you alright?'

She nodded, but her eyes were bright and tearful, and she hugged him tightly back, unable to properly explain what had happened. She wept, recalling it. 'There was a shoe, Matt. I could see a shoe lost somewhere, and someone was crying for it, but it was dark, and they could not see it. I don't know why it upset me, but something was wrong.'

He got up and went off to make her some tea, came back with it, gave her a kiss, and put his arm around her, thinking how beautiful she was in her nightie, even when her eyes were red and hair was messed up. He lay back down, holding her close, and she gradually relaxed, fell back to sleep and slept the rest of the night. Khanyi seemed to have forgotten about it by the morning, and over breakfast he asked her, 'Do you remember what you were dreaming about last night?'

'Hau! Me, Matt? Was I dreaming! What did I say?'

Matt gave her a look and glanced at PJ, saying he would explain it later. PJ had sharp little ears and he didn't want her to hear about the dream in case it upset her too.

Khanyisile followed him out a few minutes later with a cup of tea, taking it to him in the workshops. Standing in his overalls, he explained to her what she had said. He played down how upset she had seemed, but told her about the shoe she had described seeing. Pieces of her dream came back to her as he spoke, but in the bright sunshine the images seemed less intense and much less fearful. She was puzzled about why he hadn't wanted to ask her about it in front of PJ.

That question nagged at her and added to the air of uncertainty swirling around her, wondering what this odd dream could mean, but she trusted her husband and for the next few days felt better. It seemed for a while as though the cloud had been lifted from their home.

Two weeks after this, the Bartons had been out for an evening with friends, leaving their home in the care of Knox and the roaming dogs, and had driven back quite late, after a pleasant dinner with Tarryn and Frikkie. They drew up in front of the house and Matt gently lifted Pumi Jacqueline, fast asleep, out of the back of the car and carried her into her bedroom. She barely stirred.

They were both feeling content, full and tired and, after making love until they were too tired to continue, the young couple drifted off to sleep easily, satiated, close together and happy. In the early hours of the morning, the dream came for a second time, but this time it was stronger and more intense. Khanyi awoke, feeling unsure of what had happened, unable to tell reality from her dream for a few moments of terror. The disturbance woke Matt, who was watching her, deeply concerned.

'I must tell you before I forget, before everything becomes confused. I saw her shoe Matt, one of PJ's little sandals, the ones with flowers, one of her shoes, one of them is lost!'

She seemed to be upset out of all proportion to the event, and Matt put his arm around her shoulders and pulled her closer. He tried to rationalise the dream to her, a good intention that quickly went awry and did anything but calm her down.

'You have probably been thinking of all the times she loses them because we went out? She's always losing her shoes, Khanyi. Remember she left them once at Joao's house, and she left one at pre-school, and lost one somewhere in the garden until Ndephete found it. I'm sure you've just been thinking about that.'

'No, it's not that, no!' Khanyi replied, heatedly. 'The shoe is on its own, it's alone, it's just by itself somewhere. She never lost it, Matt. It's just one by itself lying somewhere. She didn't lose her shoes. One of her shoes is somewhere. Why is it there, how did it get there? Why is it there?'

She could not see where it was lying. It felt to her as though it was shrouded by a heavy mist, and she couldn't recall or describe the surroundings with any clarity. She was only certain that it wasn't any place that they had been to together, and that something in the atmosphere around there had scared her and felt wrong. The surroundings swirled vaguely around her mind with half discerned images of hills and trees, but it was shadowy and dark. She could not feel anyone there or perceive anything properly. She was not even sure about what she thought she could see but sensed that she needed to be careful. She just felt strongly that it was somewhere bad, and something about it felt wrong: a place steeped in evil, or with some harmful presence nearby. The image had frightened her.

Matt gently tried to get her to talk about it more, to understand better, but he could not get her to provide more details than what she had tried to describe. It was obviously upsetting her, and he had grown to respect these inexplicable omens, even without understanding them, whenever his wife had them. He could also remember some strange dreams he had experienced in the past: the feeling of seeing something through someone else's eyes. For a second time he tried to calm her down, and offered to go and make a drink, but this time she refused to let him leave her. She wrapped herself in a blanket like a Mosotho and padded along behind him into the kitchen, standing close to him as they waited for the kettle to boil. She snuggled up to him and talked into his chest, tapping on his shoulder to emphasise each point.

'Matt, it feels like that time when the owl came. It felt like that time…' She could not talk any more or unwrap the vision any further than that. It reminded her of that fateful day. Eventually they tired of talking about the dream and began randomly discussing various normal day things. Her fear gave way to tiredness and, as the deep mauve sky began to lighten and the wild birds of the bushveld began heralding the dawn, they returned to their bedroom, kissed each other and fell asleep again.

For a few more weeks after this, Khanyi was left undisturbed, and life continued uneventfully. Then the dream returned for a third time, in its full malevolence, this time invading her mind at two in the morning, far more intensely than before.

Matt was woken abruptly by a high, keening noise, and once again, Khanyisile was crying in her sleep beside him. But she didn't wake up normally this time, and couldn't shake her mind free of the image she had been shown. She tended to dream in SiSwati, and in her dream state the first words she said were in her own language. She had only partially come back into the world with him and kept repeating something about '*Sicatulo ihlekile, sicatulo hlekile*, the shoe is lost, why is it thrown away? Why is it alone without the other one?' It were as though her spirit had travelled around in some other time and wandered around without her, seeing things she could not see, but teasing and tormenting her with the things it could see. She knew this time, without any doubt, that it was a message of some sort. Matt did his best to comfort her, but this time she was forceful and explained it more clearly.

'I'm being troubled, Matt. I'm being troubled at night. The ancestors are troubling me. Three times I have been troubled and woken by this dream. I need to talk with Teresinha so we can pray. She is going to help me. What I see is one of her shoes. Her favourite ones. It is lying somewhere in a forest. I can see the shoe, but they won't allow me to see anything more. I don't know what it means, but I am scared to sleep.'

She feared that the next dream would be even worse.

Teresinha was the wife of their pastor Joao, and a close confidante of Khanyi's. She trusted her wisdom and her spirituality was strong and pronounced. She was a wise, gentle and beautiful woman and Khanyi confided in her over many things.

'Matt,' she said. 'Matt, I am sure now. I know this thing exactly. It is one of PJ's shoes. It's her favourite sandals, those pink ones with flowers on them. I can see it lying in a forest, somewhere dark and green, but there are some beams of light shining down. It is not supposed to be there, there is something to do with PJ in that place.'

She could not lie still, too disturbed by the strength of her vision, by something unseen and creeping, corrupting the air around her family. She was restless and walked quietly into their daughter's bedroom where the little girl lay sleeping peacefully, unaware of the drama surrounding her. Khanyi stood in the doorway, leaning against the comforting solidity of the painted metal door frame, watching their beloved daughter and listening to the soft noises she made while sleeping. Why was her sleep being disrupted?

The comforting, peaceful sound of a young child's breathing in a deep sleep affected her unexpectedly. It made her heart ache and brought tears to her eyes, thinking of what she had lost those years before: the two children she had loved then, almost as her own, and the life she had been used to and emerged from, something almost forgotten now.

PJ's golden-brown hair was spread like a tangled glowing wave across the pillow. Her mother walked noiselessly across the carpeted floor, gently opened the cupboard and saw the pair of favourite sandals visible in the dim glow of her night light. One lay on its side where it had been kicked off and come to rest, the other was lying on its sole where it should be. She kissed her child, watched her stir slightly in her sleep and felt strangely reassured that both shoes were there.

She found it hard to explain to Matt why this dream mattered so much, but she knew it carried a message that in some way affected them, but could not see how it connected, or what it meant to them. The message that came to her was not in any words, not even in the language of her childhood, but there were words associated with this dream, and in some way she believed there were people connected to it, and there was something about these people that upset her. They floated, distant and defiant, lurking in the dark shadows of her worst memories. It felt like a threat, as though they were waiting for an opportunity to bring some harm to the family. As a Christian, Khanyi would no longer consult traditional healers, but she felt sorely tempted to do so and believed that they would be able to explain to her what these dreams meant, by consulting with her ancestors. Even Teresinha could not do that.

She could not go back to sleep that night, but instead woke up completely, bathed and dressed and started preparing breakfast while the household was still sleeping. There was a nagging premonition that something far off was moving towards their home, and that it would affect them. Something unclear, evil and frightening was hanging onto the edges of the images she was troubled by, tangled in them like a creeper choking a tree, and she was deeply troubled by it. There was no way of preparing for it, and no way of knowing what it was. Something had disturbed the peace of her house.

Matt had learnt to respect these messages she occasionally received. He had stopped being sceptical several years back. He could not understand them, but he understood her, and loved her more than he would ever love anyone. He figured that, whilst he couldn't address the problem, what he could do would be to support her, reassuring her that he would always be there for her. In a way it did go some way to making her feel better. He did his best but felt blindfolded.

Khanyi also took some comfort from the dogs. Most of them had been there as youngsters when she received that fateful phone call, all those years ago. She would reach down and stroke one of the dogs, holding its warm body between her hands and stroking its ears and head. They would look up and she would gaze into their warm eyes. They stared back at her with their soft brown eyes, not sure of what they were supposed to be doing but enjoying the sudden display of affection. The older ones wondered what was making her behave like this; it was unexpected. She was always kind to them but was very seldom sentimental over them.

Chapter 8

Wilmot Mawelela

THE WELDING WORK WOULD STILL come in from time, but there were gaps when Matt found insufficient work, and he began to worry about the periods between jobs with no income, and started to look around for other kinds of work, putting out the word that he was keen to assist businesses in any way he could. Khanyisile helped, making use of her extended family network, and they created an email flyer together, and sent it to many different companies.

One morning, he got a call from a farm manager in Malkerns, a Mr Nelson Nhlengetwa, who sounded young over the phone, politely asking if he would come and look at some spraying equipment that had been broken or was badly rusted and needed replacement. The caller's voice was polite, educated and rather plaintive.

'Hello, Mr Button?'

'Yes, Matt Barton speaking,'

He had long since stopped trying to tell people he was Mr Barton, not Button.

'Okay yes, aah thanks, Mr. Button. We are facing a problem here in Malkerns with many of our crop sprayers. Some of the spray booms and mountings are becoming old now, and apparently they are also corroded' (he pronounced the word with great distaste, as though it was something unclean).

'Now, we keep repairing them, but they can easily fail at any time, then we cannot spray on certain days, and we fall behind the spray schedule and it is affecting the crop. If we fail to adhere to the application programme, it reduces the crop size.'

He hesitated, then went on, clearly troubled. 'We have to find someone to make some new booms and replace them, but it is not easy to do this properly. We are failing to find the right somebody who can build them for us. Sometimes our own workshops try to repair them, but then they become too heavy, and then also leak and they give other problems. We have heard that you might do this work and are hopeful that you can come and inspect, then see if you can make replacements for us?'

Matt looked at the blank pages in his diary and set a date and time, then rang off, thinking ahead already to take a tape measure and a few other items to help him make suitable measurements. He wasn't familiar with the agricultural equipment that Nelson was describing and wanted to see these booms for himself before deciding if he should repair, or try to rebuild them. Metalwork, piping and fabrication did not worry him, but he suspected they would not have any proper drawings to work from, so he might have to take many measurements and make his own versions to size. He only had a vague idea of what Nelson meant.

He asked Khanyi if she knew the things Nelson was describing, but she had not heard of them.

Malkerns was a long drive from the lowveld, and he reached there after a few hours. When he reached the gate, the Security guard took down his details and summoned Nelson from the offices for him, and a young, slim, rather elegant gentleman in expensive trousers and very shiny pointed shoes came into sight wearing a pained expression. He introduced himself, extending his slender hand, and invited Matt into cool, air-conditioned offices. He explained that he was an agriculture graduate from the University and had been trying to improve the reliability of the spraying equipment for some time, but they were struggling with tired, old, corroded equipment that kept breaking down. He explained the process of spraying on fertilisers, ripeners and selective herbicides and the need for accurate and regular applications. He offered Matt a delicious, ice-cold glass of pineapple juice, something he had never tasted before. Then, suitably refreshed, they went out into the yard to see the equipment.

It was, if anything, even worse than Nelson had described. There were dozens of broken and bent booms, some lying in deep grass on old stands, and many old International tractors parked about on flat tyres or blocks. He seemed almost apologetic, but explained 'these are the old ones, the equipment we don't use anymore but we keep it for spares. Let me take you to the newer ones.'

The newer versions were somewhat better, each neatly parked in designated bays, but most of these also needed repairs. The years of exposure to fertilisers and chemicals, the effect of being exposed to the elements every day, and many seasons of working on bumpy fields, had fatigued the steel and, although they were originally well designed and strongly built, they were now badly cracked and in some cases there was precious little of the original steel left to repair. They were simple enough structures, with different sizes of stainless steel tubing, made up from sections that fitted together and stainless steel nozzle holders set at regular intervals along their length, with cables and turn buckles suspending them along their reach, enabling them to spray chemicals right to the middle of a pineapple panel and drench every plant thoroughly.

Matt looked carefully at the way they had been designed – the joins and careful gusseting, the support framework of square tubing and strengthening around the high stress areas – and began taking measurements and photographs with his phone. He could see where the problems lay.

Nelson helped him, pointing out the main weaknesses, but tip-toed through the grass and kept well away from the oil spills, pointing at the machinery at arm's length, keeping clean and avoiding ever actually touching any of the old equipment. He went on to explain some of the details about how they worked, how they would be towed out onto the estates and assembled in the field, and how many spraying cycles they had to do each day. He drew a pristine coral handkerchief out of his pocket and meticulously wiped any particles of dust from his fingertips.

There were nurse tankers and spray tankers, each numbered and with different jobs to do, and they made use of reservoirs and filling points scattered around the extensive estate. He was responsible for a fleet of these machines, all varying in age and used for applying many different farm chemicals. All the tankers and equipment had a distinctive smell, not unpleasant, but an odd mixture of water and years of fertiliser and farm use. None of them were new and finding someone local to build replacements had become problematic.

Matt found out that they were hoping to order five new boom sets and tractor mountings for the foliar fertiliser sprayers, and two others for herbicides and hormone applications. They differed in detail and in their nozzle sizes, and application rates, and were designed for different tractors, with a hydraulic framework mounted on the left side, and a stack of heavy counterweights on the opposite side to keep the machines level. It was a great deal of heavy fabrication for a one-man business to take on, but Matt knew that by now his assistant Musa would be able to help with a lot of the initial measuring and cutting, and could complete much of the down hand and straightforward mild steel structural welding work. When they went back inside, he asked Nelson what they had paid for the last replacement spray booms, and was surprised when he calmly took down a file and looked up the invoice amount, showing him that they had paid almost 154,000 Emalangeni for those particular boom replacements. He looked at the invoice and identified exactly what they had bought for that amount and felt they had been somewhat overcharged.

Matt finished writing down the plant numbers, the main details and quantities, and explained that he would need to do quite a lot of design work and material cost calculations before arriving at an accurate price. He promised to provide Nelson with a formal quote as early as possible the following week. Nelson stressed the urgency of the replacements, as their programme had fallen behind due to breakdowns, and he wanted to table an answer for a management meeting a fortnight away. He explained that he now had to leave and attend a budget meeting that would take up most of the remainder of the day, but stated that he would hand him over to the tractor yard foreman who could help him, a certain Maxwell Mawelela.

Nelson sent a driver to call him from the workshops. Mr. Mawelela arrived, a short, pleasant, weathered man of mature age who was duly introduced. Matt then thanked Nelson for his help, and they shook hands and parted on friendly terms. He had enjoyed the meeting.

Maxwell habitually wore a faded John Deere cap, and proved to be a quiet, rather subdued, but very willing man, his greying hair and curling moustache evidence of his years of experience. He proved extremely helpful, understanding quickly exactly what information was needed. He had an impressive knowledge of each item of his plant and equipment, and would readily point out to Matt the weaknesses and problems with each one, in detail. They took a great many accurate measurements together, Matt recording each dimension and design in his book. He took dozens of technical photographs, wanting to be sure he had fully understood all the different requirements, and noting onto which tractor plant numbers the different boom types and sizes fitted.

Over many years of service, the equipment had been modified and altered many times and they were no longer all the same, although they had started out as a pattern fitment. They now had a mixture of different pipe dimensions, and the details of their underslung mountings, hydraulic cylinders and cables varied from unit to unit. Some had been very badly repaired and patched.

Initially, his guide behaved very formally, being highly respectful towards him but, as he relaxed and opened up, Maxwell, although helpful and informative, was also proving to be an untapped well of the deepest gloom and despair, able to see the worst-case scenario in almost every possible conversation. Here was a man who seemed to thrive in a state of almost endless misery, and who was eager to point out to a new, unsuspecting victim every one of the many problems he faced. He had a slightly hoarse, high pitched voice, used to shouting to be heard over the noise of machinery in the field.

'You see these cracks, Mr Button?' He would point towards some of the worst offenders. 'This boom and the mounting is all fucked up now because of our drivers. They refuse to slow down when going over bumps, and they are too rough with them when taking them off. They just don't care. They are very kiddish in their behaviour.'

'Yes, Maxwell, I certainly can see the problem. The metal is very badly fatigued here, and it's been repaired too many times; that's why it's cracking. I wouldn't even be able to weld this again, the metal is too weak now, there is no good steel left,' replied Matt.

'Aish, Button, things here are bad, they are bad, very, very bad. It's almost hopeless for us now, Mr Button. In fact, on my side, from what I can see, it's really a disaster. It means these tractors cannot spray, and now they will just waste the soluble urea, which cost us a lot of money to buy, then the crop is going to be ruined and will fail to grow because it does not get enough fertiliser, even if the weeds can be controlled…'

'Yes, I can see that it would be a big problem', said Matt, unsure what comment was expected of him but hoping to stem the flow. Maxwell, however, was only just getting started, relishing the opportunity of pouring out his troubles to this new, understanding and evidently sympathetic visitor. Maxwell was still warming to the task before him.

'Button, then it means even when it comes time to harvest, we cannot harvest, why? Because there will be no fruit for the harvesters, not even golf balls, then it means the crop will be lost and will be a disaster. It will be a complete failure. Then you can imagine our bosses are going to be even more angry towards us and the company will be closed, because we no more have pineapples. So, it will be terrible for the region, the jobs will be lost and all over the region there will be desolation. In fact, Button, it will be a catastrophe.'

Matt nodded in sympathy and agreement, thinking the diatribe complete, but Maxwell continued, slowly but inexorably building up to a full head of steam, revelling in his melancholy theme of impending doom and expanding it to depict a life of constant wretchedness and despair.

'Even when we visit our homes in the rural areas, then it means our wives will come to us asking for money, but we will have no money because we have no income. Then they will demand money from us and quarrel with us and they will always be barking like dogs. There will be conflict in the different regions and even in our homes. Others may leave, or will run away with their boyfriends and it may happen they steal our furniture, our blankets and even our double mattress, even TVs, and our children will also be starving, those still remaining alive, because we have no money for food, then it means they also can never survive because they need food for nourishment. Nobody is going to be there to cook for them. You will find us sitting at home like a chicken looking at the trees, with no children, all because of these drivers. They are the ones to blame for our misery.'

Matt was by this stage, beginning to feel a bit lost and disheartened himself, caught up in all the mayhem and chaos, adrift in the tumult, drowning slowly in the dark angry seas of despair and hopelessness that Maxwell was describing with such relish. Clutching at a straw, desperate for a glimmer of light in the gloom, he forced himself to struggle to the surface, against the relentless onslaught. He cheerfully tried to muster some semblance of hope.

'Well, that's why I'm here, Maxwell, to try and sort them all out for you and make new ones so that those things won't happen anymore!'

But Maxwell shook his head despairingly, as though suddenly filled with woe at the visitor's failure to grasp the extent and full history of machinery abuse.

'Aah, Mr Button, it's good to be ever hopeful, it's good you are here, but many others have tried before, and all have failed. It will never last. Our farm manager Mr. Edmond Carmichael used to work with us here. He tried many times in 2003 but then after some time he left. They want to destroy everything, even before you complete repairing one you find they have destroyed another one. When I ask them to be more careful, they tell me I must keep quiet because I am not a driver. They don't want to listen to me and tell me to stop making noise. We are all of us going to die here because of this. Others will starve. Soon there will be no more pineapples and all of us will be sitting at home looking at trees. Some may also become mad. Even if we sell our cattle we will still be left with nothing.'

He shook his head even more hopelessly, as though the very worst outcome was inevitable. Sitting around looking at the trees, prior to dying of starvation and neglect seemed to be a recurring theme of Mr Mawelela, a calming vision of his that mentally encompassed his personal world view, aligning perfectly with his two key topics: despair and utter hopelessness. It was an ethos that he lived by.

He reminded Matt of the gloomy gardener he had inherited from his late brother's household, the old man Ndephete, who took a similarly dismal view on life in general. Matt smiled to himself, thinking that if ever the two men were to meet, they could be miserable together, swap notes and become good company for each other, comparing respective levels of despair. Thinking about such a meeting lifted his spirits somewhat. Ndephete would grizzle about worthless, unreliable, falsehearted Chinese lawnmowers, and Maxwell would complain about drivers ruining tractors, breaking pumps, starving the crop of valuable nutrients and taking away their livelihood.

He tried to change the subject as they went around the machinery, still carefully noting down layouts, dimensions and plant numbers, making detailed sketches where necessary to record the pulley heights and hydraulic cylinder fittings. He kept noticing other faults – oil leaks, damaged rims, broken seats, weeping seals and different problems that were nothing to do with the sprayers, but issues that also needed repairing – and wondered if he should mention these to Maxwell. He quickly thought better of it. Maxwell was wholly focused on the damage caused by drivers, age and neglect, and it wouldn't be helpful to make him aware of any other problems he had missed. In a moment of inspiration, Matt changed tack, venturing hastily towards what he hoped would be a safer, more positive topic. He asked bravely, 'So anyway, Maxwell, have you got children yourself?'

He nodded. 'I'm having children,'

'Are they schooling and how old are they?'

'I'm having three, two are still schooling down in Shiselweni, the other one is pregnant at home and left her education now in Form Three. They are very troublesome children, very much problematic. They are not clever, and they don't want to listen to their teachers. Both the girls only like boys and TV, and the boy one he is interested in football and music only. The other one is standard seven, the other one is standard five.'

Then he stopped. 'But why do you still call me Maxwell, Mr Matt?' They were on first name terms now.

Matt looked at him, taken aback by the change of direction and rather startled. 'But, but Nelson said, when we met, he said you were…'

'I am not Maxwell, Mr. Matt, that is not my real name'.

'I'm very sorry…er, Mr. Mawelela, but when Nelson introduced you to me this morning in the office, that was the name he gave me, and that was what he called you, so I sort of understood it to be your name.'

'Yes, Mr Matt, what you are saying it's a true, but Maxwell is not my name. Here on the farm they call me Maxwell, but I am actually Wilmot. My true name is Wilmot, but here they are used to calling me by Maxwell.'

This seemed to be another grievance in his life, and he explained with a mournful expression that when he came to work there at first, on Monday the 3rd of August 1987 (he remembered the exact date), the clerk writing names of workers for some reason recorded his name as Maxwell, even though he was Wilmot. Then, when he tried to ask them to change it he was told by the Personnel and the Farm Manager Mr. Pierre Van de Walt (who was now late after dying in 2002 from a snake bite), to keep quiet or he would not get any job, so then he became Maxwell. The clerk did not want to mess up his register and admit to a mistake. He still felt aggrieved by this and had never forgiven Van de Walt.

'But have you been to see Nelson about this? Can't Nhlengetwa change it now you are the foreman?' asked Matt.

Wilmot began again, his voice rising in heated indignation as another sore point had evidently been disturbed and poked. 'If I make that utterance it means they are going to punish me. They will make a big hoolabala and tell me to go home, because the drivers already they like complaining about me. Many times, they say I am too harsh (he pronounced it hush) and because I am hush the unions no more want me to stay here, claiming I frequently make noise against them which is not true, it's a blue lie! Even Nelson himself, even if he is the manager, you can find he is the same one who can refuse if I tell him I no more wish to be called Maxwell. He will argue and tell me that I am supposed to be Maxwell since I have long been working here as Maxwell. He claims it will confuse the workers if I become Wilmot.'

Matt decided suddenly that, no matter what he might have missed, he had taken enough measurements, and felt that he could no longer survive under the African tsunami of Wilmot's depressing outlook on life, although he had grown to like the man. What he didn't know he would have to guess at, but one way or another he was finished and had had enough. He asked for Wilmot's phone number, in case he needed any further information about the ageing tractors, tanks and sprayers.

He wished him well, trying to hide his relief, and asked as they parted near the car park, 'What would you like me to call you, Wilmot?'

'It's still better if you can call me by Maxwell,' said Wilmot dejectedly. 'But if you come again, if I am still alive by then, maybe you can bring me a size 8 Gumboot. They always issue me with a size 9 here which is not my size, I use a size 8. I have told them this many times. Every year I tell them to write it on that paper, but they refuse giving me my correct size if I ask them. They say I am supposed to take size 9 since I am a man and it's written size nine on those papers, from last time.'

He then embarked on a whole new narrative, explaining that ever since 2007 he had been asking for a size 8, and a thirty-eight inch overall, but Matt really didn't want to start a fresh conversation about this new issue involving protective clothing, so he just said he would try.

As he drove out of the valley, the strong smell of citrus hung in the air near the canning plant, and he could see bright coloured long yellow and orange piles, hundreds of tons of fruit lying in the sun waiting to be processed, juiced or segmented and canned. He looked out across the rolling fields of thousands of evenly growing pineapple plants, vigorous and strong, so healthy looking that their long leaves shone almost blue under their deep green, and realised that he had a new respect for what went into growing the spikey plants and their spectacular fruit. He hoped he could win some of the business and began thinking ahead, his mind racing over several different options, and how best he could approach such a big piece of fabrication work. He began to think about making up a jig. They all fitted onto similar tractors. Once he had made up a jig for the first of the five booms, he felt that he would be able to build the remainder quite quickly, even with his small staff of one. The technical side of his mind began to furiously think about different materials, the positioning of gussets, the welding techniques he would need for stainless steel pipes, the wall thickness needed for the tubes and how to seal them off and embed them neatly into one another.

Cutting and drilling materials like that was going to be hard. It would mean importing a lot of special steel stock, and some materials and gases he seldom used, some of which were costly. He thought of his connection at the sugar mill, the highly competent store manager Amos Gule, and how he would revel in handling an order as complicated as this. He decided, as he drove along, that it would be best to leave the complicated matter of handling the purchase, importation and delivery all up to Amos, as he would know best what was entailed, and where to source such specialised things from. He would have to spend some time drawing up a detailed technical list of items required.

He began to feel confident about how he could fabricate the booms, each to the right dimensions and in a fairly short time. As the afternoon faded away behind him, he drove along the same quiet road he had first used, the very first time he had driven from the airport to the house. Seeing it under the headlights again reminded him of that tormented trip, the sense of the unknown, the sorrow, the foreboding, and the feeling of loss he had been carrying with him that evening, all those years ago, flying out to the Kingdom as a single man to finalise his older brother's affairs and close up the household, and deal with the sale of his assets and any other matters arising.

He remembered going through the files and documents in the study and finding that Galloway Consulting had been a thriving concern with considerable value tied up in property and investments. He thought of how he had marvelled at the house they lived in, so much finer than his own, and had admired the well-tended gardens that surrounded their home.

He had never expected to meet someone like Khanyi, or to fall in love with her. Had never imagined that in his new life he would meet and befriend unusual, colourful people like Joao, or his beautiful wife Teresinha, or the booming, capable and always upbeat Gabriel Dlamini, who had become like a combination uncle and father to him. He had driven into an unknown world that evening, with no inkling that he would one day become a father, or would one day have had his settled life turned upside down by a daughter, who had effortlessly changed all his priorities. He drove along slowly, carefully watching for straying zebra, cattle and guinea fowl along the roadside. Finally he turned into the familiar dirt road, and driving between the neat sugar cane fields with their tall stands of perfectly even stalks, he soon heard again the lazy tsk… tsk… tsk… sound of overhead sprinklers, making their endless circular sweeps of irrigation and splattering onto the sides and windscreen of the bakkie, drumming loudly on the roof, the warm canal water washing away clean patches in the dust. He began thinking about seeing Khanyi again, and how just being away for one day he had missed her. They were steadily working at their small business, something of value that they were building together. There were moments when he would still occasionally sense his late brother's presence near him, but it was a reassuring presence, and he had begun to feel as much a part of the homestead as they had been, when it was their home. He missed Patrick often and wished he could talk to him again.

Chapter 9

Cold Amos

MATT WORKED ON HIS LIST for a full day, at one stage even calling on his old storeman Salikh in the UK, to ask for his advice and check on some complicated welding rod specifications. He had all his measurements and made some allowances for inevitable wastage and unused lengths of pipe, gradually assembling an accurate list of his requirements, so that he could arrive at a bill of sales and a costing. Most of what he needed to buy was mild steel plate, in various thicknesses, but he also had to have some bushes machined, and pins turned for him on a lathe, and for this he needed the cooperation of a machine shop. He knew that some of what he needed would probably be materials that Amos and his buyers had never ordered before, but he had learned to put faith in their diverse list of contacts and suppliers. Amos was buying for agricultural stores, mechanical stores, several small villages, and a whole industry with its own specific needs, and there were relatively few items that he had never ordered before. His list of contact numbers was long, and his knowledge of suppliers immense. Situated where he was, miles from any hardware suppliers, Matt had no other option. He made an appointment, and the following morning drove into the tiny town and parked outside the stores for his meeting.

He was asked to wait in the office while they called Amos, but was surprised to see him emerge from the darkened stores interior, as tall and lugubrious as ever, but looking far bulkier than his usual self. He was wearing a full-length padded jacket with a furry collar and a thick long sleeved jersey underneath, and with his heavy trousers seemed to be dressed for severe cold. They greeted each other and he asked politely, in the English way, if the stores manager was feeling cold.

Matt had barely noticed it, but Amos explained that, with the changing of the seasons as they moved into Autumn (a barely discernible change of temperature in the warm lowveld), he sensed that the weather had taken an unexpected turn for the worse.

'Extreme precautions must be taken, Mr Barton, proper precautions, to prevent the onset of critical diseases and winter chills. Hence warm attire is called for. As it grows colder, I am protecting myself by maintaining my core temperature at all times.'

He folded his long slender fingers over each other and rested his skinny clasped brown hands on a pile of no less than six desk calendars given to him by suppliers, a symbol of seniority that he rotated every month. He was ready for business.

The thermometer had indeed dipped below eighteen degrees C sometime before the dawn that day, for the first time in the season, and to Amos this bitterly cold snap required special precautionary measures, so he had dressed for the intense cold. He was extremely fearful of flu and other ailments, and detested taking time off for illness. He took various medications each day to keep the virus at bay. With little spare flesh on his body, he felt the cold acutely and seldom moved far away from a heater during winter.

Matt was wearing a lightweight short sleeved shirt, and had only put on long trousers that day out of respect for Amos, specifically for their meeting, and he could barely comprehend how hot he would feel under several thick layers of clothing and a full-length winter jacket.

Amos, however, still seemed to feel chilly, despite his layers of clothing, and had closed all the windows in his office to prevent any chance of fresh air penetrating his personal cigarette smoke atmosphere. The office was close, smoky and warm, and Matt subtly peered under the desk to check if the three-bar heater was on, as Amos often had it switched on, radiating immense heat towards his crotch all day, but to his relief found that it was not 'that cold' yet.

The stores manager kindly ordered Matt a tray of tea, and asked how he was doing, and then gave his usual business greeting with a smile, 'and how may I be of assistance to you, Mr Barton?'

Matt explained the situation, and the nature of the client, and presented him with the neatly typed list, with carefully tabulated dimensions and thicknesses. Amos Gule ran down the items with his little finger, finished at the end with an extremely long fingernail that he used as a marker.

He went down the list, 'this material, those pipes, these nozzle holders I have in stock, these items I regret I am unfamiliar with and will need additional clarity from yourself, these other items I am aware of them but we have not had them in stock; they will require a special order.'

He also explained that he would have to add a small surcharge as the purchases were external and being made on behalf of another company. There were some sales tax implications.

Matt explained that he was working to a difficult deadline, as the client wanted his quote as soon as possible, and Amos understood fully. He would prepare all the pricing as quickly as he could.

'Do not be overly concerned Mr Barton, you will have my full cooperation. I will apply my mind to the task at hand and will also call for the efforts of my buyers, so that we can respond with urgency to your needs. It will be a pleasure to assist you.'

He went on to explain that, unless there were delays, he anticipated having all the pricing complete by the following day and, owing to the complexity of the items and the rarity of some of them, suggested that Matt return in person the following afternoon, confident that by then he would have secured pricing for all the items, and would have checked on their availability.

Matt was delighted and thanked him profusely, then eagerly escaped, gasping for fresh air as he emerged from the warm, smoke-filled office.

He knew Amos Gule and trusted his abilities implicitly. He knew that the phone lines would be heating up already as he contacted a number of key suppliers simultaneously, ruthlessly tasking them with getting back to him very rapidly with prices and threatening to contact alternative agents. He had once been a silent witness in the office when Mr Gule phoned a steel supplier from Middelburg who had failed to deliver some special steam piping on time, delaying a major upgrade in the mill and setting an entire capital maintenance project back by several weeks. He remained scrupulously polite and never raised his voice – if anything, speaking even more softly than usual – but had slowly, eloquently, and formally torn the unfortunate man to shreds. Matt recalled that they had ended the conversation with the supplier, a Mr Labuschagne, accepting a 20% reduction in the agreed price, waiving all delivery costs, and undertaking to ensure that the pipe steel was delivered on Saturday afternoon, even though he would have to drive the truck himself.

Matt could think of no one better to secure him the best possible pricing, and arrange the fastest delivery, and he drove back, remembering the other Amos he knew, throwing off his inhibitions, joyfully dancing at their wedding, and how pale his skin was under his long sleeved shirts and baggy straight cut trousers. He decided that if he were awarded the contract, he would have to buy him a present to thank him for all his efforts. He knew Gule loved all things British and began thinking what a suitable gift might be.

He obtained all the quotes by the end of the week, as promised, and was able to supply the farm manager Nhlengetwa with firm pricing for the replacement booms. He was able to offer keen pricing, having realised that all but one of the tractors' mounting brackets had almost identical dimensions, with their securing bolts and pins in the same positions. To speed up the production of replacements, he had devised a jig that would enable Musa to help him produce a universal boom mounting that could be fitted to several tractors, with only minimal dimensional changes. This meant he could produce them fast, probably completing one every three days if the machined bushes came on time. The booms themselves were relatively easy, it was mainly the spacing and drilling into stainless steel that was difficult, but he could get around that.

He factored in some time for delays, and felt he could back himself, knowing what he could achieve in a day. Musa had become a skilled assistant, fully capable of handling all the cutting and preparation work, much of the more straightforward down hand welding and fabrication, and much of the initial assembly, leaving Matt to handle the vertical and overhead welds, the unusual materials, and the stainless steel pipework and trunnion mountings for the hydraulics.

Nelson Nhlengetwa was delighted that he had pricing in time for his meeting, and phoned back immediately afterwards, advising Khanyi that they were awarding the work to Galloway Consulting. With that news to hand, Matt initiated the large order, and Amos began ordering all the materials he had priced, stressing the need for urgent delivery, and the local supply chain and small workshops swung rapidly into action.

Matt worked on the fabrications with Musa for several weeks and sent the finished items up to Malkerns on a truck, then drove up there again to help install them. They all fitted, and he stayed to commission them, pleased and relieved that they were put straight into work, replacing the old, corroded, original mountings and spray booms. Nelson phoned to inform him that he was delighted, and that the work had been very well received. He even remembered to take Wilmot a pair of size 8 gumboots and was convinced he saw muscles that had seldom been used before come to life, when the man briefly smiled.

Six weeks later, after Galloway consulting had the best trading month ever, Amos Gule received a package, hand delivered by Musa, covered in British stamps. This contained a big box of Yorkshire tea, Scottish shortbread, and a set of DVDs of the best of British scenery, stately gardens and historical buildings.

Chapter 10

The Missing

IT WAS A DAY LIKE any other. Warm, balmy, with scattered clouds, their bushveld life meandering along its usual path under the sun. It was three months to the day after Khanyi's last dream. PJ and her best friend were playing in the garden outside. The dogs had been banished from the children's game, and had retreated, deeply offended and in some disgrace, finding shady places or digging hollows and lying close to the workshops at the rear of the house, near to their master who was busy grinding and cutting steel under the shelter, making a very loud noise. The animals were fuzzily aggrieved at being excluded from the girls' game, but they kept trampling over all their carefully built arrangements, knocking over miniature trees carefully stuck into the soil, and destroying the miniature homes and paths the girls had carefully created next to the driveway. Then when they lay down on the picnic blankets and refused to move, PJ had become cross with them, admonished them sternly and sent them all away. They'd gazed at her mournfully and moved. Usually they liked to lie where they could see her.

When PJ's young nanny, Nomsa, went outside to call the children in from the sun, wanting to give them both some juice and a snack, normally both little ones would arrive quickly, but this time only Charmayne came to the kitchen. She was PJ's dearest playmate and friend, Tarryn's daughter.

Young children are infuriatingly vague, and when she was asked where Mpumelelo was, Tarryn at first shrugged and said she didn't know, because she was thirsty and wanted her drink, then, when she did begin to explain, she left out the most important part of what she had seen. Nomsa wanted to go and call Khanyi, who was busy working in the office, but Charmayne told the nanny solemnly that PJ had told her Auntie Khanyi was, 'Busy doing her office work today and they mustn't 'sturb her'.

The nanny then began again, asking Tarryn more seriously where PJ was but, when she could not explain this exactly, Nomsa thought she must still be playing their game outside somewhere. She went out again, to look properly, and when she realised that the child was nowhere close by, that was the first any adult knew of PJ's disappearance. At that point, Nomsa decided to interrupt and notify Khanyi anyway, once she was sure she could not locate PJ, but she was a little frightened to tell her. The two women first made a quick search all over the house, then jogged around quickly outside, in separate directions, going right around the house because sometimes the girls played under the shelter of small trees and in the flower beds, and they thought PJ might have fallen asleep somewhere. Then Khanyi checked with the gardener if he had seen her, as she sometimes used to visit him and talk to him. He had not seen her since earlier that morning when they'd both came out to play. In the way in which these things play out, Khanyi ran around to where Matt was, asking him, more urgently now, 'Matt, is PJ with you?'

But she was not.

She sat down and asked Charmayne to tell them all that she knew, but this proved to be difficult. She began telling her version of events in a roundabout fashion, unaware of how serious it was, or what it might mean. Then, as she began to explain further, frustratingly slowly, in the vague sporadic way of most small children, some disturbing elements of the story emerged. The two women hung on every word, trying not to interrupt.

The two girls had been playing together all that morning, ever since Charmayne was dropped off by Tarryn, and they were in the garden together, walking around under the shady trees, building imaginary homes and dragging around behind them an old picnic blanket, filled with all their dolls and toys, and some precious stones, special sticks and leaves. They were playing a little distance from each other, talking to each other, and putting on different voices for the characters in their make-believe world, but Charmayne was closer to the house than PJ, who was playing down near the gate. Her dolly was very tired and needed to sleep, but she was being naughty, so she was putting it to bed. She was busy covering her in leaves and ticking her off.

She heard a vehicle driving up slowly on the road outside, and a man had got out, who had called softly to PJ and spoken to her over the gate. She went towards him, then before the dogs could even run around from the workshops at the other side of the house, PJ had turned round and called to Charmayne that she was getting some vetkoek for them both. He had some in the car.

She knew they were not allowed to open the gate, and they had not done so, but when Khanyi asked her what happened next, desperately trying to keep the panic out of her voice and trying to stay calm, the little girl explained that she saw a big man suddenly reach over, grab her arms and quickly lift her over the gate and into their bakkie.

Khanyi felt as though her heart had suddenly stopped, her blood grew cold and her skin prickled. She looked at the nanny with flashing, accusing eyes, 'Where's my child? What has happened to her?' her voice rose, and became sharper, and their questioning switched languages, and quickly became too rapid and intense for the little girl. She began to feel scared of Khanyi and started crying. Then Nomsa started crying too. Khanyi could not contain her sense of fear and foreboding and it was coming out in her voice and her body language. She couldn't blame anyone but needed to be angry with someone. She stood up, terrified and increasingly exasperated but realised she could get nothing more meaningful from Charmayne, who kept talking nonsense about all her sick babies and bears going to hospital.

Charmayne was also weeping now, loudly, because she sensed something bad had happened but didn't know what she had done wrong. Khanyi gave her a hug and walked outside, her hands shaking and heart racing. She could not stay in the room there for another minute. She ran outside to call Matt and told him that Pumi Jacqueline was missing, and Charmayne knew something more about it but wasn't explaining properly.

Matt dropped everything and came in, took in the scene rapidly and surprised both women by immediately picking up Charmayne and carrying her out of the house and into the garden, away from both the crying women, trying to keep his voice steady, talking away to her calmly and softly about trivial things, and trying his best to stay clear headed and not let the fear or tension show in his voice.

'Charmayne, my lovely, please show me where you were playing with PJ,' he said. She sat cradled in his left arm, her legs around his waist and her little backside resting on his forearm, clinging onto his shoulder. Then she wiped away her tears and led him to where their dollies, toys and bears all lay in a carefully arranged scene. She showed him her special 'hopspital' for sick bears, and then showed him where PJ had been playing, and all her dollies and the house they were making. He tried to keep his voice casual and gently asked her more direct questions. Gradually, a little more substance began to clothe the bare bones of the abduction.

The little blonde girl thought indistinctly that the man who first spoke to her might have had a small beard, but when he asked her for more details she just gazed up at Matt with her serious blue eyes, then shrugged her shoulders, and couldn't tell him if he was tall or short, pale skinned or dark, or what he wore, just that the other bigger man had lifted PJ up very fast, pulling on her arms.

They had put PJ in the bakkie, slammed the door and then driven away even before the dogs started barking, and when they all came galloping up, panting with excitement after running round from the back of the house there was nothing to see but dust and the faint noise of a vehicle driving away. They lay down around her, unsure of what had happened, then soon after that Nomsa called them inside for juice.

Charmayne, with a small child's logic, asked Matt why PJ had gone somewhere in a car by herself, and then, sensing that she had maybe mentioned the bad thing, this triggered a new chain of thought and she told him that all her babies were sleeping under some leaves, and maybe PJ was there too, but because they were sick they mustn't be disturbed, and she then told him that one of them was very sick and had to have medicine, and that PJ was being the doctor because she was the only one who could cure them. She was rambling, as though by saying more she would make the grown-up feel better.

Matt surmised that it had all happened very recently. It seemed to be shortly after the car had gone, that the nanny had gone outside to call them in for their juice. Nomsa, when she was questioned said she ran around the garden outside, leaving Charmayne to her juice, and looked under all the big shrubs, then called the old man Ndephete from the vegetable gardens at the back of the house to check if PJ was with him. He had not seen her. She had not heard the dogs barking and had been keeping an eye on the girls from time to time, as she always did when they played outside. She could not see them from where she had been ironing.

There had been a further delay because the nanny was scared to tell Khanyi she didn't know where PJ was at first, but after checking in the gardens she went to her in the office and explained. At first, she still thought she must be sleeping somewhere, or had maybe been picked up by someone they knew.

Khanyi asked Matt and Musa to check again if Pumi was maybe out in the workshops, playing there. She was not. They quickly double-checked the bathrooms and bedrooms.

She had gone.

They were lost, captured in that agonizing moment when uncertainty begins to give way to an awful surety, and it felt as though the world has slowed to a standstill, something holding back time for a brief period, before everything becomes still and a hideous clarity emerges as reality sets in.

They could not find her and, as a last resort, began searching right around the property with a sense of rising panic, in case she had wandered off and fallen asleep somewhere, although that was unlike her. She was not in the garden anywhere, and her dollies and bears were still lying in the grass near the gate. Charmayne was at the centre of all this, but it took some time before she could explain what had happened, and she was too young and innocent to understand the significance of what it meant. Several minutes had passed before they all realised without any doubt that what Charmayne was describing to them was a kidnapping. That their beloved little daughter, Pumi Jacqueline, had been abducted by two unknown men in a vehicle. The description was unclear. Matt gathered the information and pieced the story together and decided immediately to phone the police. He was lucky enough to be put through to Detective Inspector Rennie.

Chapter 11

Detective Inspector Rennie

When a child abduction has happened, and there is a witness to it taking place, there is no reason to delay the search, and the sooner it starts the better. DI Rennie was well used to dealing with members of the public from all walks of life and could hear by the tone of voice and what Matt told him that this parent sounded like a responsible man who had already checked in all the usual places. He asked the usual things, knowing nothing about who the Bartons were or where they lived – could she be at a friend's house? Could she have walked off to some shops nearby? Was there anyone in the area who might have asked her to visit them, had she had any disagreement with her mother, might some relative have taken her somewhere? The indications were all ominous. It looked as though she had been selected earlier, had been watched for some time and then snatched from the garden while playing, in sight of the other little one. He shuddered to himself as he thought about what it might mean.

There seemed to be nothing to indicate that any other possible explanations could apply, but in some of the most horrific cases he had solved, sometimes even the parents themselves were involved. He needed to interview them both face to face, and explained to Matt that he would leave immediately and would need to question them both that afternoon, and the other child, and would need some pictures of their daughter, and to get more details. PJ was taken during the morning, and Rennie left as soon as he was able to, reaching them later that afternoon.

He emerged from his double cab, flicking some dust off his sleeve: a lean, muscular, fit looking man in his late thirties. His short, dark hair was cut close to his scalp and he was clean shaven, with a handsome, intelligent-looking face, tending to look a little serious most of the time. He wore a lightweight grey suit, but left the jacket hanging in the car, and had a certain understated style of his own. When he smiled, his face transformed with a wolfish grin, his teeth remaining pressed together, and one gold cap gleaming unexpectedly, his only bodily adornment. He was slightly taller than Matt, and gave the impression of alertness, of untapped energy and great intensity, like a compressed spring. He seemed to be a man who knew exactly what he was doing.

Richard Rennie had come through the Royal Eswatini Police ranks very quickly and, after graduating at the top of his year in Police College, he had been singled out for fast track development and intensive training, and had been sent on a lot of courses. He was a career policeman, who had spent some time working and studying with the British Police and was already an experienced and highly regarded senior detective in the force. He did not tell Matt what his special area of work was.

It was a rather tense, investigative visit. Rennie found the household in a state of deep shock. He knew, but did not want to say out loud, that with small children, if they are not found within the first two days, they are rarely found alive or ever seen again. This had played on his mind as he drove towards the lowveld from the station in Manzini.

He carried out three formal interviews, with Nomsa, Khanyisile and Matt, and left with several photographs of the missing child and a nauseous sinking feeling in his stomach. Such a child would be worth a lot to those who deal in infant body parts.

The Bartons had arranged that before nightfall that day, her playmate from that morning, Tarryn's daughter Charmayne, would come over again and be available in case he needed to talk to her. He valued this opportunity but knew how difficult it could be, questioning a young child.

When he reached their homestead, after spending time talking to the adults, he first asked Charmayne to show him where they were playing, then sat down on the grass with her, in his smart suit pants, and to begin with, deliberately avoided asking her anything about what had happened, even though he was desperate to know as much as possible and time was critically important. He needed her to relax and trust him.

She was nervous at first, but gradually told him all about their game, and where they usually played, and what the game entailed. Charmayne relaxed and began to feel at ease with him, so she had to show him where the dragon lived, and where the magic bush was that made medicine and chocolate milk and, using his sharp intellect, his instincts and his training, he slipped serious questions in amongst the fantasy ones, as though they were of equal importance. He sidled skilfully up to the really important questions, making them sound innocuous, careful to prevent the little girl from becoming scared and clamming up on him.

He questioned her very gently, with her mother close by, within sight all the time, but not within earshot. The little girl was brave and confident and only got upset once, when she stopped rambling and described the way PJ had been pulled over the gate, but she proved to be a superb witness. She was a little vague, as small children usually are, but having grown up on a farm she could describe certain things very accurately, having noticed and remembered some details that actually mattered a great deal. As he sat with her, he managed to glean several distinct facts, each one a vital piece of evidence.

Charmayne had no idea how important her information was and Rennie, knowing young children, questioned her very slowly, with great patience, calmly and gently. She had seemed a bit frightened by him at first, and he did not want to scare her into silence. He skilfully befriended her, then obtained more information from her than she had provided before to anyone, even her mother.

The vehicle was a bakkie, not a car, and it was definitely blue. She even showed him the precise shade of blue using one of their doll's dresses. It didn't have a canopy on the back (she knew what a canopy looked like) and she noticed that it didn't even have any back door – she meant that the tailgate was missing. It also had tinted windows.

PJ had said she was going to get some magwinya. She had called to Charmayne that the nice visitor said he had some in his van, and he was going to share some with her. They used to sometimes go out with Nomsa to buy the delicious little brown vetkoek from one of the old ladies nearby. But they always asked PJ's mummy first.

She had seen her friend walking towards the gate to talk to that man and had seen what happened. She was putting her dolly to bed under some leaves, that's why she didn't go to the gate, she explained to the nice kind man, because her baby was very sick and she was waiting for the doctor to come and visit, and PJ was the doctor in their game. The conversation veered between fantasy and real life, but Rennie knew exactly when she was relaying facts, and he weighed her evidence, testing it in subtle ways by coming back to it, and her key testimony was solid and unvarying.

He kept his face at her level and he was left with no doubts concerning what she had seen. The story rang agonisingly true.

He thanked the Bartons, tried his best to comfort Khanyi, politely thanked Tarryn and the little girl Charmayne, and Nomsa, then got back into his car and began making calls. He passed on the information about the vehicle and the missing girl immediately to Police Headquarters, so that it could be scheduled with national news broadcasts and put on air, and the whole country could be alerted. They handled the information quickly and efficiently and, far away in Mbabane, a police communication staffer began putting together a short statement describing the child's appearance, the blue vehicle, the two men and the event, as far as they were able to. It would start being broadcast on the National radio station early the next day, or even later that same evening if he could arrange it. He tried to hide the fear he felt at what had happened. He arranged with Matt to be back the following morning at 5.00am to pick up Knox, as he wanted someone with him that the girl would recognise, in case this proved important, but he had no idea where to start looking.

His mind jumped back to the phone call he had received from Matt Barton that morning. Matt had been surprised at how quickly they had sent an officer to visit them, but he knew nothing about muti murders. Rennie had raced down to the lowveld from Manzini. The Detective Inspector had listened attentively and asked for a picture of the child. They had many. She was a beautiful little girl, with the most extraordinary green eyes. He had seldom seen such a stunning looking child.

Charmayne was collected by her parents, and Tarryn spoke to her in Afrikaans as they drove home trying to pick up any more details, but did not get anything further from her. She had told Rennie everything she knew.

Tarryn's friendship with Khanyisile had grown closer over the years. They had given birth to children within a few months of each other, and their two little girls often played together. She had helped Khanyi with their wedding. Tarryn's loneliness had helped to draw them together, her close friendship with Khanyi becoming an inexorable force that eventually also brought the husbands together.

Frikkie, Tarryn's husband had initially come across as a rather dour, silent man, but had slowly emerged from his shell and begun tactfully showing Matt how to braai properly, a skill that he knew instinctively and could do very well. Frikkie was shy and respectful among those he considered more learned or wealthier than himself, and that included Matt who was a professional welder, and had worked all over the world. But Frikkie could cook a whole meal on an open fire, from bread, to main course, vegetables, and even dessert, and he often wondered why a kitchen was even necessary. He was more at home speaking Afrikaans than English and always joked to Matt that he only used English in self-defence, modestly apologising for his pronunciation.

He was the regional manager for a fertiliser agency, and he would both manage the sales and invoicing, as well as drive a very sophisticated and complex low ground pressure four-wheel drive fertiliser sprayer, tracking its own application rates on satellite. He spent much of his life in the fields, his skin burnt dark by the sun. His work involved long, hot, days working with tankers of liquid fertiliser and pre-emergent herbicides, accurately calculating application rates, and meticulously calibrating his equipment to ensure that it was applying at exactly the correct rates. He always came home smelling of farm chemicals. He operated with one assistant, but otherwise toiled on his own and it was lonely, hard work out on the huge estates for days on end, attending to all the problems that would inevitably arise from time to time. Out in the cane lands, he would rely on his own initiative and usually resolved breakdowns by himself.

He was no mean mechanic, and after Matt had done some emergency welding repairs on the huge American spray rig one day, and refused to charge him, Frikkie in return had helped him repair a problem with the brakes on one of the farm bakkies. He came across as a quiet, serious man, but he had a wickedly funny sense of humour that he kept well hidden, a facet of his makeup that would only come out after a bottle of good red wine or a few beers, in company that he felt he could relax in and really trust. Matt had become very fond of him.

Frikkie had started a tiny herd of milking cattle, and he and Tarryn were selling fresh milk from their home. He loved life in the bush, and would look across at his sophisticated young wife, glamourous and tanned, with her modern clothes and fashions, and sometimes wonder at his fortune, and how he had successfully got her out of

Bloemfontein and her cappuccino and muffins student lifestyle. She still effortlessly made most other women in the area look painfully dull and drab.

Tarryn and Khanyi, spurring each other on, had become increasingly ambitious in the foreign dishes they cooked, and tried these out on the men, with varying results. Frikkie had to overcome his innate distrust of the English to befriend Matt but had, over time, warmed to the *Engelsman* and now regarded him as a friend. They were of similar age, and both cared for their families deeply, worked hard, and were exceptionally good at what they did. Their wives turned heads when they went shopping together, both attractive young women and clearly close friends. Tarryn's husband had to overcome some deep seated problems with her family, who felt she had married beneath her, and refused to ever visit her, and he always remembered how Khanyisile had helped her to overcome her loneliness, something she'd suffered from deeply when they'd first moved to the lowveld as newly-weds. They had slowly become close friends, 'house friends' as South Africans would say. They were as shocked as the Bartons when PJ was taken. She had been to their house many times to play and was beloved in that household too. Tarryn looked at her own little girl, Charmayne, hugged her tightly and imagined what she would be feeling if it were her child.

Chapter 12

The vigil

WHEN IT BECAME CLEAR THAT the child had been taken, Matt and Khanyisile gathered the few staff they had and formally told them, then asked them to spread the word in case anyone had seen her nearby. The small gathering sat around the dining room table in shock and despair as the afternoon ended. Khanyi and Nomsa were both crying, holding each other, the old gardener sat shaking his head, deeply shocked, and Matt, after a few minutes began phoning close friends and a few customers, just asking them to be alert about what had happened and to pass on anything they might have heard.

The first to arrive were Joao and Teresinha Dos Santos, the Barton's pastor and his wife, closely followed by Tarryn, and then her husband Frikkie who had driven in from the fields, coming straight from work, still in his uniform. Other friends living nearby started arriving, deeply shocked. PJ had been playing with Tarryn's daughter when she was taken, but it could have been anyone's child. Over two-way radio farm channels and cell phone calls the word spread quickly, passed on rapidly through the shocked rural community. It was unimaginable. Many local families had young children, and Matt and Khanyi were well known and liked in the area. Charmayne fell fast asleep in one of the spare bedrooms, exhausted and unaware of all the activity.

Gabriel Dlamini arrived at dusk with his wife and some family members and, as the daylight left and the real darkness swept over them, a number of people began steadily arriving at the house just to be with the family, offer help, and to show their love and concern, wanting to intercede for the beloved child's safe return. Khanyi felt her mind flying in many directions. Maybe Charmayne was confused. Could PJ have fallen into a canal and drowned? Had she wandered off to play with someone? What if PJ was lying hurt somewhere, or bitten by a snake? Why did she go outside the gate? What could she do?

Her thoughts were like a wild bird, trapped, panicking and fluttering against a window, trying one way then another to escape. But her little girl was gone. The people who had arrived during daylight had walked the whole area again before darkness fell, searching in every conceivable place she might have been, spreading out, right around the homestead and calling into the bordering stands of sugar cane to make absolutely certain.

There was no trace of her. Mpumelelo, the beloved one, was gone, taken from them by unknown men. Khanyi was sobbing, gulping for air, struggling to draw her breath and unable to talk, and could not call and tell people. It fell to Nomsa, who bravely took her cellphone and began making a series of calls, each time checking the name and nature of the contact with Khanyi first, then one by one calling her extended family members and friends, families scattered all over the Kingdom, notifying them that the little girl, Mpumelelo Jacqueline, had been abducted. Some of them already knew her. All of them were deeply shocked and promised to either come and offer support to the Bartons, or to keep an eye out for the child and listen for any rumours.

They came on foot and in cars, mostly unannounced, and they came in numbers, quietly making their way up the drive to first greet the couple, then gradually dispersing around the home to seat themselves in a kind of unofficial ranking determined by closeness. Some arrived later that evening, having driven long distances. A few aunties and friends, emotionally nearest to Khanyisile, would briefly sit alongside her on the sofa to comfort her, or settle on the carpet near her feet, or take up positions elsewhere but in the same room, and everyone else, less well known or of lower standing in the family, settled some distance away. It was enough to show your presence, greet, shake Matt's hand or hug him, and then take up a position and somehow share the burden with them.

Some of the visitors insisted on visiting Pumi Jacqueline's room, to be able to feel something of her presence, and they would stand in the room silently, taking her spirit into themselves and thinking despairingly of the stolen little one, sometimes standing stock still and weeping in silent agony. Others would immediately go and find a suitable resting place outside in the garden to think about the event. Many visitors bought with them money, which they contributed, or containers of food or drinks, and these were all added to trays of hastily prepared snacks and quietly offered to the growing number of new arrivals. They fast ran out of cups and plates.

As the numbers grew and all the available chairs from the household were used, the women sat gracefully on grass mats, with their legs bent at the knees and folded to one side, knees and ankles together. They sat there quietly, resting on the sides of their legs, leaning their weight onto one outstretched arm in that unique way African women have, able to sit for long periods on the ground, waiting patiently without complaint. As they sat quietly, chatting in low voices, in one community of spirit, they would pluck at pieces of grass and pick at the small weeds and flowers in the lawn with the hand that was free. Many would gaze vacantly at the ground, slowly shaking their heads from time to time, wiping away tears and making that soft clucking noise from the back of their throat when something is unbearably sad and painful. There was a continuous low murmur of unusually subdued conversation floating around the house and garden. Voices were seldom raised, there was no sound of laughter, and few sudden movements. It was as though the world had been muted around their home.

Some visitors arrived who were barely known to the Barton couple, and even some local customers made the effort to come by, either staying to remain in community with those attending the vigil, or to explain apologetically that they could not stay and just wanted to express their sympathy. They would make their way into the lounge, and briefly express their sorrow and assurances that the Barton family and the missing child were being covered in their prayers, squeeze Matt's shoulders and then leave promptly, many of them leaving behind even more food or drink.

That night, at around 8.30pm, a small delegation had even arrived after driving all the way from the Nkomati farmers' cooperative, one of the first organisations Matt had done work for in the area. The elderly men climbed stiffly out of Timothy's double cab, knocked the dust off themselves and politely made their way into the home to find Matt and Khanyi and express their sorrow.

They assured them that all their employees would be told in the morning and would all be on the look-out for the first-born child. The men shook their heads, and Ngomezulu rubbed at his greying hair, unable to find words to explain how sorry they felt. They offered their prayers and knew that some of their members would burn sacred herbs and perform certain rituals that night to discern answers from their ancestors. They did not share this with Matt, and it was unnecessary to tell Khanyisile.

Some of the visitors barely saw either Matt or Khanyi, but would merely ask someone in the house to inform them that they had visited, that they had been there with them to pay respects, and many local people simply came in with mats or blankets, laid them out and stationed themselves without fuss in the garden.

A few of the younger women, without being asked to, boldly took over key roles and started taking control of the kitchen, despite it all being new to them, and together with Nomsa began to handle the tasks involved in catering. They were evidently unhappy about the Mnumzane doing anything in the kitchen at such a time, and gently absolved him of such duties, as they did not like to see him doing domestic work. But for Matt, a little shell shocked and overwhelmed, it was something he could keep busy with while Khanyisile sat in shocked silence on the couch, almost immobile, surrounded by friends who tended to her every need.

The men would come up and ask Matt what they could do to help, a question to which he had no answer, and in the absence of any other demands on their time they would be seen strolling around the garden, using their phones, gesturing with their hands and calling everyone they knew, contacts all across the land, asking them to be alert for the child, and describing her or telling people they knew to watch out for the blue bakkie. DI Rennie had shared the vehicle's description.

Matt felt lost without Khanyi, and out of his depth. He felt inadequate to play much part in the spiritual warfare that seemed to be raging around him, but busied himself as best he could, answering phone calls, checking on his wife, and relaying messages. He was kept busy greeting and thanking people, making occasional hot drinks and insisting on taking trays of tea, or cold drinks and water out into the garden to thirsty visitors. He was constantly saying goodbye to visitors, many of whom he had never met before, a process he repeated again and again. He barely had time to think it all through, but the pain was growing inside him, feeling like a cold knife turning in a deep wound. He felt as though his heart was breaking every time he saw anything belonging to PJ.

Neither Matt nor Khanyi realised at the time that Joao and Teresinha had begun planning things as soon as they were aware of the abduction, or that they had notified Gabriel Dlamini, the booming presence who had given his blessing to their union and became one of Matt's closest friends and an honorary uncle. He had stepped in swiftly and taken care of numerous arrangements in his inimitable style, to such an extent that huge aluminium pots full of chicken and beef stew, boiled cabbage and pap, began arriving on the back of various bakkies a few hours after nightfall, along with hundreds of spoons, paper plates, cups and many crates of cold drink. Everyone who came and stayed was given something to eat.

The Bartons were finding it difficult to do anything for themselves. Khanyisile had willing helpers keeping her supplied with drinks, but she felt nauseous and was unable to eat, so her carers stayed close to her and comforted her, holding her hands as they sat talking quietly to her, or just keeping her company in contemplative silence. It was barely necessary for her to do anything, other than to get up, bathe herself and change, and then come back into the lounge and sit in a warm tracksuit. She barely moved, keeping still, mostly remaining wrapped under a thick Sotho blanket, feeling alone with her worst fears and thoughts, while two of the most faithful dogs resisted any efforts to remove them, and occupied prime spots, filling spaces directly at her feet. Efforts to move them were met with snarling disdain.

Sometimes, when a well-meaning visitor expressed their sympathy, she would be overwhelmed by more tears and a runner would quickly be sent to summon Matt, who was the only one able to comfort her. She was remembering what had happened to her before they were married, and could not help but be tormented by thoughts of whether their daughter would ever be restored to them. During one of these times, she managed to talk to him, gulping in air between her sobs, determined to explain what she was feeling.

'They've taken her, Matt, they have taken my little one. This was my dream. They have taken my child from us. It was in my dream, Matt! This is what I was shown that time. I saw it. I saw the place. PJ has been taken and now her shoe is lost somewhere. She is in a forest; they have taken her into a big forest. It was in the dream Matt!'

Her voice rose, intense and forceful, and he listened intensely as she explained to him. 'Remember the last time I dreamt Matt, the terrible one about her shoe? Those ones she likes too much.

Remember, I saw it in the forest. I saw it lying somewhere by itself. The ones who took her must be close by that place.'

She grew silent, tortured by her thoughts. It made her feel sick. She could not quite put across the intensity and clarity of her vision. Matt took it in and believed her, because he had great respect for his wife's intuition, even if he seldom could understand it. But he was feeling inadequate, a *mlungu* adrift in a sea of doubt, unsure of what it meant or how best to respond. There were forests all over the Western side of the Kingdom, running almost unbroken, right from the cool highveld and the endless rolling hills in the north, all around Piggs Peak and Bulembu, down towards the bulging western borders of the Kingdom and the immense Usutu, then in huge tracts of land all the way down to the forests and plantations around the town of Hlatikulu and almost to Nhlangano.

She could be anywhere, in any of them if she were even still in the country. Khanyi could be right, but where, in which forest? Where to start searching? The more he thought about it, the more he despaired, feeling useless and powerless to find her, and not knowing where to begin looking.

The dogs were confused by the large, unexpected invasion of strangers suddenly being allowed access into their homestead and were initially deeply suspicious. But then, as sensitive, intelligent creatures, they recognised that the group was mostly made up of women who seemed to conduct themselves properly and were being welcomed. The animals concluded that there was no immediate threat. In some strange way the visitors, although smelling new to them for the most part, all seemed to have their credentials and access endorsed by Khanyisile, Nomsa or Matt, and were thus permitted to be absorbed into the household and automatically afforded protection, even if they were still viewed with some suspicion. They had never encountered so many visitors at once.

Rather than threatening the thronging visitors or barking at them, they simply increased the area that they usually guarded to include a much larger space, and then eventually settled down, mostly lying curled up just beyond the edges of the little groups on the lawn.

One of the older female dogs, tiring of the noise and unusual sounds of so many strange voices, retired to the workshops, dug a shallow den in the ground and walked round and round, finally settling into a tightly wound circle, her black muzzle nestling under her back paws, and slept there in peace. The bigger dogs were unusually subdued but roamed around the unusually busy garden, sniffing new people occasionally and leaning against the ones they knew. The exceptions were two old animals, raised from puppies, that never left the side of their mistress. Those two dogs always stayed with her, getting up and following her whenever she moved but always remaining close to her, barely leaving her side throughout the vigil. They would even growl softly at people coming up to her whom she did not seem ready to see.

Some of the others, especially the spoilt little terrier, would occasionally seek out Matt for reassurance, or to establish where he was, but otherwise they remained just beyond the edge of the throng, curled up and dozing at the edges of the garden beyond the trees, or sitting quietly and looking out into the darkness with noble expressions. They were aware that some bad event had happened, sensing in some canine way that something like this had happened once before. They tried to comfort their owners as best they could.

Knox had come to work at sunset and was his usual massive presence, slowly walking around, unused to having such a large throng filling in the garden during his night patrols, when he would normally stroll around alone, guarding the property. He continued as usual with his normal pattern, with his two favourite Swazi dogs leaving their resting places and following him around, as they usually did. After a short time, Matt told him he should leave early and knock off for the night. There were more than enough people around to prevent any trouble and he would be needed early the next day to go with DI Rennie.

Knox loved PJ and had spent the evening staring intently across the fence line into the bush for any trace of her abductors. He was desperately hoping for a lead to follow, to have something definite to respond to. He had been off duty and at home when PJ was snatched but carried some of the pain of her disappearance on his shoulders, and still felt responsible, as though he had failed the family in some way. He missed the child and felt her loss deeply, desperately wanting the opportunity to take full revenge on those who had taken her from their midst.

The vigil party gently but inexorably invaded two rooms in the house, and much of the garden, like water spreading over land in a flood. They kept arriving throughout the evening and sat around outside and held a vigil throughout that night, staying awake, praying and suffering with the family even through the coldest hours before the first light of dawn. When the dew began to settle, they just pulled their shawls or emahiya over their heads or pulled their blankets tighter around them, but continued to sit with their thoughts, quietly praying.

Occasionally out of the darkness, a lone voice would tentatively begin humming or singing a well-known tune and one voice would immediately be joined by others, singing very slowly and instinctively taking up three- or four-part harmonies. They sang old church songs from memory, verse after verse, until one hymn would gradually peter out as they tired of it and was replaced when another song began. Many of them seemed to know the old songs, line, verse and chorus, and their voices would gather, rising up and drifting out gently through the serenity of the trees, silver moonlight casting the garden into peaceful shadows. Eventually, they mostly slept.

Others remained silent, just pulling their covers more closely over their heads and sitting still in contemplation, staring out at the darkness and cold starlight, wondering where she was. Several of the visitors knew Pumi Jacqueline by sight only, others had children who had played with her, others had never seen the little girl, but were relatives of Khanyi, or knew the young couple from church. The underlying connections to the family varied but, shared between them all was a sense that something unspeakable had happened. Such events were not unheard of, and small children were the most at risk. But this most shocking and fearful act had taken place on their doorstep and they were outraged. As one, they believed that the combined power of good must be harnessed, unified and sent out against the powerful forces of evil.

It was the traditional response in times of great loss or tragedy, this gentle influx of souls. Mostly rural people whose hearts were bleeding with the family over the loss of their child. Children were innocents, for most parents the most beloved and precious beings. Some of the faithful spent the whole night awake, fervently praying for her safe return. Some thought with horror about what might be happening to her, praying to God and to their ancestors that she should be returned unharmed. What had happened was unthinkable, and what it might mean could only be spoken of in hushed tones.

When it grew dark, Matt turned on the outside security lights and collected all the candles and lanterns he had in the house, sending them outside to all the people. These were whisked off him, carried away and distributed all about the lawn and under the trees, the yellow gleam of hurricane lamps and candles in weighted bags affording glimpses of sombre faces and solemn features, an occasional smile of thanks or recognition. The soft light gently illuminated the house and the garden, forming oases of light, each surrounded by a small group, mostly women, but with a few men standing in quiet groups discussing the abduction, and even a handful of young children, sleeping around them.

The used plates and spoons were collected, as if by magic, and swiftly washed by dozens of hands, and some of the elderly folk wrapped themselves in bed covers and blankets against the dew fall, then leant against tree trunks and slept, heads nodding forward. The number of visitors kept changing as various groups arrived and left, coming and going even late into the night, but there was always a core of the most faithful who remained.

There was little noise apart from the low murmur of conversation and the singing, which died out sometime after darkness fell, leaving just the weak light of candles and lanterns surrounded by bodies, mostly sitting or prostate.

Matt had never seen anything like it. He had attended a few wakes in England and Ireland, and had spoken at the sparsely attended services for his elder brother and his family after the tragedy, but had seen nothing like this. The people came, stayed throughout the long night, made no demands, drank no alcohol, asked for little, took nothing, and poured out their love and concern over the family. The kitchen was in constant use, but being continuously cleaned and wiped down by volunteers, and at one stage he was even able to persuade Khanyi, grief stricken and in deep shock, to have a short rest next to him during the night as they held onto each other on the couch. She would not go to the bedroom in case the phone rang and she was needed.

Teresinha and Joao stayed with them until very late, praying with them, and Gabriel also stayed until he had to go out to check on the harvesting night shift at 10pm. Joao reminded Khanyi how she had found the teddy bear in the sea, the last remnant of the original Barton family, against all odds, and how God was able to work miracles that were far beyond our understanding. He prayed fervently and passionately, rising to his feet and beseeching the Almighty to keep their beloved little girl safe and return her to them. His strong voice seemed to tremble with power and suppressed emotion. Inside the house, highly regarded family members and other church friends moved around to be near to Khanyisile. They were themselves mostly covered in shawls and blankets, but many remained seated on the floor out of respect, and had to be asked many times to sit on the sofa or to occupy the armchairs. Tarryn and Teresinha stayed on either side of Khanyi unless Matt was there.

Tarryn didn't say much. She found that every time she wanted to talk to Khanyisile her voice would choke up, but she stayed as long as she could, then left at around eleven. Frikkie and their sleeping daughter had already gone home. He had the animals to feed.

There was, in the packed lounge a rich, mingled smell of humanity, sunlight soap and candle smoke and through this fog, either whispered words of people talking quietly, or the ebb and swell of voices lifted in prayer, intercession and supplication. A random, swirling torrent of gentle African voices, as believers prayed, both speaking in tongues and their own languages. The sound eddied and flowed, breaking like waves across the room. Joao was speaking Portuguese, Teresinha prayed in Shangaan, Swahili and English, and even Tarryn, unused to praying aloud or indeed praying at all, found herself reciting very softly old snatches of memorised Afrikaans childhood prayers, words she remembered hearing her Ouma recite on her Free State farm. But above all this there was SiSwati, its sound continuous, melodious, tumbling richly around the room, the exquisite range of different clicks, loud and soft words punctuating the long sentences and filling the dark corners.

Somebody would start to pray, and another would join in at the same time, then a third person would start as well, each raising up the little girl's safety, mentioning her name and praying for protection for her, and her safe return. Their voices would rise together and then roll away to be replaced by others, and the sound in the room would lift and fade in the darkness. Dozens of people interceding with whatever being they held most sacred for her return. The strength of their belief seemed to offer hope, binding them together and holding the worst fears of the darkness at bay. They prayed that angels would gather around her and protect her from harm, and that those who had stolen her would be captured.

Matt felt a mixture of being oddly comforted, but also disturbed and uneasy. He sensed that the people gathered about them were lifting him and Khanyi in some way, but he was not the spiritual being that his wife was. His perception was confused and distracted. Somehow, in the air about them he could feel that there was some secret strength gathered in the home and filling the surrounding gardens, something of immense and incomprehensible power that he had never experienced before, but it was unclear to him what he was feeling.

He felt as though his late brother Patrick and his wife Melanie were there with them, watching from the periphery of his vision and somehow there to comfort him too. Not in a ghoulish sense like in a spooky film but drenching his soul with an inexplicable feeling of heightened awareness. Wherever he walked through the dark garden, there was the sense of strong emotions, of different souls reaching out and caring for him, and he felt uplifted by them and strangely comforted, despite being surrounded by strangers, but his thoughts tortured and tormented him. They ran along like snakes in a deep, dark channel, seething, churning over themselves and writhing, spitting up onto the surface, again and again, conveying whatever his little girl might be going through, coupled to the agony it was causing Khanyi. The combination made him feel like he was carrying two burdens, his daughter's terror and the evident suffering of his young wife, whom he loved totally. The pain was unbearable. The sky felt huge above him, the stars vivid and bright, scattered like jewels thrown across the blue darkness. He felt as though it was pulled taut, stretched across from horizon to horizon, and thought of his little girl PJ, her beautiful face and trusting smile lost somewhere under those same stars, somewhere alone in the darkness. The sense of her absence was sharp and intense, a blade cutting deeply into him, driving itchy and dull into parts of his soul he had never known existed.

The long night slowly passed.

Chapter 13

The witness

THE NASTY MAN WITH HARD hands was gripping her very hard while he ran. She had never been handled so roughly and he was hurting her. When they took her, no one had lifted her so hard or so roughly over the gate before, or ever pulled on her arms the way he had. She was thrown into the footwell of the bakkie and held down at their feet, and the other man's feet were stinky. She tried to stand up, to turn round to see Charmayne, right after they took her, but the shorter one pushed her down, keeping her out of sight and below the windows. It all happened so quickly.

It was hot and dirty in the van and she had cried aloud and struggled at first, and again when they eventually stopped and took her into the house that night. But the man was much too strong to fight against, and when he shook her and told her to keep quiet, she was so scared she felt as though she couldn't breathe. It had been a long and painful time, driving along, cramped on the floor, forced to stay below the dashboard and out of sight, and she had no idea where she was.

She spent the night locked up and alone, crying quietly by herself for Khanyi until exhaustion overwhelmed her fear and she slept. The previous evening, when she still had enough energy left to fight, just as the horrible one was pulling her out of the footwell of the bakkie, she squirmed and wriggled, trying to get free. But he grabbed her very tightly and hurt her again, and she wasn't accustomed to being handled like that. No one had ever done that to her. She fought spiritedly, as much as a little girl can, and even tried to scream out loud.

'Let me go, let me go!' kicking and struggling as best she could, but the smelly man hissed at her 'Keep still and be quiet or I'll beat you.'

She was so shocked by this that she did try to stop crying, but she couldn't and continued to squirm and struggle whenever he clamped his hand over her face. She hated having her mouth covered, it felt like she couldn't breathe. She remembered driving for a long time, then stopping somewhere, and she heard one of them kicking open a metal door, one that scraped on the floor. They carried her quickly into an old building, a foul-smelling place without proper lights, and she had to lie on pieces of old cardboard in a dirty room that smelt like a toilet. It had newspapers taped over the windows. There were broken bottles along the wall and lots of rubbish and horrible things lying around, and it was full of ants. She was terrified, trembling to herself in fear. She had to try and stop her teeth chattering in case they heard her, because she was so scared that they would come in and beat her.

After a long time, left in the room crying to herself, it grew completely dark and the smaller man came in with a short stump of candle, burning weakly and casting deep shadows, and put a torn chunk of bread and peanut butter and a can of cool drink on an old piece of wood on the floor, but he didn't look at her or say anything. He glanced at her briefly, then went out and locked the door behind him. She sat watching it for a while, in case someone else was going to come in and do something bad to her, almost too scared to move. After she had decided they weren't coming back, she drank the cool drink and ate a few bites of the bread, and lay down, thinking about home, her mummy and daddy, and began crying again. Eventually, utterly exhausted, she fell asleep. All night long she was tormented by mosquitoes, and kept waking up bitten, itchy, dirty and afraid.

She awoke fully when first light came into the room and felt her whole young body flood instantly with despair. It was nothing like waking up at home and knowing that she was going to see her beloved Nomsa, or her pets and her parents, and everything else she loved. It was just like being in a bad dream, except she knew something bad had really happened to her. She could not fight them and thought that no one could ever know where she was, so they wouldn't rescue her, which broke her child's heart.

They came for her again early that morning, when it was still cold outside and only starting to get light. Then they forced her back in the bakkie, handling her roughly, and drove off again, for another long time. She had to sit up near the shorter man's legs, next to the stick that she remembered Daddy using to make the car go faster. They stopped once, somewhere near the road, and the big man went out and came back with a plastic bag, something to eat and some cool drinks. They didn't give her any, and she wasn't able to look outside to see where she was. Then they carried on driving and after what seemed like an unbearably long time, bouncing around next to smelly feet with nothing to hold onto and feeling a bit sick, but hungry and thirsty and scared all at the same time, they slowed down and stopped. One of them took her out again, this time in a different place, somewhere far away in a forest. She didn't know the time, or even how to tell it, but it felt sort of like the middle of the morning, sometime between breakfast and lunchtime, and it was somewhere much colder than home.

They had climbed steadily as they drove that morning, and were now in the west of the country, over a thousand metres higher than where she lived, and the air was noticeably cooler, especially in the shade. They hid the blue vehicle with branches, then walked quickly away from it, waited to be sure no traffic was coming, then ran across the dirt road, pulling her with them. After a short while, they lifted her up, not in a nice way, and all she could see around her was brown pine needles on the floor of a forest, and tall trees. She had no idea where she was.

When the big man began jogging, carrying her under one arm, she soon just wanted the bumping to stop. It was really sore, but it went on and on, with the strong man crushing her body too tightly under his arm, squeezing her hard. The smell of his body was strong and acrid in her nose, and his hard hand was mostly clamped over her mouth. Sometimes he would stop and change sides. She'd thought at first that maybe someone wanted to steal her to be their little girl, because maybe they didn't have one, but she couldn't understand why they were being so cruel to her. And she was really thirsty. Being carried and bumping up and down was hurting her side. She felt lost, alone, frightened and forgotten and her tiny innocent heart was beating faster than ever before.

Ginindza had been an old man for as long as anyone had known him. His greying hair and wispy beard and moustache gave witness to his many years. His first names were uncertain, and he had not heard them spoken for such a long time that he was by now even unsure of them himself. His hair was long and unkempt, in the style of rural tribesmen from long ago.

He knew, from being told, that he had been raised near Mankayane, in a village close to the Ntabamhlope hills. He had long lost track of his real age, and he was unsure of who his parents had been or even what clan names they had given him. He was just known as *Mkhulu* or Ginindza, the one who lived in the forest. He was an amiable, shambling figure of a man, often dressed in a disreputable looking old brown overcoat. He had found it in a shop in Matata that sold second hand European clothes, after one of the longest journeys he had ever undertaken. He disliked towns and busy places and preferred to barter and trade goods rather than use money. Money confused him and seemed to have no value.

He lived mainly by finding, collecting and selling the young, tasty Boletus mushrooms that grew wild in certain parts of the pine forest, but occasionally he would also find and sell combs of wild honey. He would also set illegal game traps and catch in them duiker, porcupines and small animals that live and roam freely in the pine forests, especially in those bush areas that are too steep to be farmed for timber or used by the foresters as loading zones.

He used to sometimes listen to the radio, but once the batteries died he would go for many weeks without hearing it, until he had saved enough cash or had enough money left after buying mealie meal to buy a new battery, so he knew little of what happened outside of his world. As far as he was aware, not much had changed since the days of the Protectorate, except that food had now become scarce and was more costly, new clothes were unaffordable, and the forest lands were harvested more quickly than before, so his favoured places for trapping, wild bees and mushrooms were often disturbed and threatened. He eked out an existence unseen and unknown by officialdom, one of the uncounted and undocumented, but he was well liked and respected in his home area.

Ginindza would locate hives in rock faces and hollow logs or fallen trees, and smoke out the wild bees to steal their honey, using a mixture of eucalyptus leaves, pine needles, traditional herbs and dagga, in blissful and flagrant disregard of all the regulations forbidding open flames in the forest. The bees were attracted to the sap from the pine trees and the sweet-smelling fragrant eucalyptus plantations, and he alone knew of many hives that had been active for years in secluded sections of the forest.

He also knew from experience how much smoke he could risk making before it might be seen from the look-out towers; and knew exactly how long it would take before the forest security men could hike to wherever he was, trying to seek out the source of the smoke. Once you were in the forest, you could no longer see the sky, so they had to be guided by radio, which was difficult. With his skills and knowledge of secret paths and short cuts, he had seldom been caught. He had his favourite swarms of bees, and he knew and named them, and could feel when the weather was right, avoiding hot days when they would be aggressive. He used to talk to the different swarms and respected them all, and he could sense instinctively when the time was right to carry out his raids. Both how he felt and how the bees were behaving on that day had to be synchronised. He had been stung hundreds of times but regarded this as just punishment for stealing their honey. He did not begrudge them their stings, regarding them, like hunger, as part of his normal life. He was a fit old man and could walk for hours up and down the hilly terrain of the forests without tiring.

Ginindza had spent most of his life living close to the edges of the Usutu forest, and could find his way through near darkness back to his village, following the sounds, rocky outcrops and subtle landmarks as clearly as if they were signs and pathways, often with his backpack stuffed with honeycombs and, if he were lucky, some fresh mushrooms, or perhaps a trapped buck or hare that could be eaten or sold. He had settled finally in the Siphocisini area, close to the region they call Mushroom Valley. He knew some secret parts of the forest intimately, and knew many of the small paths, finding his way even when the scenery and vegetation changed with the seasons, but he was always careful to avoid unplanned contact with forest wardens. He spoke infrequently, but when he did speak it was in a deep, pure form of ancient SiSwati from the rural south that urban youngsters could not always follow. He found it equally hard to follow their slang, a strange way of speaking mixed up with words from other languages.

He was only friendly with a handful of people, those he trusted or knew by sight from trading with them, sometimes exchanging whatever he had harvested for eggs, snuff, vegetables, shoes or foodstuffs instead of cash. He was at home in the gloom of the forest and its darkness held few fears for him.

Ginindza's eyesight was no longer as sharp as it had been, but he could still see further than most people in the low light of the forest, and his hearing was still acute. He could follow a honey bird for many hours, singing and whistling back to it as he walked, and could always pick up his own tracks and the pathways he had used, discerning them quite easily. Often, he was the only person on a particular path, so he usually picked up the spoor quickly if any strangers had been walking along one of his little known trails, many of which would eventually detour and lead close to reliable sources of drinking water.

The morning it happened, Ginindza was walking slowly into the forest for his day's work, his mind peaceful and quiet, alone with his thoughts, when he heard the sound of rapid footfalls, crunching on the bed of pine needles, then a distant cough followed by someone hawking and spitting, and gradually the very faint rumbling sound of low voices. An indistinct conversation coming from somewhere unseen, echoing faintly through the trees and muffled by the thick layer underfoot and heavy forest covering overhead. The two men's voices seemed to be arguing.

Sound was always muffled in the forest and, as it echoed off the trees and through the valleys, it would dissipate, weaken and die out, making it difficult to determine what direction it came from. Voices were not uncommon. There were sometimes workers moving along in teams, spraying weed killer for firebreaks, or clearing roads, and often tractors running as they extracted timber, but the sound of people running was something unusual, a sound alien to his heightened awareness of that remote section of the plantation, and to all his experience of the area. Usually, he was alone on this path.

The little girl's captors could not keep this steady jogging up for long periods, although they had done it before. It is difficult and tiring to carry a child who does not want to be carried.

Boy, the smaller, lighter-skinned of the two men, jogged ahead with a small bag over his shoulder containing a change of clothes, plastic bags and the sharpened tools they would need. Even he was tiring now. His job had been to lure the chosen one in the first place.

Now, it was to ensure that no one saw them, and to keep them on the barely discernible path, picking up the faint trail marks and always staying slightly ahead. If he were seen, he could quickly use the contents of the bag to deal with the witness himself, silencing them if they became inquisitive, or make up a convincing lie and claim that he was looking for wild honey or checking his traps.

During that morning, after leaving the shack, stopping once to buy some food and driving slowly so as not to draw attention to themselves, they had driven their blue bakkie right off the road and left it there, in the forest, breaking up its shape and hiding its unusual colour by covering it with small branches, limbs and striplings. They had used bunches of weeds pulled from the verges to sweep away and cover the tracks marking where the vehicle had driven across the verge, over the low bank, well away from the road and out of sight. Boy had held onto the child, while his stronger partner tore low branches off the young trees, set back from the road. He had tried to help until as he'd attempted to break a fallen branch by stamping on it, he'd misjudged how strong it was, and how soft the ground was underfoot. Instead of snapping and breaking cleanly, it had broken off and sprung back at him. The jagged stump had cut him above his ankle painfully, and he'd almost dropped the child. The wound had bled into his sock and the sharp pain, stinging with sweat and dirt, was making him limp.

They'd left the vehicle well hidden, almost invisible unless you knew what you were looking for, and had then turned away, taking up the child again and setting off in the opposite direction, starting out on the other side of the forest road, some way back from the van, following the little known paths that they knew, trails that gradually became less and less evident, jogging steadily towards the special flat rock. Boy was hampered by his injury, and his partner Ndzinisa was complaining bitterly about having to carry the burden of the child all the time.

They both believed that witches and ghosts moved around the forest at night, hiding there undisturbed in daylight, and were fearful of what might be lurking in the darkness beyond the tall trees. They hated the cool shade and noises of wind; they preferred the bustle and movement of towns and wanted to complete their business in daylight. They were intent upon finishing what had to be done that afternoon swiftly, completing an act of great savagery and evil, removing parts of a living child in a secret way that can never be written. They had to complete several unspeakable mutilations and deeds that would be well rewarded by the powerful Sangoma; the one who had given them the detailed instructions and told them what kind of child to find. She needed the strongest muti to change the life and business fortunes of an influential and powerful client. Much depended on them completing the work quickly and bringing her the ncccssary parts while they were still fresh.

They had done such things for her before, when a Malawian albino child had disappeared from a holding camp for illegal immigrants, and secretly they both feared what would happen to them if they failed her. The work was always allocated in secret and rewarded handsomely, but any disobedience to her or failure on their part would result in them both disappearing. They would simply not be seen again, and their remains would never be found. In the quietness of the vast plantation they kept moving, stopping only seldom and then briefly to sit and draw breath, all the while keeping the child silent and holding her captive. Boy was limping slightly and stopped periodically to wipe at his wound. The shady gloom and darker patches of the forest made them both uneasy, so they kept moving, each one always in sight of the other in case of betrayal.

Ginindza stopped walking and listened intently, trying to gauge the source of the sound. Once he was sure of what he had heard, as was his habit, he immediately left the overgrown path – what little trace there was of it. Stepping quietly and easily away off to one side, the old forest man disappeared effortlessly, blending into the background. Very few people would ever have noticed his tracks. The sun was climbing now, and he needed to find shade to hide in. He found some deep, dense natural cover behind a low bank and settled down in a shallow depression, sheltering behind a strong-smelling tall stand of bug weed. He tugged his greasy brown woollen balaclava off his head and pocketed it, then slowly raised his gaze, like a gecko after a moth, and watched silently from his hiding place.

Across the small clearing, between the path and his hide-out of natural cover, a man came into sight, walking and jogging along unsteadily, his short strides stepping over the fallen branches and ridges with some difficulty. He was short and stocky, and looked a bit tired. He was breathing heavily. As he watched, he heard again the same cough followed by a spitting noise, and heard the runner muttering to himself. He seemed to be angry about something, complaining about his thirst and having to run with an injury.

Ginindza remained hidden, still listening intently, and a few minutes later a second, taller man emerged over the rise, labouring hard and moving more slowly, the weight of a burden seeming to make his feet land more heavily and distinctly. He was panting with effort. He was stronger and trotted a little more slowly along the path, some distance behind the first man. This one was bigger and carried under one arm what he gradually realised was a small child, a little girl.

One of the man's hands was clamped firmly over her mouth while the other tightly gripped her small body around the waist. He was cursing her and sweating as he ran. It was difficult to see everything clearly through the stand of weeds and scrub, but he saw that the child was wearing a blue dress, and had golden coloured hair, like honey. Her skin was neither white nor black; she had lightly coloured skin. She seemed to be trying to cry, with her eyes wide open and frightened, but the sound was constrained, muffled and choked off behind the tall one's cupped hand. This big man carried her, not as one would normally carry a child, but as one would carry firewood, luggage or a sack of maize.

Ginindza only saw them for a short time, being very careful not to reveal his position. They passed across the clearing before him, heading downhill, then turned and began climbing uphill again. He sensed something cold around the two men, following them like a great cloud of darkness. Evil accompanied them. He could feel it in his body and his waters, sensing it in the air, and the child did not seem to be well in their company. She seemed fearful.

He only saw some of her light blue clothing, but as she was carried under one arm, her legs were sticking out and flopping about behind. As they passed, he noticed that on one foot at the end of her short dusky leg there was a small sandal, an object of an odd bright colour, while the other foot was bare. The tiny sole of her foot was a paler colour than her skin. As he watched them a short distance away, her feet came into full view and his sharp eyes missed little, and he caught a flash of several vivid colours he would later struggle to describe, a kind of artificial brightness that he never normally saw in the forest. The second man went up over the hillock and slowly out of sight.

After a short time had passed, the great forest's serenity returned and he dug out his old brown, smelly balaclava and replaced it on his head, rolled up above his ears; a comforting, familiar feeling. He was greatly upset and disturbed by what he had seen. There was something about it that tormented him, and the vision left in its wake a strong sense of menace. Once they were completely out of earshot, he still did not rise immediately from his hide, but remained seated on the forest floor, thinking. He instinctively reached into his ancient coat pocket and located his little red and yellow round plastic tub of snuff. He sat back, thinking about what he had witnessed, and placed a pinch on his left hand, in the natural web between thumb and forefinger. Sniffing sharply, he took this into his nostrils, feeling the slight rush as the drug entered his bloodstream. He gazed up at the shafts of sunlight shining through the gaps in the tree cover, gently illuminating the green bower and pungent bug weed around him, sneezed a few times and considered if any action was necessary on his part, and if so, what he should do about what he had seen. Certain things seen had somehow lodged in his mind and upset him. He was deeply unsettled, left unhappy by the image.

Why was the child being carried in such a way, when she was clearly old enough to walk alone? Usually, an adult walked a bit slower, their cupped hand pressing on the back of a child's head, gently guiding their direction and urging them forward. Normally, they would be discussing life. Why did they not allow her to walk? Was she drugged or perhaps sick? Why was she being silenced? What were the two men doing with such a child, and from whom were they running? Who was chasing them? From where had they come? It disturbed him and even the soothing effect of the snuff failed to calm his fears. The intent of these men troubled him. It troubled him deeply.

Ginindza knew nothing of the hideous modern perversions of child pornography, or the industry of sex trafficking, or even the kidnapping of children for ransom. He had never even heard of such things, but he knew about witches, and muti murders, and he suspected deep witchcraft was behind what he had witnessed. He had no children of his own but knew that they must always be cherished and cared for, not carried like something without life.

He sensed that something dark was sweeping in, some hunched and slimy evil presence coming to threaten the peaceful calm that prevailed over the rolling hills and dark valleys he loved. He feared he had seen something that needed to be spoken of to others. He shook his head and pondered over what he had seen. In a distinct flash of clarity and vision, he thought suddenly of one of his favourite customers, Lindiwe, a certain young woman whom he would see quite often, that talkative pretty one who seemed to know much about what was happening in the country. She usually bought his mushrooms and often gave him more in return than he was expecting. He would tell her. Relieved, with a clear intention in his mind and a resolution made, he stood up, regained the pathway, and resumed walking. He headed directly away from the two men, a sense of urgency adding haste to his steady pace.

Chapter 14

Lindiwe – the friendship

LINDIWE MAVIMBELA WAS A BUSINESSWOMAN. She traded in second-hand clothes, cheap Chinese imitation branded *takkies*, cabbages, fruit and some vegetables. She was known to extend credit to those who could not afford to pay for garments at once, charging extortionate interest rates for this. She kept a secret and valuable notebook, with all the names of those who owed her money. She also, more discreetly and for much more money, grew and sold *dagga* from her extensive private and deeply secluded plantations, mostly fields well hidden in the highveld. From these, she supplied regular buyers from outside the country, most of whom would travel long distances to purchase her bags of specially nurtured, highly potent marijuana heads. The quality of her dagga was well known. She had done this for many years, and sold it to people that she only ever knew by their Christian names: M'griza, the dirty one who used to fix cars; Mushtaq, the half Indian; Spokes from Natal; Innocence, the dark skinned Zimbabwean; and the one they called Slender, the immensely fat government man from Limpopo. They used to drive right up to her homestead late at night in their big cars and vans with shaded windows. They were the ones who always paid in cash, and treated her with respect. They would phone from different cell phone numbers each time, greet her, ask her if she had stock, then arrange the collection, always at night. They respected her, and never asked where the product came from.

From these varied sources of income, she had put two of her intelligent, focused and well-brought-up young daughters through nursing college, and was paying to educate her third child, about to complete high school. She was a large, shapely woman, pleasant to talk to, with a round, pretty face, and sharp sense of humour. She always wore big shiny earrings and a brightly coloured *doek,* and she had an intriguing gap between her teeth that was revealed every time she flashed her quick smile. She was flirtatious and funny, popular among her many clients, and was a recipient of a surprising amount of confidential information. Various men professed love for her from time to time, but she mocked and rejected them all, believing that they were interested only in sharing her bed first, and then stealing her money. The worthless drunkard father of her children had been with her for some years but had beaten her up once too often. In the last and final assault she was ready for him and had fought back, hitting him repeatedly with her iron and punching him in the ribs and stomach. He had not been expecting resistance and was too drunk and off balance to properly fight back, and that last time he had lost the element of surprise.

She eventually beat him to the ground of their hut with the old fashioned black metal stove iron, gouging big chunks out of his skull, then dragged his senseless body out of the hut, some distance away, to leave him in a drunken stupor, covered in mud and bleeding under the incessant rain of a bitterly cold dark night.

Some weeks after this, he had come back to their home, rather sheepishly, his head wrapped in a dirty bandage, and had collected his clothes, his expensive shoes, a gold lighter and his Supersonic radio and left for good, taking back his surname from her. She had then forged a successful and happy life of her own, raising in the process three small children, alone. She was strong enough to laugh uproariously about how badly she had beaten her useless man, that worthless government plumber who had never even finished paying *lobola*. This story was quite well known in the area and gave her a certain standing in the community. She was raising her daughters to respect themselves and to reject the many attempts to impregnate them while they were still studying to become nurses. They feared and respected their mother and obeyed. None of them knew about the other source of income.

What was known to very few people was that MaLindiwe also kept detailed notes of all her business transactions in a second small notebook, one she kept hidden in the wall, and she had amassed a surprisingly large savings account that earned her a considerable monthly interest. Managing this required some careful planning. In the manner of the people of the area, she had made certain discreet enquiries, then crossed the border into South Africa one day. In exchange for a large cash payment to a Home Affairs clerk, she had returned later with a new name and surname, and a new barcoded South African ID document. This, and an easily-established false address and Post Office box in a small town, soon enabled her to open a South African savings account, so most of her dagga income was stashed away in Piet Retief, earning better rates of interest than she could obtain in Eswatini. Only her income from the stall remained in Eswatini and local currency.

Whenever she visited the bank in Piet Retief, she would always feign stupidity, appearing to be an uneducated rural woman of great naivety, a simple person needing assistance to bank cash, apparently the proceeds from yet another successful sale of one of her imaginary cattle. The bank had eventually issued her with a bank card, and she loved the power this gave her, knowing she could draw cash whenever she needed some, without needing to see anyone.

Ginindza had emerged from the forest, blinking in the sunshine that morning, with the sun moving towards midday. He was feeling deeply burdened by what he had witnessed and walked immediately to MaLindiwe's roadside stall. They greeted one another, spoke briefly and then, to her surprise, he requested a private discussion with her. She looked at him quizzically – he was too old to want to propose love to her and had never done so before, but he clearly needed to discuss a special matter, and it appeared to be urgent.

A woman of action, she summoned a young boy to mind the stall, and retired with the old man some distance away for a discreet conversation. He looked intently at the ground, scratching at it with a twig. 'I have encountered a problem, Lindiwe,' he said. 'Ever since that time, up until so far, it is disturbing my thoughts.'

She suspected that he had been caught by forest security and had to pay them a bribe to be released, so needed to borrow cash or something similar, but then he went on.

'Today, I was coming from the western side of Mushroom Valley and I saw something strange. Now it troubles my mind.'

She nodded, her gleaming earrings moving slightly and catching the sunlight, and smiled, her open face encouraging him to go on. '*Yini Mkhulu, yini Inkinga*?' What – what is the problem old man?

He shook his head, looking away, and she thought she saw a rare emotion welling up in his eyes as they filled with tears. 'Lindiwe, I saw men carrying a child this morning, moving deep in the forest in the direction of that area we know as Engwenyameni.' He looked down, and in a very low voice continued. 'They were two, Lindiwe. The other one was smaller, he was running ahead, the other one was big, he was strong, he was carrying a little girl like this…' he imitated the man.

'He was holding her mouth to not make noise, but she was fearful of these men, and they were in a hurry, trying to go fast, as if going somewhere.' He coughed and spat, as though the mere telling of it had left a sour taste in his mouth.

Lindiwe felt a cold shiver run down her back, instantly on alert. She had heard three times that morning, in a special announcement following each newscast, that the Royal Eswatini Police were seeking a young child, a girl who had been abducted from the lowveld the previous day, thought to be in the company of two men travelling in a blue bakkie. The girl was said to be aged four, and was light in complexion, with curly golden-brown hair. She had been wearing a pale blue dress. Ginindza had no watch, but as he described where he had seen them, and how he had walked quickly to find her, she thought this must have happened over an hour earlier.

Her mind racing, and nerves suddenly on edge, she asked him, 'Ginindza, how did this child look?'

'She was a light-skinned somebody,' he replied without hesitation. 'Her skin was very light in colour, like brown sugar, and she was having golden hair, and she was putting on a blue clothing like the sky in winter.'

'Are you sure her hair was definitely golden, but how did it look? Was it long?' questioned Lindiwe, looking at him sharply, every nerve in her body buzzing. He replied that it was so. It reminded him a little bit of the colour of a blonde weave. There was a certain, very promiscuous, young woman living locally who had such extensions in her hair, but he said it was not so light as that. Lindi knew the girl he described.

He said about the child's hair, 'It was like golden in colour, but not bright, and when there was sunlight, it shone like the fur of a puppy'.

He looked away and went on, 'She was only having one shoe. It had different colours on it, almost like flowers. They were blue and red and yellow, and I could see her legs and both of her feet, but the other one had no shoe.'

There is no true SiSwati word for pink, but there are descriptions of many different shades of red and ochre and he likened the shoe to the inside of a cows lung when cut open for roasting, or a piece of old red fabric that has been left in the sun and washed many times. But it was even brighter than that. He could not describe luminous pink other than 'ipinki'.

For Lindiwe it was enough. She was certain this must be the missing child and had been strongly moved by the news and her suffering, feeling deeply for the parents that morning. Children could disappear so easily. She thought of her own three girls when they were small, and how she had watched over them so carefully, like a hawk.

To his surprise she suddenly turned on him and startled him out of his rambling recollections to bluntly ask him one more question. 'Ginindza, could you show someone quickly where you saw this child being carried today, and which way they were going?'

He replied that he could do so easily and could guide them exactly to the place. He knew without any doubt the direction in which they were running.

Time seemed to come to a stop as she processed all that he had told her. She stood close to him for a long moment, touched by the old man's sincerity, but deeply shocked by what she had heard. She needed to take a moment of time to collect her thoughts. She did not want to become involved with the police but knew in her heart that they must be given this information. It was urgent and could be especially important. There was a child's life at stake.

Lindiwe was a big woman to see running, something she seldom did, but she ran back to her stall, grabbed her cellphone from under her cushion and breathlessly called the police number, explaining urgently that she had some important information about the missing girl from the lowveld. She did not want to just give this to anyone.

For once, thankfully, the number was answered quickly, then swiftly and with surprising efficiency they explained to her what they were doing, patching her through to the officer in charge of the case. Then there were a few odd noises and a ringing sound, and suddenly she was put through directly to Detective Inspector Rennie's personal cellphone. The signal was patchy because he was driving his car at that moment towards Mhlabanyati.

He had been at the Barton's home again early that morning, in case there were any new leads, and had picked up Knox Mkhize in case a situation developed where they needed someone PJ would know and trust. The Barton's powerfully-built security guard was a big man she had known her whole life, utterly devoted to Pumi Jacqueline and determined to find her alive, or track down her captors and kill them, even if it meant trouble with the policeman. He would assist in whatever way he could. Rennie had turned round and left with him, driving off at high speed, heading to investigate a tip off near Mafutseni.

Chapter 15

On the spoor

DETECTIVE INSPECTOR RENNIE CONSIDERED THAT they would probably be taking her deep into the bush, or some secluded area, somewhere remote but near to a stream, or some body of water, to remove the parts they needed. In previous cases he had investigated, they always washed themselves and the rocks after completing the hideous cutting. They also usually washed the body after removing the body parts but would then leave it, often uncovered. They would try to collect and save the bloodied water used for washing, as this also had special powers and would be sold as it supposedly afforded invisibility to thieves. It had a high value on the illegal market.

That morning, he had already been following a tip off from someone who had phoned the police about a blue bakkie. He had driven to a grubby, run down area near Mafutseni, where they established from neighbours, all rather reluctant to talk, that a blue bakkie had been parked there overnight outside an old abandoned farm house. One of the young men staying nearby told them that it was missing its tailgate, it had arrived late, two men had got out, one shorter than the other and that morning it had started up and they left early. The windows were darkened, and the witness had not seen much more, but noticed the blue bakkie. He heard them getting inside because the pressed steel door of the derelict house made an unmistakeable screeching noise when it was opened. It was a dirty place, where skelms and criminals lurked, an old house they would use for drinking, sex and taking drugs. Sometimes stolen items were found there. He was too scared to go closer and see what they were doing.

During that frantic morning, after the first meeting with Rennie, the Bartons had also received a call, and Matt had promptly handed the phone to Khanyi. One of her sisters, the first born to one of Khanyi's uncle's friends, lived in Malkerns, and she had introduced herself as Beauty Simelane. Beauty phoned because she needed to tell Khanyisile something. While she was preparing their breakfast porridge, she had heard over the radio a few times that the police were searching for a blue bakkie, last seen near Mafutseni, and there was a search on for a kidnapped coloured girl thought to be linked to this vehicle. It gave details about her age, appearance, and clothing. She had not known Khanyi's number but knew her slightly and got her details from her father. Beauty and Khanyi had once met during a church music festival, when she had loved Khanyi's singing and had spoken to her afterwards. Her father had told her that it was Khanyi's child.

There is a beautiful road that leads up into the dark green, conifer-covered hills, running from the north western edges of the pineapple fields in Malkerns, climbing up into the cooler air and heading towards the wild area known as Engwenyameni. Beauty's story then followed. She lived nearby, close to this little-known road, and had been out early that morning with her two grown brothers, collecting firewood from the edge of the pineapple fields, where old dead trees had been piled into rough windrows, from which firewood and small logs could sometimes be harvested.

The boys were busy cutting with a bow saw and loading firewood, and she (the only driver) had been sitting, leaning against the windscreen and relaxing on the bonnet in the shade, when she had first heard, and then seen, a blue bakkie driving slowly out of the pineapple fields and heading towards the forest along that same road. It was just near the place where the neat rows of pineapple plants and inter panel roads lap up almost against the very outskirts of the Usutu forest. She could see that it had two men inside, but the side windows were darkened. She thought that it did not have a tailgate as she could not see clearly what make it was. Usually, such vehicles have the make – like Mazda, Ford or Toyota – painted on the tailgate, and the tailgates often rattle.

This was not a frequently used road. It was slowly falling into disuse and was not easy to find among the neatly contoured pineapple lands in the valley, but she and her brothers had noticed the colour of the van as it emerged after driving steadily through those rarely used roads. All three of them had seen it. The two boys had both looked up at the noise and after it drove out of sight they'd discussed it together, because they had all heard the newscast about the abduction and the blue vehicle. Beauty thought she had seen it shortly before nine that morning.

The Bartons had received many phone calls following the item broadcast on the news, although they hadn't been named as the parents, and Matt, desperate to be doing something active, had decided to chase down one of these possible leads. He had driven northwards with Gabriel and was searching small villages in the highveld for a blue van supposed to have been seen there recently.

Rennie had driven quickly up the main road to Mafutseni. They had identified and entered the derelict house, inspecting it for any clues. The two men quickly went in and searched the filthy building. It looked like two rooms had been used recently. There were fresh candle stubs lying around, several new stompies and three empty quart beer bottles in one room, still smelling of beer. In the other, someone had slept on cardboard, and there was a coke can, still smelling of coke, with a few breadcrumbs on the floor that the ants hadn't found yet. Some of the window frames had been boarded up with old newspapers and cardboard.

They had just left there when he received a phone call from Khanyisile. She was now sounding even more distraught, despite all the well-meaning people around her. He spoke to her very calmly, without raising his voice, quietly and unemotionally encouraging her to relay the information to him carefully, and exactly as Beauty had given it to her. He listened carefully, then thanked her and asked her to pass on his thanks to Beauty, knowing that this was potentially a crucial lead. He kept the excitement out of his voice.

The pace was hotting up, and he could sense it. He was certain that this was the van they were looking for. The tip off meant that the blue bakkie must be in the edges of the Usutu forest by now, heading up into the highveld, probably north west towards the old Transvaal and Lundzi border post. Perhaps they were aiming to cross the border with her. Rennie had already been driving for some time and was still working through this second lead, thinking about how he could locate the vehicle, suspecting that they might have hidden it somewhere or changed cars when, shortly after midday, Lindiwe's call, the third and most important of that fateful day, was put through to his cellphone.

He had Knox Mkhize beside him in the double cab, listening, when the call came through. Lindiwe explained what she had just heard, while catching her breath, relaying the information the old man Ginindza had given her. Her voice was strong, clear and distinct, amplified through the vehicles sound system, and he glanced at Knox beside him, listening intently, the big man drawing in his breath and tensing his shoulders and arms as though preparing for battle. He kept tightening and releasing his meaty fists, cracking his knuckles.

Lindiwe Mavimbela introduced herself briefly as a stall owner near Mhlabanyatsi, from Siphocisini, and then explained that two men had been seen in the forest that morning, jogging and walking together and carrying a child who seemed to fit the missing child's description. She thought this was around an hour and thirty or forty minutes back. The little girl was still alive.

The witness who had seen this was well known to her. He did not have a watch, but he had come straight to see her and was there with her now and could show them the place. Rennie listened to her message with acute concentration. He felt a familiar surge of excitement as soon as she mentioned the golden hair, and the specific colour of the dress. He felt as though his blood had grown ice cold and was suddenly coursing through his body with extra speed and power. He knew this unique feeling, when he would suddenly gain an acuity of vision and great clarity of thought, like a moving picture coming into sharp focus, and he sensed immediately that this was a crucial lead and a vital breakthrough.

Now it had become a matter of timing, speed and finding the child still alive. He quickly and precisely made an arrangement to meet this Mavimbela woman, and to pick up the witness, the old man called Ginindza, from an exact spot close to where they were. He asked Lindiwe to describe herself and what she was wearing so that there could be no mistake. She in turn listened acutely and could hear by his accent that the policeman was a coloured man. He spoke SiSwati fluently, although with a distinct accent. He thought Lindiwe sounded bright and intelligent, and very willing to help. He had picked up the urgency in her voice: sincerity, not excitement, not thrill seeking but real urgency.

He made sure that he had the exact details describing where they would meet him, cut the call and then focused on driving. He and Knox sped up and he raced on, overtaking all other traffic, even against oncoming vehicles. As they began nearing the town of Manzini, he switched on his flashing lights and siren in the double cab and they drove through town, jumping all the robots. They raced out of the town centre and hurtled up the hill, passing Matsapha at great speed, heading towards Mahlanya market and the second Malkerns turn off. He was often driving on the wrong side of the road, crossing solid white lines, but he kept going, foot flat on the accelerator, headlights on full beam, passing everything else and cursing at the trucks, buses and taxis getting in his way.

Knox held onto the roof handle tightly with his left hand, and clutched his fighting sticks with his right, absorbing the excitement and the entire experience as preparation for hot pursuit and a battle, praying to his ancestors that they must find the child alive, and aching for the chance to kill at least some of her captors before the policeman stopped him. He was longing to take revenge and make them pay for their actions, but he knew that the law tended to see things differently, and this policeman seemed to be a powerful, thinking, fearless man.

DI Rennie was deep in thought, calculating as he drove, working out the remaining distances and available time. He suspected that the two men would be hurrying through the forest to some specific killing spot, but they would be slowed by carrying the child. He was a skilful driver, used to driving fast. Driving with one hand, he radioed ahead to the police in Mhlabanyati, ordering them to assemble some specialist officers, and some young, fit men, preferably with tracking experience, and to make a vehicle available immediately to meet him on the road coming from Siphocisini. If anyone was closer than that, they should start looking near the main road for a blue van, or for tracks.

He stressed the urgency of the situation, and that he was now in pursuit, explaining what he already knew. He had deduced from Mavimbela's call that the van had probably been abandoned already, as the captors were seemingly on foot. He prayed that what this old man had recounted to Lindiwe was true, and that he was not fabricating anything.

His urgent voice and radio presence, a command coming with great intensity over the two-way radio from a senior CID officer with rank, carried weight and authority. Instead of the usual delays and feeble excuses about breakdowns, petrol or the lack of transport, he was advised after twenty minutes that a 4x4 vehicle, fully fuelled up, manned with several young policemen, would be ready and waiting for him by the time he reached there. They were also speaking to the regional police station further up the road to get someone onto the same route who would begin working their way back along the road from the Lundzi border post, heading south east, and they too would be searching for signs of the blue bakkie. The problem was that there were so many unmarked roads in the forest.

Detective Rennie was beginning to fear they would be too late. All the time he had been with the Bartons, and then investigating the house at Mafutseni, precious time had been passing. So much was still unknown.

From other violent abduction and murder cases he had investigated, he hoped that the men who had stolen the child might need to pause and steel themselves for the final act and, if they were tired from running, this might take a bit of time. He thought that they would probably sit and rest for a bit, catching their breath, recovering, maybe drinking or using drugs to numb themselves up before starting what they had to do. He prayed it would be so.

Through gritted teeth, swearing vehemently at the hopelessly slow traffic and tractors delaying him, but taking all the gaps between them and driving flat out, as fast as the powerful pick up would travel, he thought of the little girl, terrified and held captive by strangers, and sought the protection he remembered from his school days, calling on St Michael the Archangel, softly saying under his breath a faintly remembered prayer: 'Defend us in battle, be our protection against the wickedness and snares of the devil. May God rebuke him we humbly pray, and do thou, O Prince of the Heavenly host, by the power of God, cast into Hell Satan and all the evil spirits who prowl about the world seeking the ruin of souls, Amen.'

He quickly crossed himself.

Knox looked across at him, unclear about the prayer but understanding the sentiment and joined in. '*Enkhosi,* Hallelujah, Amen! We are going to find them today, we two together, and then we kill them.' Rennie glanced across at him and nodded, too busy driving to discuss the rights and wrongs or legality of his passenger's heartfelt response.

He somehow felt strengthened and encouraged by this divine intervention and could almost visualise an archangel, wielding a long fiery sword, flying away ahead of them, streaking across the clouds. Detective Rennie, a doting father of two little girls himself, and a devout Roman Catholic by upbringing, pressed his foot even harder to the floor. The powerful vehicle hesitated, kicked down a gear and accelerated again, surging effortlessly back to top speed. Malkerns Valley and the next turn off was looming quickly into sight. They had one more road bridge to cross.

The arrangement they had made to meet Ginindza worked well. He and Lindiwe were waiting by the road, exactly at the agreed place. Rennie spun the car round and briefly thanked Sis Lindiwe. The old man got in and then they streaked off, continuing up the road that leads towards Mushroom Valley. Ginindza had hardly ever been in a car of any kind. He greeted Knox faintly, then, fearing imminent death, closed his eyes and began communing with his ancestors in case his life was about to end suddenly. He wondered if he had even done the right thing in telling Sis Lindiwe. Despite everything he was feeling, the wild ride, being jolted around and thrown violently from side to side, he could not get the image of the terrified little child out of his mind.

He wasn't sure if it usually felt like this when moving in a 'private', but he much preferred walking and did not even want to look out of the windows. He desperately wanted to take some snuff but was too fearful to even consider releasing one hand for a moment, let alone both. The cornering forces and bumps terrified him. This coloured man driving them was clearly insane. He clung tightly onto the seat top in front of him, and to a handle in his door, his two wizened old hands gripping onto the upholstery like a vice, and just kept hanging on in quiet desperation. He was barely able to answer the questions that Rennie asked him but understood clearly when he was told that he must indicate when they came to the place nearest to where he saw the men. He began opening his eyes briefly, glancing at the country flying past him, amazed at the blur and how soon different landmarks he recognised had begun passing by.

He knew that, travelling with this young madman and big Zulu, they would very soon be at the hidden entrance to the path and he tried his best to concentrate, frightened almost out of his skin by the sheer speed. They raced on, flying over the bumps and humpbacks, scattering gravel behind them, a long dust trail left hanging in the air.

Barely half an hour after leaving Lindiwe, he muttered to Knox that they were coming close, and risked releasing one hand to indicate a faint opening coming up on the right. Rennie could discern nothing, no visible break in the bush alongside the road, but he reduced speed. Suddenly, at a slight turn in the gravel road, Ginindza asked him to stop. He skidded to a halt in the gravel, pulled over onto the bank and switched off, the din of hours of fast driving replaced with nothing more than the quiet movement of air in the trees, and the tick … tick… ticking sounds of the hot engine and exhaust as it began to cool down. There was nothing to see that indicated a pathway, and for a terrible moment Rennie thought the old man was lost or confused.

But Ginindza, delighted to be getting out of this insane death machine alive and in one piece, gathered his ancient emahiya and greasy coat about his spindly legs and, after pulling ineffectually at the wrong handle several times, leapt out. He moved surprisingly quickly. Muttering a few words, he then headed straight across the road and indicated a barely discernible opening in the weeds and grass where the vegetation had recently been pushed down.

'This is the way,' he announced. 'I will show you where I saw them. We must show speed.'

They did not hesitate or waste any time looking for the blue bakkie, hidden by branches a short way off the road on the opposite side. There was no time. They didn't even notice the crushed plants, flattened and pushed over where it had been driven off the road.

Rennie quickly checked that he had two full magazines, holstered his firearm and grabbed his two-way radio and a torch. Knox gathered his fighting sticks and a favourite, deeply notched blackened iron wood 'Kerrie that had eaten several skulls before, and they set off, following Ginindza along the path.

The spritely old man was fit and knew exactly where he was. He was able to discern a pathway that neither of the two other men could readily make out. His eyes adjusted quickly to the familiar gloom of the forest covering and he moved lightly and more quickly than usual, not worried about making a noise and not quite running, but either jogging along or moving at a fast walk. He had left his backpack in the police car. Rennie called up the nearest police on his walkie talkie and found out that they were a few minutes behind them. They would see his car and follow the tracks they had left. Rennie tried to describe the landmarks at its entrance.

Now there were three sets of footfalls: Ginindza, gambolling along lightly and easily on his dusty, thin, scaly old legs; Rennie, young and fit, steadily loping a short distance behind him; and a short way back the bulky form of Knox, just easing his long legs and big body into movement, shaking off long hours in the car, taking big steady strides that he could keep up for hours, always keeping the leading two in sight. They covered the ground fast, moving down off the road, into the rolling terrain of the forest and along the path, clambering over the ridges and stumps left by previous tree plantings. Rennie could feel his heart starting to race.

They stopped to draw breath briefly where Ginindza showed them he had seen the men, and where he had lain, hidden from them, then continued along the path, moving as quickly as they could. Ginindza was old, but he had stamina and could still move fast, and Rennie kept urging him on. Twenty minutes further on, Ginindza slowed, then stopped and pointed out in the distance an empty blue and silver packet of chips. There were clear depressions in the pine needles nearby. Their quarry had stopped there to rest and had eaten something, throwing the empty packet down onto the forest floor. A little later, they found a cold drink can, still clean, droplets of the drink still inside. It had only recently been dropped there.

After running along for some time, the shadows lengthened as the afternoon wore on and they came to a place where they could hear the faint sound of running water in the distance. Ginindza signalled to them to slow down and quieten their footfalls. He gestured ahead, beckoning to the two men and explaining to them that there was a stream and a rocky place nearby, a little way ahead and to the left. He did not want to go there, as it was bewitched, a dangerous place. He sat down and said he would not go further, but he thought they could find the men there by the stream.

Knox and Rennie continued along the path towards the stream, stealthily and more cautiously than before, treading carefully. Rennie took out his gun, flicked the safety off, double checked the spare magazine and holstered it again, loaded. They were both still panting heavily from their long run through the forest, and he tried to slow his breathing.

DI Rennie led, and Knox followed him, staying slightly off to the right-hand side, reliving his younger days as a warlord and using the natural cover to stay almost out of sight. They noticed the type of vegetation changing as they neared the secluded stream, and both crouched down as they approached the bank, hoping to surprise the men who had PJ. Both prayed she was still alive.

As they breasted the top of the bank and looked down, they knew they had found them: two men with a little girl spread on the rocks between them. This was where the deed was to be done.

Chapter 16

The end of innocence

THERE ARE CERTAIN MEN AND women who, even when they know they have lost everything, know fully that there is no chance of them escaping, even when there is nothing to be gained by continuing in their course of action, will sometimes cause pain to others for the sake of it. They will see through to the end their intention of doing evil for their own motives.

They may feel a twinge of regret but proceed with the act anyway, despite knowing they have caused someone else pain, or caused abject misery and despair. The sense that they have broken a home, taken a life, or ruined someone else's life, fills them with a perverted satisfaction. Why should they suffer alone? A kind of evil sometimes lurks deep in the mind of a person who can rationalise almost any action to themselves – as though thinking, 'Even if I won't get the money, I don't care. I'm going to kill the child and take that from the parents. That is something precious to them and I will take that from them.'

They can close off the normal feelings of sympathy and may not even experience the human sensations of normal people.

When he encountered the two men crouched on the rock – one of them holding down the child, hand clamped over her mouth, the other with the skinning knife preparing to cut into her, to start removing the private parts, the breasts, the lips, the eyes and earlobes – Detective Inspector Richard Rennie knew in his heart that these men were not going to stop. He had seen such creatures before.

Rennie did not believe they were God's children, and that was how he justified what sometimes had to happen.

The men looked up, startled but slow to react to the sudden intrusion into such a hidden place. They started and glared at Rennie, seeing him through glazed, deadened eyes. After reaching the killing spot, they had been very tired. They had rested for a time, eaten something, and then smoked three pipes of dagga laced with nyaope, with the greater amount smoked by the bigger man, and this had made them feel brave and immune to any feelings of sympathy. The drugs had dulled any conventional sense of simple humanity. Boy had spittle dribbling from his mouth but could no longer feel it on his face. They no longer clearly understood concepts like risk, threat or reward and had become partially immune to pain. It would be exceedingly difficult to arrest and subdue such men.

The little girl splayed out on the flat rock had become to them a field to be harvested, a beast to be slaughtered for money. Boy held her down and the other would cut. They had deliberately avoided any interaction with her during the abduction because they knew that this made the task more difficult, tending to weaken their resolve. They had no hatred specifically for her, but equally had no concern or feeling for her life or body. She was simply the chosen one, a means to an end.

The drugs coursing through their bodies affected their judgement differently, and Ndzinisa, stupefied, decided to take the child's life anyway. The Sangoma would protect him and the threat of imminent arrest would not prevent him from at least killing the child. He had driven far, taken risks, gone without food and run all this way – his mind was on a course now, it was deserved, nothing was going to stop him at least taking part of her for himself. His rational mind was broken, disengaged and disconnected. His grasp of events, and innate fear of witchcraft and punishment, meant that he was unable to comprehend clearly or grasp the risk that Rennie posed. He even wondered briefly if the intruder would also want some of the muti.

His partner Boy reacted differently and his brain, although slow to engage, thought it best to flee. He suspected in his dulled mind that Rennie might be coming to stop them, but his unfocused thoughts would not clear and churned over slowly like molasses in his mind. He stood up and made an uncoordinated attempt to dash for the bank. Reminded painfully of his cut ankle, he was unaware that Knox had circled around and was standing at the top of it, hidden in the dark shadows.

From the hatred and darkness emanating from his stare, a sense of wrongdoing and the stench of evil that shrouded his whole body, Rennie knew instinctively that the crouching one would kill the child out of spite. There was, in his eyes, somewhere behind the drugs, a barbaric threat of violence, some strange unseen presence corrupting the natural beauty of the place. He would have preferred to take him prisoner, but once he turned again to face the child lying prostrate before him, and began to bend her head backwards to expose her neck, he knew there was no chance of the child surviving. He knew that he had to make a split-second decision.

He shouted one warning: '*Phakamisa izandla, Phezulu*!' put your hands up!'

But instead of surrendering, he saw the kidnapper's hand moving downwards, the grip on the knife changing subtly, the sinews and muscles in his body tensing, preparing, stiffening himself to cut into the soft, pale exposed throat of the child. Instinctively, Rennie drew back the slide of his 9mm automatic and, in one quick movement, exhaled, aimed and fired, gripping his firearm firmly in both hands. In the split second before pulling the trigger (a deliberate act he would admit to no one, other than his priest during confession), he edged his shot fractionally down, away from the shoulder he had intended to aim at, and aimed straight for the heart, a man-stopping shot at a larger target, easier to hit, centred on the target's upper chest.

The heavy bullet went through the upper right quadrant of the heart, tearing it to pieces and tearing a great wound in the chest cavity. Like an injured bird, or a half-shot animal, the derailed nervous system still issued random instructions and the muscles still tried to obey, slavishly remembering the intent. His arms flailed at the child, stabbing at her even as he began to topple over backwards. The knife cut into her soft little arm, and Rennie fired a second time, deliberately aiming higher up.

The second heavy bullet caught Ndzinisa in his gaping mouth, open, surprised and about to cry out. It passed straight through his throat, shattering the bones and exiting through the lower part of his skull, then ricocheted, whining off the rocks, embedding itself deeply in the trunk of a pine tree. It separated his brain from the rest of his body instantly. He was knocked backwards by the impact of the bullet and fell awkwardly with a grunt, still holding the knife in one hand. He landed heavily and settled, twitching, quickly becoming motionless on the rocks, bleeding profusely.

Pumi Jacqueline turned and fractionally looked up for a moment, then shut her little eyes tightly and lay still, too terrified to move. Unable to prevent it, she wet herself.

Rennie took in the developing situation quickly, one man down, shot and killed, the child still looking alive, although slightly cut. He saw that the second man, having released her and taken his hand off her mouth was turning and scrambling up the bank, heading for the forest.

He knew that if the second man managed to get into the trees, there was a good chance he would make his escape because the bush was dense, the forest dark, and the afternoon light fading. With only the three of them there, two to give chase and one needing to stay with the child, if he made for the forest there were too few of them to cover the crime scene and he might escape. These men were fast of foot and wily; they were used to being hunted. The detective was still breathing heavily from the long run along the trail.

Rennie shouted a second warning both in English and SiSwati, but Boy continued trying to get away, scrabbling frantically for grip and handholds in the low hanging shrubs, lantana and foul-smelling bush weed that grew along the bank. He was making his escape, desperately crawling upwards, fighting his way up, over the riverbank and into the gathering darkness of the forest. Rennie wanted him alive, but the firing angles, the shadows and shrubs made a wounding shot difficult. He fired a third time, deliberately high. He spent a lot of time and his own money on the firing range. He knew he was a good shot – he had practised hard enough – and although he seldom had to discharge his weapon, when he had to he knew his own capabilities. But the golden rule was you should not shoot unless you had a clear view of the target. He did not have a clear view.

But he had forgotten momentarily about Knox. Boy had not even noticed him, focusing entirely on Rennie, and thought he was escaping into an empty forest. As he gleefully pulled himself up onto the riverbank and reached level ground, he stood up, feeling triumphant. Without warning, a very large man suddenly stepped out of the shadows, grabbed him by the throat and began choking him to death, cutting off his breathing, crushing his throat with a powerful hand and preventing him from crying out.

All the rage and hatred rising within Mkhize powered his grip and, as he crushed the windpipe, he could feel the vermin beginning to weaken in his hand. Knox squeezed even harder and then lifted him off the ground, one hand still choking his throat, the other clenched in his shirt front.

Boy's hands flapped at him ineffectually, then, with great force and violence, Knox suddenly threw him backwards down onto the rocks, hoping this would break his head and kill him. He knew that police tended to disapprove of such methods, or he would have dealt with the matter more permanently, then and there, using his fighting sticks to crack the worthless one's skull. His blood was up for revenge and he thirsted for a killing.

Boy, still feeling high from the drugs, was disoriented by the sudden turn of events and had barely seen the big man. He just felt an enormous hand grabbing him and cutting off his air supply, then a sudden force lifting him off his feet and hurling him backwards. He lost his footing and was thrown into the air behind him, his senses fading and hands clawing helplessly at nothing, trying to prevent himself overbalancing. They found only emptiness, and he fell backwards, falling a long way down and landing heavily on the uneven and unforgiving rock face. He hit the outcrop hard, breaking his right arm in two places on impact and spraining his left wrist as he landed on it, still flailing away, desperately trying to break his fall. He tried to scream, but to his confusion found that he couldn't. He was unable to make any noise because his larynx had been crushed. The only sound that came out was like a choking dog attempting to bark.

With surprising speed and agility for such a large man, Knox followed Boy, leaping off the grassy earthen bank alongside the stream, landing hard down on the rock face, taking the shock on his knees and legs. Then, without pausing, he ran straight up to PJ, grabbed her and lifted her quickly into his arms. He had heard but not seen the shots that had hit Ndzinisa.

PJ was screaming now, out of fear and in panic, having heard the three shots at close range. After having been kidnapped by strangers, forcibly held down, silenced and then having been carried, jerking and bumping through the forest, she was lost in a place somewhere far beyond sheer terror.

She suddenly smelt something familiar, saw a face she knew and liked, raised her child's arms and hands, beseeching. As he lifted her off the rocks, her tiny body melted into his arms and she buried her face into his neck, pushing her face into his shoulder to hide and cry, her heart beating like a trapped bird. Her whole body was trembling like a puppy's.

The detective, in a more dignified way, cleared and holstered his weapon and climbed elegantly down onto the rocks, dusting off his slender hands. He went swiftly across to Knox and asked, 'Is she alright, Knox?'

Knox untangled her hands and placed her very carefully down on the rocks, still holding her gently at arm's length and then, in the African way, felt and examined each limb, her feet, the calves, her thighs and knees, the legs, her hips and sides, the stomach, and her little arms, her dainty hands and fingers, the forearms, shoulders and tummy. He looked at her neck, checked all around her head, looked at her ears, touching and examining every part of her thoroughly and briefly lifted her skirt, then said to the policeman, 'Aah, she's okay, this one, the little girl is alright… our child, the first born, she's alive but just frightened too much.'

Boy was by now attempting to rise again, making a sort of harsh gasping sound, struggling and squirming as he tried to let them know how much his arm and shoulder were hurting. Some way behind him, his partner was lying dead, bleeding profusely, bright red flowing across the white rocks and congealing into a darkening mess. Knox did not want PJ to see or hear this anymore and gently turned her head back to his shoulder and walked away from the scene, just happening accidentally to trip heavily over Boy's broken shoulder and arm and grinding it underneath his boot as he walked past him and away. Boy again tried to scream as the ends of his broken and displaced bones ground against each other, but found he was unable to. He tapped feebly at Knox's leg. The odd noises that came out of his ruined throat grew momentarily louder, but nobody took any notice. The drugs were wearing off and he could certainly feel pain now. Things had not gone according to plan.

When they were some distance away, Knox gently washed down PJs legs and panties in the shallow stream, scooping up clean water with his hand, and he then cleaned and examined the cut on her arm. He clambered carefully up the riverbank and into the forest and carried PJ far enough away into the trees that the noise of the stream drowned any noises that her captor could still make. Then he sat down gently with her on his lap and began shushing and stroking her.

She was crying, 'Mama, want my mama, where's my mama,' and he just said quietly, '*Lalela mtanami, lalela, shushushushu, haikona, don't cry, kahle wena, kahle wena* it's alright, I will bring you to Mama, it's alright now, you are safe here with Knox, you are safe now, we are going home to find Khanyi.'

He tied a clean cloth around her arm, the red one he always had tied around his right bicep. His deep rumbling voice was soothing and gentle, and his massive chest and brawny arms around her comforted her like a warm blanket. Her breathing gradually slowed, and in between gasps and sobbing for Mama, she said something about 'my Knoxie came', and he felt her slowly calming, the trembling growing less under his massive hands. Then, still occasionally gasping for air and sobbing as a young child will, she gently drifted off to sleep, safe now but utterly exhausted.

Holding her in one hefty arm, his elbow clasped tightly around her waist, he sat with her under the shade of the trees in the surrounding glade and gradually relaxed, feeling her body secure on his lap. No one, other than her parents, would be able to take her from him while he was still alive. He regretted not killing the one who had been holding her down, regretted not twisting his head like a chicken, but took satisfaction from the knowledge that at least the other one was dead and the police would probably interrogate the weakened one until they found who had hired them.

He knew how much he had damaged the man's throat. He had crushed it and felt it give way and break under his grip. He knew the short one would never be able to speak normally again. There was still some pleasure in that at least. The big one was finished, and the abnormal, misplaced arrangement of the arm and how the shoulder looked on the smaller one after being thrown down onto the rocks gave him some slight comfort.

The child was safe, the abductors were caught, one broken and the other dead. Knox felt that he had done his job.

In the near distance he could see the other police had now started to arrive, after following Rennie's directions and, one by one, they also approached respectfully and thanked Knox too. Some of the uniformed men peeked tenderly at the trembling girl in his arms without touching her, as though she were a flighty animal. Some shook their heads. 'Hau, she is safe this little one.'

She was hiding her face, still trembling occasionally. There was much happiness, back slapping, loud laughter, shoulder hugs and camaraderie. Several of them knew Rennie and congratulated him. They had quickly located the blue bakkie hidden in the trees and were only about twenty minutes behind Rennie and Knox, having managed to follow their tracks along the path without much difficulty. They had heard the shots from a distance. Fearing the worst, several of them had arrived with weapons drawn, but they were jubilant at the outcome.

The shadowy copse and forest stream was now swarming with uniformed police and after taking pictures, as the shadows deepened and it grew cooler, they dragged the corpse of the first muti murderer up onto the forest floor with minimal ceremony, dropped it on the ground, coated in pine needles that had stuck to the blood, and threw an old blanket over the body. Then they handcuffed Boy, read him his rights, formally arrested him, and roughly forced him to walk up the bank, ignoring his pleas, and laughing at the strange, choking noises coming from his broken voice. He was complaining bitterly in a hoarse whisper about the pain of his shattered shoulder, arm and wrist, but there was no sympathy shown. One of the police constables had a small first aid kit, and he expertly dressed PJ's wound, tenderly and with gentle care. They rounded up the bags, the cutting knives, the drug paraphernalia and the pair's few belongings and bagged them all as evidence. Boy was questioned and answered in a whispered response to the officers that his partner was called

Ndzinisa. He did not seem to want to look at him. As the drugs wore off, they caused him to salivate, and he kept spitting, bleary eyed and confused. Everything they had planned had gone wrong.

Before they carried the body in the blanket and escorted the captive up the long path back towards the road, Ginindza emerged from the gloom like a forest wraith. He had sat down, taken some snuff, and was feeling at peace with the world after being startled by the gunfire.

Rennie thanked him, and asked him briefly, 'Babe Ginindza, can you identify if these were the men you saw running with the child this morning?'

He pulled back the blanket, uncovered the corpse to reveal the damaged head and torso of Ndzinisa, and then went across the clearing and gripped and pivoted Boy's head roughly to face him. Ginindza looked closely at them both, as though inspecting animal carcasses. He went right up to Boy and gazed into his face, as though looking for marks on a rock.

'Yebo, Baba, these are the ones. The big one, the one that is now late, was carrying her, this smaller one making noise was running in front and that young she one, carried by Knox, that is the same child they were carrying. I saw them all.'

He went across towards Knox and greeted him and very gently touched the sleeping child's matted golden-brown hair and honey skin, tentatively feeling her tiny toes and feet between his fingers as though testing a fabric. He looked at how still and young she was, and thought he had never seen anything so perfect as this little girl.

'Is she alright?'

Knox nodded to him and replied softly, 'She has much fear remaining within her, but she has not been hurt or raped. We reached her in time.' He paused. 'Yeh, Babe Ginindza, *Yeh Mkhulu*, we are grateful, we are grateful all of us and all of her family. It is you who saved her, this one whom we love.'

Rennie said the same thing, grasping his calloused hand and shaking it firmly. 'Mr Ginindza, what you did today was very brave. We will never forget it. You are the one who allowed us to save the life of this little girl. We were just in time.'

Ginindza nodded and his old eyes misted over as he thought backwards over so many new events and experiences that had happened to disrupt his life that day. Seeing what he'd seen, speaking to Lindiwe, going in a motor car, running back along the path and hearing shots, now seeing the dead man, his devil accomplice, and the living child. It had been a day like no other he could remember.

He suddenly recalled something that had been troubling him. 'But what of her shoe? She is still short one.' For some reason this worried him. The policeman Rennie told him not to worry, they had saved the child.

It was over. The men turned as one and started making their way back to the road. All the police in the vicinity knew they had saved the child, but there were two sniffer dogs with them and their handlers released them into the woods as they walked, to run the wider area and see if there were any others, or any signs of the buyer nearby.

As soon as he had cellphone signal, Detective Rennie tried phoning the father, Matt Barton, but the signal kept cutting out. They had reached the police vehicles that were waiting on the road, so he climbed into one of the 4x4s and used its radio. The message quickly went out to those who had remained behind, guarding the vehicles, and those men still searching elsewhere: 'We have got her, guys, we have got the child and she is unharmed.'

Some of the more religious policemen immediately stopped what they were doing, wherever they were in the forest, laid down their searching sticks on the ground, bowed their heads and prayed.

Matt was not at home. He'd had to get out and feel he was doing something to help. He and Gabriel had been following a vague lead, information that had taken him to the highveld and they were up in a bush area near Ndzingeni, roaming aimlessly around, stopping and asking rural farmers and at different kraals and homesteads if they had seen the small girl, or the blue bakkie. They had been endlessly side-tracked, mostly by excited young women who had heard the story on the radio, knew little about it but wanted to become famous, and were stitching together lies and half-truths to try and attract attention and male visitors. They had been sent from homestead to homestead after a blue bakkie that someone claimed to have seen, and had eventually found one that was a sun drenched blue, but was up on blocks, without its engine, a vehicle about thirty years old without wheels or a back axle that had not moved for decades. It had become a home for chickens.

Matt had walked dejectedly back, and was just outside the fenced kraal, about to give up, when his cellphone rang. He moved around looking at the screen until the signal got stronger then answered the call. It was a landline number; one he didn't recognise.

It was the Royal Eswatini police, a call was being patched through from a radio and he was asked to hold for Detective Inspector Rennie. There were various clicks, beeps and squelching sounds. Then he heard the familiar articulate and educated voice, softly rolling the 'r's.

'Mr Barton, Mr Barton, this is Detective Inspector Rennie speaking. I want to inform you that we have recovered your child, Mr Barton. She is safe and sound and she is in good hands. We are walking with her right now, but she is sleeping. We are carrying her to the car now, and I will personally be driving her back to your place tonight, but we will be late. We are still far from your place. Must I wake her up so you can speak to her?'

Matt tried to answer but his mouth had become dry and his body grew strangely weak. He felt a numbness overwhelm him and his balance failed. He slowly dropped to his knees as if knocked unconscious. He felt his legs giving way and sank slowly to the ground beneath, no longer able to stand. He clasped his head in his hands and wept, clinging tightly to the phone.

He just managed to get the words out, 'Thank you, thank you, thank you so much Inspector,' but he couldn't say any more.

After a time, during which the detective politely waited, he managed to say, 'No I don't want to speak to her now, Richard. I can't speak to her yet. Let her sleep. Give me a few minutes and I will speak to her. I must call my wife.' The sense of relief that overwhelmed him was so strong he could barely move his body.

Faintly echoing what had happened to Khanyi when they were in Mozambique and she had found the icon rolling in the surf, Gabriel saw his young friend fall to his knees from some distance away. He had seen him walking out of the homestead, leaving the kraal, then suddenly just falling straight down onto his knees. He ran towards him, thinking he had been bitten by a snake or fainted from stress and the lack of food, or, worse still, and what he most feared, had just received the worst news. The news they were dreading. He rushed up and crouched before him. 'What is it Matt? What's wrong?'

Matt looked up at the older man, his vision blurred through a veil of tears. 'Gabriel, they've found her. That was the police. They have found PJ, Gabriel, and she is okay. They have got her now.'

Neither of them could find words to speak and the older man looked away into the distance as though searching for guidance there. Then he somehow found some strength from deep within, blinked away a few tears himself, sniffed and crouched down, kneeling among the blackjacks, sparse thin grass and the dust beneath them.

He reached across to Matt, gripping his shoulders. 'This is a miracle, Matt. This is a miracle in your life you can never forget. All our prayers have been answered. It's a miracle. The people gathered together and we were very much strong in our faith all last night, and see, now we have been rewarded, the little one is found alive. God has guided the police and Knox to find her, and it's a blessing.'

He leant across the dark highveld dirt and they hugged, speechless, for several minutes, still kneeling. He heard the younger man drawing in a great lungful of air as he tried to pull himself together.

'We must go, Gabriel. We must go back home now. I must be there when she gets back!'

It was eventually Gabriel, not Matt, who phoned Khanyisile. Matt was still too distraught to talk to her at first and didn't want her to hear him until he was sure of his own voice. By then it was late afternoon, and she was sitting in their lounge after a long, emotional vigil and an interminable second day of waiting and not knowing. Some loyal and dear friends still stayed with her, but she was filled with a deep sense of longing and a black hopelessness that was welling up inside her, threatening to smother her thoughts.

The second night was drawing in, and among the group some were silently beginning to give up hope, though no one would utter those words. Khanyisile was at a point when grief and shock start giving way to sheer exhaustion, and she felt that she had nothing more to give. She was all cried out, prayed out, grieved out and simply shattered. She didn't want to eat or drink and felt that nothing of the old Khanyisile inside her could remain. It felt like nothing mattered any more. She just wanted Matt to come home and to be able to hold him to her and mourn their loss together. She had heard all about the five-year-old Malawian albino girl's body that was found mutilated and knew what this abduction could mean to them. The dreams that had tormented her were looming strong, lying in wait, lurking all around her in the shadows, spirits ready to pounce on her and claim her.

Everything she valued most in her life had been taken from her before: her own mother, her first child, the beloved Barton family she'd worked for, and now it was happening again, even with Matt whom she loved like no other. She was undoubtedly cursed and felt that even God had turned His back on her.

Chapter 17

Deliverance

TERESINHA, WITHOUT CHILDREN OF HER own, felt strongly compelled to stay with Khanyisile until the end, whatever outcome that might bring. They would either mourn together or rejoice, or a mixture of the two, but she would be with her. Somewhere out there in the darkness was the beloved little girl, someone she had known from when she was born and had watched grow into the happy child she had become. She adored PJ. Teresinha, Joao's wife, was a strong woman of great beauty and complicated heritage, with North Indian, Portuguese and African ancestors.

She had first befriended Khanyisile when she was still recovering from the loss of the family she cared for. She had never ceased interceding spiritually, was always physically close to her friend, and had barely left her side after the abduction. She was kept busy answering the phone and fielding all the calls, writing down any meaningful tip offs and passing them on to Matt or the police. Khanyi had a lot of relatives, and most of those who were unable to attend the vigil in person had phoned up to express support. The stress of the incoming calls was hideous, each one increasing the tension by raising up their hopes then dashing them down again, so it was Teresinha who answered the phone. Following the night vigil, she had remained with Khanyisile all day, much longer than many other visitors had been able to.

She answered the phone, and Gabriel recognised her calm, unusual, slightly Portuguese accented voice and gently asked to speak to Khanyi. Teresinha handed her the cellphone, saying in her soft voice, 'It's Gabriel, Khanyi'.

She was careful not to convey anything more in her expression, not knowing yet what the call meant. Khanyi took the phone numbly from her friend, but answered, her voice flat and without interest, feeling burdened enough and unable to cope with more bad news or more false leads. Seated in the darkened room with candles glowing, and the sense that her heart was already broken, Khanyi answered flatly, 'Yebo, Babe Gabriel, it's Khanyi here'.

Gabriel spoke in SiSwati, his deep powerful voice instantly recognisable, booming strongly across the ether. 'SisKhanyi, it's Gabriel here. SisKhanyi, they have found our child, they have found her. She is still okay, she is not hurt. Pumi is with Knox now. They are moving with her together with the police. They are bringing her home to you now, from somewhere in the forest near Siphocisini.'

There was a stunned silence. Then Khanyi let out a long wail, the intense pent-up emotions of the last thirty hours bursting from her. The desperate waiting for news and the hours of hoping, beseeching the world for her daughter's return, had entirely overwhelmed her. Teresinha came quickly to her, fearing the worst news had been delivered and simply squeezed her, holding her tightly and needing to support her as she collapsed to one side. Khanyi took a deep breath and told her the news. PJ was safe. She thanked Gabriel and gave the phone back. She felt as though everything in her body was suddenly buzzing, electric, coming back to life.

'I must speak to Matt now. Please call him for me', she asked Teresinha. For a moment she could not even remember his number, the one number she knew off by heart. Her steadfast, loyal friend placed the call, and Matt answered, driving along the remote roads with Gabriel on his way back from the highveld in the cold, empty darkness. He recognised the number and answered, 'Hi, Khanyi my love, it's me. She's safe. We are on our way home.'

Neither of them could speak for a few moments; they were both crying. Then he went on, 'They are bringing her home, Khanyi. She's coming back now. Rennie told me she is with Knox. They are all safe. What about you? Are you okay? We will be back in about three hours.'

'I'm okay now, Matt. Teresinha is still here with me, we are going to call everybody and tell the people now.'

They rang off, both feeling as though a long night of darkness had finally broken, and that the light of dawn and deliverance was on its way. The two women stood together and hugged each other tightly, squeezing all the agony of uncertainty and fear out of each other. Teresinha bowed her head, humbled by the moment, giving fervent thanks. She was the taller of the two women and her fragrant hair, long, curly and shining, tumbled about their two heads like a dark shroud. Finally, she drew a deep breath, pulled her shoulders back, gazed deeply into Khanyi's eyes and shook her head slowly, smiling. She sighed heavily, releasing a great weight. Khanyi just clung to her, scarcely able to breathe. They eventually pulled apart, silenced, stunned by the enormity of the relief flooding through them. Their hands stayed tightly together.

'I must call Joao, Khanyi. He has been fasting ever since she was taken.' She did this and they both heard his voice booming loudly over the phone, hearing the news and praising loudly, giving thanks to an all-seeing God.

'Oh, the sweetheart, oh my God, oh thank you Jesus, *a querida, oh meu amor, Obrigado Jesus*!' he repeated over and over again. His faith had been rewarded.

Khanyisile asked Teresinha, the senior aunts and some of the older women to call everyone together, all of those who had remained with them through the long vigil, and as they gradually assembled they still formed quite a large party. They all came trooping into the room, filling it, excited that there had been some development but unsure what it meant, and then the house lights were all turned on again.

With an exhausted smile Khanyi stood before them and announced to them quietly, her voice hoarse, 'Bomake, my child has been found. The police found her, and she is coming back with Knox and the detective. They say she is okay.'

There was momentary hush, then a huge chorus of delight and ululating, 'Hau Hau Hau Hau!' and many other thrilled sounds as the women rushed forward to hug her. There were tears, and someone instantly burst into song, a song of praise and joyfulness, giving thanks that good had triumphed over evil. The entire house came to life again at that moment, more lights were turned on, candles were blown out, blankets were folded away, food was put on the stove to heat, coffee was being made. It was a hubbub of activity. Joyful delight flooded the building.

Outside, under the stars, the dogs awoke, disturbed by the excitement and din, got up, stretched themselves, shook their coats and made their way inquisitively towards the source of the noise, aware that something had changed in the atmosphere, and hopeful that it might mean something good to eat or friendly humans again.

The three largest animals made their way straight through the crowded room to Khanyisile, pushing between the bodies and aware that something was being celebrated. They leant heavily against her and licked her hands, treading on her feet to be as close as possible, looking around and wagging their tails madly.

Everyone there knew they had witnessed something you might only see once in a lifetime, and they didn't want to miss any part of it. The women outside were still ululating, shrill, loud and long, and some began to stamp their feet, dance, clap and sing the old songs. Many of the women made phone calls, putting other family members out of the agony of not knowing. Word flew across the Kingdom: she had been found.

Khanyisile finally walked outside, bare footed, the first time she had been outside the house since the abduction, without the burden of uncertainty weighing on her soul and mind. She thought back to when she had been visited by the owl in the tree, all those years ago, thought of her strange dreams, seeing PJ's shoe where it was not supposed to be, and felt inside her the strength of love for their amazing little girl, the heartbreak she and Matt had suffered at the beginning of their life together, and the strength and support of her friends and extended family. She felt some divine blessing pouring upon her, a sensation that was like warm oil pouring onto her head and shoulders, as though His grace was somehow anointing her, covering their homestead for all time, and that the power of the people gathered together and their prayers had somehow defeated and overcome a mighty evil.

In the distance, at the end of the garden she could see an old lady she did not know, an old gogo with sparse, greying hair who had walked in with her sleeping mat from her village in the bush. An elder with rheumy eyes who had remained outside throughout, sleeping out on the grass, a woman who had to be shown how to use the bathroom.

She was jumping, spinning and ululating, one arm raised high above her head, waving a sprig torn from a tree, stamping her feet on the grass, making the white cowrie shell bracelets around her ankles rattle, wailing, dancing and shouting loudly, 'Hallelujah! Amen! Hallelujah! Amen!' and spitting out strong words, denouncing Satan and all his followers, bringing curses down on the evildoers. She whirled and stamped and shouted up into the night sky in her own private celebration.

Khanyi pulled herself together, took a deep breath, phoned Tarryn and told her, then called several family members across the Kingdom, asking them to tell the others. It was getting late, but she also phoned Beauty Simelane, the woman who had seen the blue bakkie entering the forest, waking her from her sleep. Beauty squealed with excitement and told her she would wake her brothers straight away, because they had gone to sleep still very much worried about that child. None of them had eaten the rest of that day. Beauty was thrilled, almost beside herself with excitement, having been an important part of the whole thing.

Matt, slowly beginning to feel himself again, called up his customer and friend Padraic, the Irish farmer he had helped years before, to let him know the news. He knew that the old man had been deeply upset by what happened. Padraic was fast asleep and irritable. Like most farmers he went to bed early and the call had clearly disturbed him. Phone calls made at night to farmers in the bush invariably convey bad news.

'Hello, is that Mr O'Connor?'

'It is himself, so it is, Jesus Christ and all the saints, phwat is it now, who's that, after calling me at this time of night? What have you broken now? Sure, I was fast asleep, so I was!'

'Mr O'Connor, it's Matt here.'

The distant voice changed, calming down a bit, the Irish charm coming back into it. 'Oh, is that yourself Mathew? Are you calling to tell me some news now? Has there been some news of your little girlie at all?'

'Yes Padraic. I'm sorry to wake you but I wanted to tell you we have just heard, they have found her, and she is safe. They're bringing her home to us now. She's with the police.'

There was a pause, as the old farmer took in this news. He hunted about noisily on his bedside table for a handkerchief, needing to wipe his eyes.

'Oh, Matt boy, that's a great mercy so it is, a great blessing indeed. Thank the saints above. Sure, I'll be after telling Kaitleen and the girls straight away. They were terribly worried, so they were. They'll want to know now. I must wake them, so I must. Oh well, that's good Mathew, that's surely good news you're telling me now.

God bless you both, God bless you. Say hello to young Khanyi now, will you? Let me go and wake the daughter. She has been terribly upset by this, so she has. She'll be after wanting to know the news straight away.'

He rang off. Kaitleen O'Connor had met Pumi Jacqueline once before, when Matt visited Shamrock farms to repair some roller frames in the packing plant, and the two had somehow become friendly, the older student, now at university forming an immediate bond with the little girl.

Driving down from Ndzingeni, along the bumpy, twisting road descending towards the lowveld, Gabriel looked across at his friend by the light of the dashboard, and saw in him a shadow, a mere remembrance of the young, tense, highly strung Englishman he had befriended those few years ago, before he was married. His big heart welled up as he thought about what they had been through.

'It's okay, Matt, you can relax now. I will bring us home together. Just rest and sleep. Don't worry, tonight you will have PJ with you at home again. Your family has been blessed.'

He drove along steadily, beginning to smell the unique caramel smell of cane fires as they drew closer to the independent growers in the north east of the country. Gabriel drove with his window down to keep himself fresh and enjoy the cool night air. The stars were bright and clear above them, and the cabin of the vehicle felt like a cocoon of security and safety around them both. Matt felt his head bumping against the hard, cold window glass, and looked up at the immense Southern African sky, black velvet scattered with jewels, hanging like diamonds of sharp, white clear light. He had a sense of déjà vu.

He remembered a time he had laid his head against the cold cabin window of an aircraft flying south towards the unknown all those years before – before he had met Khanyi and before he had ever been to their home. Thinking about his elder brother Patrick, his wife Melanie and their young family blown out of the sky and falling through freezing cold, tumbling thousands of feet to their death. He remembered the tears he had shed then and shed them again, his eyes welling up this time with relief, overwhelmed by the depth of feelings he had for his wife and daughter and grateful for his friend Gabriel, the man who had helped to bring them together and even helped to arrange their wedding. He smiled through the tears in his eyes, sniffing.

They left the cane fields behind them and, far in the distance as they drove along, meandering across the hillsides on the horizon, he could see a bush fire glowing brightly, an orange and yellow ribbon of flame snaking its way across the veld, the bushveld trees silhouetted against the flames and the grey fire smoke roiling up into the dark skies. The occasional faint whiff of wood smoke would eke its way into the vehicle's cabin and its distinct sweet smell brought him back to earth.

Gabriel sat, reliable, steady and solid, driving the big bakkie quickly and competently along the road and slowing only for wandering cattle and speed bumps, or vehicles on the road without lights. He was immensely capable, confident and unshakeable, and his strong presence was a reassurance to Matt, just as it always had been. He knew the road.

Through wet eyes, Matt gazed up at the night sky, feeling dazed and unsure, unsure about everything he thought he knew, but aware that he was somehow sensing a presence around them that he could never comprehend fully. Aware too that Khanyi's extended family had played a vital role, and that the vigil had played another, providing them with strength, and comforting them in a way he could not even begin to describe. He felt that Gabriel, next to him, was the closest thing to a father that he had in the Kingdom, perhaps anywhere. He thought of the people he must call, to let them know – a few farmers, certain customers, their friends, all of whom had been spreading the word asking if anyone had seen anything of PJ. A wave of emotion ran over him, as he thought back to who he had been, and what he had in his life then, and the person he was now, and the value of people like Gabriel, Joao and Padraic in his life. He remembered how Knox had walked into their lives, how he had saved them both once before, before PJ was born, and imagined her now, sleeping peacefully in his strong arms. Presently he fell asleep, and Gabriel glanced across at the younger man and nodded, smiling.

Chapter 18

The return

DI RENNIE HAD BEEN ON the go, chasing, detecting and driving for many hours, and as the intense emotions of the chase, the shooting, and the adrenalin drained from him, he suddenly felt immensely tired. He realised that he was now too exhausted to drive them safely all the way back to the lowveld. He explained to Knox what was happening, then phoned ahead, speaking briefly to one of his many contacts. They drove to a small dusty house on the outskirts of Manzini, where he drew up and handed the vehicle over to one of his cousins, a trusted young student called Lionel who helped him out from time to time in exchange for a little spending cash.

Lionel was a slightly built young man, with a short parted afro hair style and one diamond stud earing, and he was evidently accustomed to these last-minute calls. He came out of the house wearing red tracksuit pants and top, and a pair of immaculately clean white takkies, climbed in, greeted everyone politely, adjusted the driver's seat to get himself positioned and turned the vehicle around. He had driven Rennie many times before. They drove back into town together and stopped briefly at a fast-food outlet, where Rennie climbed out and bought the group some fried chicken, cups of tea and cold drinks. He did not eat anything himself. Then Lionel continued with the journey, after refuelling the big vehicle on the outskirts of town. PJ drank a little Fanta but didn't want to eat.

Richard Rennie, after letting his wife know where he was and that he was safe, explained in a nutshell what was happening. He reassured her that he still loved her, asked her to kiss their two girls goodnight, then climbed into the rear of the double cab, just managing to mention to Lionel where they were headed, before falling asleep. Although he was shattered, he was determined to see the whole incident right through to the end and wanted to be there personally to close the case and hand PJ back to her parents himself.

Lionel was, if anything, a young man of even fewer words than Knox, especially when around strangers. He glanced across at the little girl, and introduced himself to Knox, pronouncing his name Leonell, not Lionel. He was a studious and rather serious person and, after commenting once about the danger of black cattle roaming across the road around Mafutseni, he concentrated on driving, the powerful headlamps lighting up the road far ahead. There was very light traffic on the road that evening, and he could have travelled fast, but he drove carefully, feeling acutely conscious of the trust Richard had placed in him, and of the precious load he carried in the form of the sleeping child.

From the earlier phone call, he knew that the little girl had been kidnapped, pursued, found and then saved through the work of the police, and he guessed this big guy next to him had probably helped to save her. He was tasked with the responsibility of driving her home, with Knox showing him the way at the end of the journey. He loved the sense of adventure that these occasional exposures to real detective work brought into his life, and he enjoyed the opportunity to help his cousin whenever it came along. They drove along smoothly. He was a good driver and after a while Knox dozed off too, still holding Pumi Jacqueline securely, wrapped snugly in his arms, her head on his shoulder, leaving Lionel the only fully alert and wide-awake person in the vehicle.

He switched on the radio and tuned to a station broadcasting from Maputo, listening to the rapid Portuguese chat of the late-night DJ, the mix of classic old pop music playing softly in the cab. Occasionally, he glanced across at the big man beside him, and the sleeping girl, wondering to himself what she must have been through. She reminded him of his own baby sister. He had always looked up to his cousin Richard and admired him, and the way he lived, thinking that it must be a special feeling to be able to solve a case and return a child to its parents, a rare success story falling amidst what he knew was tough, emotionally draining work, with few wins, many fatalities and many failures. He also knew that Rennie sometimes found the work overwhelming when children were involved, especially when they got to them too late to save them and only found the remains. He was by several years the younger of the two, but they had shared much of their childhood together and had attended the same schools.

PJ stirred once or twice, looked around at the inside of the car, lit only by the dashboard lights and the police radio. She saw the strange new man driving but was reassured by the feeling of Knox holding her on his lap. She had slept almost since the shooting in the forest and was starting to feel a bit more like herself again.

She looked at the driver, decided that he looked safe and, in her clear young child's voice, asked him, 'Excuse me, Mr man what is your name, and where are we going now?'

He glanced across at her, smiled and quietly told her his name. 'Well, girlie, my name is Leonel'. He added that the detective in the back seat had asked him to drive them because he was too tired to drive further, and explained that he was taking her home to her parents.

She digested this for a while and looked back at Rennie, head nodding, fast asleep in the back. Then she asked again, 'Did he get very tired from catching the bad men who took me away?'

He answered her, 'Yes, little girl, he has been working on the case for a long time, and he was tired, but he wanted to get you home as soon as possible so he asked me to help him. I'm his cousin.'

PJ thought about this for a while.

'Do you know where my friend Charmayne has gone, Leonel?' she asked.

'No, sorry girlie, I don't,' replied Lionel gently, 'but I'm sure you will find her again when we get home'.

She felt comforted by this and, with Knox still cradling her in his arms, feeling warm, safe and secure she decided that this was probably also a nice man. She gazed wide-eyed at his shiny earing for a while, then the stars outside in the deep black sky briefly caught her attention and she drifted back off to sleep.

The young replacement driver had enjoyed the brief interlude and conversation. The *laaitie* was so cute. He didn't know many details about what had happened that day, but understood that they had been right across the country after this child. From his few brief exchanges with Knox while they'd eaten together, he had worked out that they had caught or killed the suspects before they had harmed the girl, the sick bastards. They drove on through the dark with just the radio playing and the humming of the big 4x4 tyres for company. After an hour or more, Knox stirred and asked Lionel to stop, as he needed a comfort break.

The driver pulled over onto the wide verge of the road as it cut straight across the wildness of Hlane game reserve. He let the engine idle for a long time as the turbo spun down and cooled. A wisp or two of fine white dust, disturbed by their excursion off the tar and into the veld, floated and swirled in the shafts of light from the headlamps, overtaking the slowing bakkie, and once they had stopped Knox very slowly and carefully disentangled PJ's soft arm from around his neck, and eased her off his chest and onto the front seat of the car. She stirred briefly, then her head slumped forward onto her chest, and she murmured something softly but didn't wake. Her mouth lolled open as her head dropped and she folded her little hands.

He walked ahead a short way following the beams, and then ventured out into the darkened area to the side of the headlights spread of light and did what he needed to, keeping a wary eye out for snakes and wild animals.

PJ slowly woke up, disturbed by the change in motion and sudden quietness after the steady noise of travelling, and immediately asked Lionel where Knox was, momentarily frightened by his absence. He pointed towards him, in the lights and PJ stood up on the seat and watched the familiar shape walking back to the double cab, swishing one of his fighting sticks at the long grass. The big man opened the door but then, knowing him well enough to, she pulled on his arm so that he lowered his scarred head to her level. With her hot child's breath tickling close to his ear she whispered, 'Knoxie, I need to make a wee.'

There was no awkwardness for him, he had known her from when she was born. He nodded, indicating with a subtle look the child's natural request to Lionel, and lifted her out of the seat, then carried her to the back of the van. She was a bit shy, but he told her not to worry, nobody was around and he would keep an eye for her, and then he slowly lowered her down on the road behind the tailgate, placing her carefully onto the gravel as though she was a piece of priceless porcelain. Under the bright red taillights, the little girl lifted up her dress and made her toilet, while he looked away, standing beside her, his large bulk and broad shoulders obscuring a big chunk of the night sky from her view.

'Okay now, PJ? All finish?' he enquired.

'I need a tissue,' came the reply. That he did not have, but there were clean paper napkins from the takeaway that sufficed. PJ used these, and he lifted her back up, far above the dusty grass and whatever serpents and goggas might be hiding in it, and they returned to the passenger's side and climbed back in.

'Thanks, Lionel,' said Knox, and they started off again, both feeling much more comfortable. Throughout this short interlude, DI Richard Rennie slept on deeply, used to catching up on sleep in odd places. As he slumped on the back seat he dreamt, his spirit flying off and showing him bright swirling images of a mighty archangel, covered in light, hurtling through the sky and brandishing a long sword; of two men running along a trail through the forest and slowly becoming tired; of the smell of drugs and a dirty glass pipe lying stinking on the ground; and then somehow seeing the bullet from a shot he had fired spinning through the air in slow motion and striking something evil, destroying a scorpion that had a face like a man but was really some creature belonging to the devil. Looking down like a hawk from high above, he then felt something unseen and powerful nudge the barrel of his automatic, sliding the front sight off an injuring shot to a stopping shot, a killing strike hitting the head, and of an innocent little girl spread-eagled on the rocks, held down in place and gagged. He began to murmur in his sleep.

He saw the archangel descend from the treetops in mighty wrath, revealing his strength by throwing someone backwards across a gully and onto rocks, and as the body hit the ground the van hit a pot hole, and he awoke with a start, his heart racing, aware suddenly of movement, the steady engine noise of fast travel, and the cool rushing of night air past his window.

'Is everything okay, Lionel?' he enquired. He was sweating from the dream's intensity, his pulse racing.

'It's all good, Richard,' the young driver replied. 'No problems. We are nearly there.'

Eventually, they slowed down, crossed the Mbuluzi River by the ruins of an old garage, and turned north, heading along parallel to the Lebombo range, looming vast and dark blue along their right-hand side. He began to see tall even stands of sugar cane growing on both sides of the road and could smell sweetness, cane stalks crushed by trucks on the road surface. Occasionally, in the distance, he could see the bright floodlights of harvesting equipment, moving along slowly across the flat cane fields, loading whole stick sugar cane deep into the night shift. Knox stirred too and began to look around at his surroundings, soon telling Lionel to watch for an unmarked turn coming up.

They slowed and turned onto a gravel road, wet patches shining like black puddles underneath the irrigation sprinklers. He slowed down further as the road became bumpy, and Knox guided him carefully to the gate and entrance to the house. As they stopped outside, he got out of the car with some difficulty, still cradling PJ in his arms.

The headlights lit up the line of trees and gravel driveway and a large pack of dogs came hurtling down the length of it, barking and snarling at the disturbance. Lionel started at the sight and quickly closed his window, but Knox just stretched out one huge hand over the gate, his hand open. The pack of animals sniffed it and recognised him, and began to gambol around in excitement, wagging their tails, excited to be reunited with their night-time friend again. As he climbed back in, they sniffed eagerly at PJ and licked at her legs and feet, and she woke up to the sight of her own driveway, lit up by the headlights, and all her own pets coming out to welcome her back.

In the years to come, when she was an old lady herself, with children and grandchildren of her own, she would still remember seeing that sight, but would always struggle to put it into words. Lionel drove them up to the house, let the van run for a few moments as he eased his back, switched off, and then they all got out, stiff, stretching and yawning in the cold night air, the stars bright and eternal above them.

Matt and Khanyi were already outside, waiting by the van, and Knox handed their daughter back to her parents, without saying anything. Nothing needed to be said. The Bartons clung to each other as one little unit, hugging her tightly and holding onto each other. Khanyisile was weeping with relief and shaking like a leaf. After a few moments together, Matt clasped Knox's hand and shook his head, unable to speak. His eyes were filled with tears. Knox gripped his shoulder tightly and squeezed it hard in his vice-like grip. He nodded at his young employer, understanding. He too had lost children. For the first time in many hours, he felt the muscles in his back and his massive shoulders relaxing.

DI Rennie did not intrude, but after the emotions had subsided, he approached the family and simply said, 'Mr and Mrs Barton, I am very happy to be returning your child. She is okay but she will be in shock for a long time. This man Knox of yours is a good man to have in a crisis. He helped us to save her. He is a hero, this big man of yours. He fears nothing.'

He went on, 'Knox can tell you what happened later, but you need not worry about the kidnappers. They will not be troubling anyone again.'

Something about the way he said this, and a glance of understanding that flashed between Knox and Rennie carried some hidden meaning, and Matt picked it up, and suspected that someone had been killed that day.

'Detective Rennie, I don't know what to say. We can't even explain to you how thankful we are, but can we at least offer you something to eat and drink?'

The two men, Rennie and Lionel, accepted this and came in and, as Khanyi fussed over Pumi Jacqueline and stripped off her clothes, bathed her, checked the dressing on her arm and prepared her for bed, Matt quickly brewed some good strong coffee and put together a light meal. It had been many hours since Rennie had eaten anything, and he was hungry and grateful. Lionel ate a little to be polite. Knox requested to leave and go home. He said he was now feeling tired. Matt escorted him outside.

'Is she okay, Knox? Will she be alright?'

'Aah, boss, she is very much scared, she is still full of fear, she is hungry and thirsty, and she said her arms are sore, but now she is home again. After some time, she will be alright. I see only one small cut on her arm, you will see it. The one who did this is dead; the policeman shot and killed him. The other one is broken now, there to his shoulder, but also, he will make no more noise now. He cannot talk to anybody nicely. The policeman he didn't want me to kill him. I don't know why.'

Matt looked at him, as he had once before, wondering what the man was really capable of.

'No, there's no problem, Boss. I just helped the police to catch the other one and it might happen that I did choke him just a small amount. Haayi! but this policeman Rennie is too clever. He didn't want me to beat him too much, they want to question him. He is a good man, very clever, and he can drive fast!'

They left the discussion there and parted. Knox walked off into the darkness, heading for his own house. As he walked home, he began singing to himself, old war songs glorifying bravery, coming from the deep green, rolling valleys of Zululand.

Rennie and Lionel were chatting politely to Khanyi, making small talk and enjoying the coffee. PJ could not be left alone and had fallen asleep again, wrapped snugly in a blanket on Khanyi's lap. She was sucking her thumb, something she had stopped doing years before.

Khanyi sat on the couch and asked the visitors briefly about how they had found her. DI Rennie was reluctant at that time to give too many details, and he was tired, but told the young couple that he had followed three very important leads, the first one taking him to Mafutseni, then the incredibly valuable information from Beauty about the blue van, giving them a direction to follow, and then, thanks to Lindiwe, being able to make contact with a key witness, the old man Ginindza who had actually seen the two kidnappers running into the forest carrying her, and who was willing to lead them to the place where he thought they would be. He didn't want to go into too much detail about what happened after that. He kept his eye on the child in case she was half awake and listening.

Khanyi took in the story, thinking about Beauty phoning her from Malkerns, and other people she didn't even know deciding to help them, getting involved and playing such a central role in PJ's recovery. She wondered if she would ever get to meet this old man Ginindza and thank him herself.

It grew late, some time had passed and conversation ebbed as it will, and it seemed as though time was slowing. After resting and discussing the events of the past two days in the quietness of the evening, the two coloured men stood up to leave, long after midnight, and politely and rather formally thanked the Bartons for the refreshments.

'Thank you kindly for your hospitality, Mr and Mrs Barton,' said Lionel. 'It was a pleasure to meet y'all. Y'all have got a lekker place here.'

Detective Inspector Rennie eased his back and stretched himself, preparing for another long spell in the double cab, and then suddenly asked quietly if he could have one more look at the little girl. Khanyi pulled the blanket back and he stepped across the room to the mother and daughter, looking intently at the child's sleeping face. He gently reached out and stroked her hair, feeling it very gently in his slender fingers, then he tenderly touched one of her earlobes between finger and thumb. She didn't stir. He had bent over them both, then stood upright, still gazing at the sleeping child, and crossed himself.

'Mrs Barton, she is a beautiful child, so perfect. A gift from God. You must look after her very well. She has been blessed already once in her life. One day she will forget all this happened, but for the next few months she will have some strange reactions. If you need any help, call me. I have friends who can assist with some specialised counselling – even for you two as well, if you want it. This has been very traumatic for her and you both. I'm just glad it ended this way.'

He rubbed his eyes with his right hand, thumb and forefinger passing over his eyelids. It was a characteristic gesture of his when he was tired or released from tension, a habit Lionel had seen many times before. His eyes were an unusually intense shade of hazel, and they welled up momentarily with tears, making him wipe them quickly with his handkerchief. He sniffed and gathered himself, shaking off the emotion.

'I am so glad for you both, so grateful that it ended like this. We were just incredibly lucky, Mr and Mrs Barton. A child like this is… she is so perfect that it sometimes makes men…' He did not finish the sentence, lost in his own thoughts. He wiped his eyes again, shaking his handsome head.

They stood up and he shoulder hugged Matt and hugged Khanyi, slightly awkwardly, and then gave the sleeping girl a tiny pat on the head, touching her shoulder softly, biting his lip and nodding to himself. He looked as though he were being torn by deep emotions.

The two men climbed back into the double cab, with Lionel at the wheel, took their leave and left, the powerful lights and deep sound of the engine slowly dissipating and fading into the cane fields as the van disappeared. As the dust of their passing settled over the cane fields, a night jar took up its strange cry, and Matt and Khanyi heard a jackal wailing out its loneliness and hunger in the distance.

Chapter 19

Nompumelelo Jacqueline

A CHANGE CAME OVER THEIR DAUGHTER after her ordeal, but it took some weeks before her parents fully realised how much it had affected her. For a long time, she would no longer sleep in her own room, wanting to sleep between them on their bed. She also could no longer sleep without a light on. This went on for a long time, and a few times she wet the bed and was terribly upset about this afterwards.

It eventually came out that she was scared to go to the bathroom in case the men were waiting there for her. Having a child in the bed meant Matt could not sleep well, and the couple would occasionally strike sparks off each other, both tired and worried about their beloved daughter. It were as though something of her experience, unclean and foul, had tainted the home.

PJ had been trusting, chatty and confident, but they noticed that she was much quieter, and that she would no longer play outside, at least not in the garden, and then only if she stayed close to the front door. She seemed to be less keen to see her friends. The moment anyone she did not know came close to the house, she would run either to Nomsa, Khanyi or Matt, and would cling to them like a kitten, hiding her face. She had never done this before.

One afternoon, Nomsa asked to talk to Khanyi in the office, quite tearful, announcing that she needed to tell her about something she had seen.

The little girl had been playing in the driveway, close to the front door, pushing one of her dolls in a pram and a bakkie had arrived at the gate. She saw her throw the pram down and she'd rushed inside screaming for Nomsa and burst into tears. Nomsa picked her up, thinking she was hurt, but it was apparently the sight of the van that scared her. She took a long time to explain but it eventually came out that she thought they had come to take her away again.

The other thing Nomsa had seen had deeply frightened her, and she seemed to be very unwilling to divulge the details. Khanyi had to gently coax it out of her. She had seen PJ take a small doll out of her bedroom, take it outside and then begin hitting it with a stone again and again, saying it had been a bad child. She kept hitting it until she had broken its face. She feared that PJ might have been bewitched. The way she described what she had seen horrified Khanyi. This was not her child.

Khanyi called Matt and they talked about it and called on Teresinha and Joao for advice. They came round that same evening, as close friends do, but could not talk within earshot of the girl and had to be careful about what she heard. What Nomsa described fitted in with a few other things Khanyi had noticed. PJ would often have nightmares, waking up in terror during the night, and nothing they said seemed to comfort her. She would sometimes be half awake, screaming about being carried somewhere, and this was very frightening to watch. She was frightened when people came to the house, even people she knew, and was terrified whenever a van came to the house. Matt felt out of his depth. Khanyi did not know who to turn to. Their child had changed.

Joao and Teresinha suggested that she perhaps needed to see a specialist, but to be safe they prayed over her and over the house, banishing any evil spirits. Matt remembered Richard Rennie's last words, and the next day he phoned him, explaining the situation. Richard's quiet voice was comforting and calm, and he gave him two numbers to call, both people he had used previously. He told Matt that such reactions were to be expected and were completely normal. These were specialists who could help.

Matt made the call, making sure that the doors were closed, and PJ was nowhere near him. The lady he had been referred to was a child psychologist, specialising in trauma cases, but did not normally make house calls. She agreed to have a first consultation with Pumi, and then decide how best to approach the problem. She was willing to come out to them for the first meeting but was heavily booked, and this could only be in two weeks' time.

In the meantime, Matt tried something of his own. At least three times a week, after breakfast, he would walk with PJ to their bakkie, and he and Khanyi would climb into the front with PJ safely sandwiched between them. All the dogs would jump into the back. Then they would slowly drive down to the gate, Khanyi or the gardener would open it, and they would drive around the property, with cane fields on one side and their own garden and the surrounding compound on the other. Then they would arrive home again five minutes later, drive right up to the house and all get out. It was a short drive for no particular reason.

They did this for two weeks, and then one day Matt planned that Khanyi would stay behind, leaving only him and PJ on the bench seat. The two of them did the same short trip, and PJ asked why they were doing it. Matt said it was to see how the sugar cane was growing, and she seemed to accept this. He took her on his own for another two weeks or so and then one day, when it had become routine to them both, and PJ was beginning to stand up and point out birds and guinea fowl, he explained to PJ that he was very busy that day, and would it be alright if Musa drove the car, but with Khanyi coming too. She seemed to be happy with that arrangement, and each morning the three of them, plus a pack of dogs would climb in and go for their short healing drives.

It went on for a long time, sometimes with her dad, sometimes with her mum, and then one day, when she seemed to be enjoying the tiny outings without anxiety, they went a little bit further, down to the nearby canal. She seemed anxious, wanting them to explain to her exactly where the house was all the time, but it went okay. There were no tears.

One day, when he thought she was ready, Matt asked PJ if she could show Musa and Nomsa where the canal was, but both he and mummy were busy so it would just be her, Nomsa and Musa with the dogs. She shrugged and said she could go with Musa. That morning she went off in the bakkie without her parents for the first time. She was worried when the house was out of sight, but both adults had been primed and knew what to say. Her job was to tell Musa which way to turn to go home, and that seemed to take her mind off things, and they came back a few minutes later. This time she jumped out of the car and ran inside wide eyed, and breathlessly told Khanyi, 'Mummy, you know what? Musa forgot the way home *and* Nomsa forgot the way home!'

She excitedly explained that she'd had to show them which way to go, and she brought them all the way home by herself! She was thrilled by the adventure and it was as though a tiny ember of the old sparkling PJ had come back into her soul. Matt, who adored his daughter, was working on a plan. He knew that one day she would need to get back into a vehicle with someone other than her family and would have to overcome her fear of this. The dogs were enjoying their daily drive, barking at everything and everyone they saw, and she seemed to be growing in confidence, telling them all about it each time they went out. One morning, he discretely asked Nomsa to stay behind, with only Musa in the bakkie. PJ on her own in a bakkie with a black man, not family. Musa played along superbly well, pretending that he was not sure which road to take, and chatting to his little passenger all the time.

While all these daily drives were going on, PJ had her first meeting with the child psychologist, and they seemed to hit it off. They arranged a series of six initial sessions together. The first three would be at their home; thereafter, Matt would need to drive her to Manzini.

The specialist was a consulting child psychologist, a lady Doctor, Miss Magda Viljoen, and she was a loving, clever woman, deeply perceptive of suffering of any kind. She was extremely sensitive to the needs and trauma affecting young people and had a vehement hatred of seeing children suffering because of the cruelty of adults. She always wore jangling bracelets on both her arms, and deliberately practised from rooms filled with fascinating objects and artwork that she would sometimes use to draw her patients out of themselves. The children didn't realise it, but she had several rooms in the practise, each decorated differently for different ages, human needs and assessments.

Magda dressed unconventionally, often hiding her wild bush of dark hair under a bright doek or a soft crocheted hat, rather than trying to control it. She wore long dresses covered in stars and planets, or wild animals, and sometimes even maps or African pots, and her garments were all brightly coloured, unusual enough to often be a source of interest. When she turned her dark eyes onto one of her children (she always called them her children) and encouraged them, they felt as though she had somehow stopped the whole world just to listen to them. She would skilfully lead them along, meandering aimlessly up to the problem they faced, and then gently and sensitively tease it out of them, sometimes without them even realising. The time they spent with her flew by and the young, hurting patients would tell her about things that they found themselves unable to speak about at home. In some cases, they had, until meeting her, never been able to express their true feelings aloud. She dealt with a lot of difficult, painful cases, abused children, traumatised children, as well as more straightforward ones, but her love for young people burnt brightly, an unquenchable flame. Most of her young cases grew to love her over time.

Magda first got to know PJ, getting her to relax, and only then slowly drew out of her young patient some of the poison left from the events that had frightened her so deeply. PJ didn't really tell her parents much about what she and Magda did together, but from what the doctor told them, she was getting her to draw pictures of the bad men who'd hurt her, and talking about some of what happened. She had not been raped or molested and seemed to have blocked out some of the worst images. She did not understand why they had taken her or what had been about to happen to her, but she was very aware that Knox had rescued her and that he and the police had made sure that the horrible men went away.

In her child's mind, she also understood that one of them had been killed, but that Knox and the nice policeman had saved her. She was slowly letting go of her memories of the shooting. She still had nightmares about the filthy room she had been held in, and the long run through the forest, and being pulled over the gate and not being able to breathe. Some of these things would take years and years to overcome. She had developed a fear of gates, or being near to them on her own.

The Bartons learnt that they had to be cautious about letting her watch TV at all. Where before she would often just ignore grownups' programmes, the sound of gunfire would now scare her badly, and they were careful to avoid her seeing any violent scenes, or scenes of people being held against their will. She had started occasionally going to sleep in her own room again, but if anything woke her, she needed to be with her parents. She was certainly not ready to go out to anyone's house to stay yet, but a few friends started coming to visit her. There had never been a repeat of the incident with the doll, but sometimes, when she was crying and inconsolable, she would go and look for the old gardener in the garden, even straying far away from their front door, and tell him what upset her.

The gardener Ndephete was generally a grumpy, irritable old man who disliked any interruptions while he was working. He was gruff, blunt, often rude to strangers and unused to children, and he hardly spoke any English, but between him and the little girl they formed a unique understanding, and he secretly used to enjoy her visits while he was working outside.

Although she spoke SiSwati well, she would seek him out, then stand explaining to him whatever had upset her in English and he, barely understanding her, would respond in his language, often saying something that was in no way connected to what she had just told him. This reaction from an adult, although rather strange, served to calm her down again and she would often forget what had happened to made her go and look for him. He would just look at her and say 'okay' to her stories, or her complaints, nodding his head with almost no understanding.

Her visits gave him an excuse to stop working and roll himself a smoke with his potent mixture of *imbhoza* and home-grown tobacco. Then he would find and pick her a perfect guava, or a handful of mulberries, or a perfectly ripe tomato, or present her with a roasted mealie and, as she sat in the sun and ate that in front of him, he would set fire to his home made cheroot. Once it was well lit, he'd disappear behind a shroud of fragrant smoke, talking to her about the weather, all about the different trees and herbs, how to catch caterpillars, all his chickens, the naughty dogs, a big shongololo he had seen, some blight weakening the potato plants, how his maize was growing at home. Once, he made her laugh, describing how a certain mouse had eaten his shoe. He complained to her about how expensive batteries and paraffin had become, and randomly told her about the things going on in his life. It mattered little to him whether she understood it all, and she liked the gravelly sound of his voice and the odd words that he used. He would smile at her, showing the many gaps in his teeth, and she would smile back at him because he had listened to her grievance and not judged the rights and wrongs of it in any way.

She would sit and gnaw at the fruit, or her mealie cob, and tell him all about the bad behaviour of one of her bears that was very rude, or one of her children that wouldn't go to sleep, or the latest highlights from a story being read to her each night, and he would listen vaguely and nod his head, completely baffled. Something about his presence was oddly comforting and familiar to her. He was part of the garden, part of her home, an unchanging part of everything she had grown up with and, despite the age difference, there was a strong tie binding them together. He knew all about what had taken place when she was abducted, and felt that there was in some way a healing for the child in these little exchanges. He would present her with a flower most times she visited.

During one sunny afternoon, Ndepethe lifted PJ into his wheelbarrow, and put her on top of a pile of grass, wheeling her slowly down to the tree where the Zionist boy had tried to fly, and told her all about him in such a funny way that Khanyi and Nomsa suddenly heard peals of delighted laughter coming from the garden, the first time they had heard the little girl laughing like that in a long time. She was also standing right close to the gate, which neither of them had ever seen happen since she had been taken. Something in the old man made him sense that these exchanges were good for her, and over time they had become close, in a strangely distant way, and he tried to listen to her stories, albeit with very little understanding.

He was deeply fond of the child, and still felt that he had failed her in some way by not preventing her from being taken. He often berated himself for not having been nearer to the gate when it happened. They had a unique, unlikely friendship and he had grown to enjoy her distractions and interruptions, even though he still preferred plants to people. The visits made a change from gardening work. She would occasionally return to the house with a secret message for Nomsa, asking her to make a cup of tea for Ndephete, or to bring him a glass of juice. Being part of these little domestic conspiracies took her mind off the terrible images that lingered, helping in some way to drive them into the further reaches of her mind. They were no longer at the forefront of everything, and with Magda's help she was slowly but steadily returning to the untainted little girl she used to be, finding herself again. The unseen, subtle efforts of many people around her were all slowly helping her on a difficult road to recovery.

She restarted attending pre-school and painting pictures to bring home to her ever-admiring parents, and she would sometimes also create special ones for Ndephethe, Knox or even Musa. They would take them from her gravely, with both hands, bow and listen to the full explanation and then thank her very solemnly for making them a picture, and for the treasured gift, although Ndephethe, she noticed, often tended to hold them upside down.

She would try and explain to the old man what the picture was, but then he would nod and ask her again what it was, and then she would show him the tree and the birds, and the sun and house, the stick figures of people she had drawn. After pointing out all the things she had painted, he would gaze at the images, unseeing, nodding his head, but often suspecting to himself that the child had perhaps lost some of her senses in the forest. He seemed to most enjoy the pieces in which either he, or his old lawnmower, featured prominently.

He could seldom make the imaginary leaps forward that were necessary to convert a child's priceless piece of art into the picture she was seeing, but Knox could. Khanyisile would have been surprised to find that Knox kept every one of PJ's paintings in a precious plastic file in his house, and that he would write the date and time on each picture, and sometimes the content. He would occasionally take them out and page through them, before falling asleep with tears in his eyes.

Chapter 20

The letter

SIX MONTHS AFTER PJ HAD been saved, on their way back from a routine local shopping trip, they cleared their post box. Matt had to sign for a thick, weighty, registered letter, posted from his attorneys. It was covered in British postage stamps, plastered on both sides in air mail stickers as though someone overseas had thought that, by applying more of them, it would make the post faster.

Matt's attorneys were working with his letting agents and handling his property in the UK. There was apparently an issue regarding the management of surface water from his neighbour's property, and these neighbours had requested permission to excavate a wide drainage ditch across his driveway, to join it up to a local main drainage line. It would eventually flow from their property into his, and written approval was needed for this, as it would affect surface water flows on his property, and require digging up his driveway, changing its appearance. The process required a specially lined trench, made to specific dimensions and built to approved building standards, with a suitably strong steel grating, in a material that conformed to various local safety standards and regulations, all properly installed over the trench. The entire process could not be started without written County Council permission, and his signature was required on several forms and documents. These included a building application form, a detailed plan, and there was a great deal of other paperwork involved, as his house was let, and any neighbours affected by the construction had to provide confirmation indicating that they had no objections thereto, plus there was an ancient, and well-loved Plane tree growing close by, protected by a preservation order, and its roots would have to be trimmed in order to cut open the drain.

The documents were extensive. They referred to the relevant section of an act covering sustainable drainage systems, and explained that a representation had to be made, followed by formal application to the Town Clerk's office. There were certain fees to be paid, with building contractors to be selected and contracted in writing to carry out the work to the applicable County and Town building standards. One of the civil engineers from the town council would have to be engaged to come out and verify the construction and dimensions of the drain, then sign off the plans, and this would require a formal site survey and detailed inspection. It was all terribly confusing.

But the attorneys also seemed to be telling him something, in their arcane, mysterious and flowery language. One part of it read 'wherein, apropos the aforementioned matter, we hereby seek from you as the lawful and uninhibited owner of the described property, your written permission and unconditional approval to proceed,' and it carried on in that vein for a full page, without ever unequivocally mentioning exactly what they suggested Matt should do. Later that evening, he showed some of it to Khanyi, and she tried to read it, could not, and then asked him if he thought it was possible that the one writing had perhaps been bewitched.

After reading through it several times and deciphering it as best he could, Matt decided it meant that, ideally, they wanted him to visit his house, see the work for himself and approve what needed to be done and, while he was there, sign a great many forms and documents, in person, and before a witness, all to do with giving permission for contractors to build this trench, about six metres in length and thirty five centimetres deep, to run from a collector box next to his driveway, across to another, larger one, terminating under a metal manhole cover that would intrude slightly into his driveway, and involve knocking down a small section of wall.

The sheaf of documents they had sent included several different forms and an indemnity agreement to be completed and signed, and a document authorising the agents to initiate the process of applying for planning permission. The attorneys politely warned that there was no way to simplify or shorten this process and that it could take several months.

He sat in his car, parked outside the post office, under the shade of a flamboyant tree, the sounds of the mill clearly audible nearby, and the heavy smell of dust and crushed sugar cane drifting through the window. Reading through it, he felt the cold, bony hand of officialdom and bureaucracy slowly reaching out from the past and clasping his shoulder, like walking into a dark, cold, empty house after being away from it for many years. Against his surroundings now, it seemed strangely incongruous, something oddly disturbing that left within him a peculiar sinking feeling, as though he had done something wrong, even though he had not.

The timing, although strange, was not all bad. He had been thinking for some time that it might be a good thing for them all to have a complete change of scenery, partly to show Khanyisile where he had come from, and to take her and Pumi Jacqueline on their first aircraft flight. They were both worried that their daughter had never quite returned to the joyful, carefree little girl she had been before the abduction, and he wondered if seeing some completely new places and sharing the experience of going on a plane might help her. Doctor Magda had advised them to wait for at least six months, always following a regular routine, and had asked to see PJ again before she would give her advice.

She had seen PJ again and told him she felt that the timing was okay, and that she was probably able to handle the trip, but that they should never, ever let her out of their sight. The child had made good progress.

He broached the idea over supper and found that Khanyi was enthusiastic, but deeply worried about the cold and their exposure to potential illnesses. She had been warned by several friends and relatives who had worked in England – mostly schoolteachers, students and nurses – that the cold was something unimaginable, almost impossible to describe. They said that your skin became pale when you stayed there for a long time, that the sun was seldom seen, it rained almost every day and, among various other terrors, that people were impatient. Many supermarkets had unmanned tills, which were deeply confusing to use, and there was seldom anyone to help you if you did something wrong. She did not want to be the one who caused bells to ring and have strangers come and berate her in public for not understanding where to put a shopping basket. These aspects of the trip worried her most.

Overall, she was keen but fearful, convinced that she was putting her daughter at risk. She was also conflicted, because while she knew Matt would know what they needed, and would keep them warm, and protect them from these dangers while they were there, it was all going to be new. He was reassuring but just as when he'd tried to explain to her about the Indian Ocean before she saw it for the first time, she remained unconvinced.

She had truly been longing to see where he used to work, and she also wanted to meet this man Brian Pearson of whom he'd spoken so often when they were first together. He seemed to respect him almost like a father, and she remembered how he had given them both a very generous wedding gift. They had equipped their kitchen with the money those pounds represented. There was a whole life that Matt had lived before that she knew little about, and deep in her heart she knew that it would be good for them all to go there for a visit, but not for too long.

She began her planning, starting off by finding the type of warm clothing that you cannot buy anywhere in the warm lowveld. PJ had never worn anything like a vest before, or a heavy coat, a hat (except a bonnet against the sun), a scarf or gloves, or even lace up shoes. All these items had to be found somewhere. She had spent most of her young childhood in panties, a frock and sandals and not much else. With Matt's help, they found some shops selling mail order children's clothing and then, after making enquiries, located some second-hand warm clothes at a big shop in Big Bend. She slowly began assembling a small wardrobe of warm clothes, both for her and for PJ.

Shoes were going to be an issue, as PJ had never worn closed shoes before and hated the feeling that they gave her feet, kicking them off at the first opportunity. Khanyi tried to explain to her daughter that her feet would get cold where they were going, but PJ refused to accept this idea, and would only wear them reluctantly for a few brief, uncomfortable minutes before kicking them off again. She did not like the sensation. When they explained the plan to their daughter, PJ was dead set against the idea from the first moment it was suggested, and it was only after a few days that Nomsa managed to find out what was worrying her.

Pumi was very frightened that they would go somewhere where she might get separated from her mum and dad, or that she would have to sleep in a different place from them. She feared they might be parted. She confided this to Nomsa one tearful afternoon, after behaving unusually badly all day, and they realised that this was the biggest fear she faced. She was also worried about leaving Knox, Ndephethe and Nomsa behind.

Matt and Khanyi needed to find a way around this and began showing her pictures of where they would be staying, emphasising the rooms with three beds, or interjoining rooms, and fold-out sofas, and promised her that such a thing would never happen. They would never be separated. She was still worried though, and, like her mama, not entirely convinced about these arrangements.

Matt had phoned his old workplace and set up an appointment to see Brian Pearson with the lovely Emma, sounding just the same, telling him she was 'dead happy to hear his voice again'. He found out that Salikh was still there, still working in the stores, but that he had got married and had a baby in the time Matt had been away. Emma told him some of the other news, but many of the people he had worked with had moved on.

As he had once experienced before, he felt as though he had come into sudden contact with a huge spinning piece of machinery. That he had somehow stretched out and let his hand touch on a whirling frenzy of activity and deadlines, of men flying across the world to conduct highly specialised repairs, of urgent backroom activity keeping them supplied with all that they would need. A world of reports, boarding times, hotel bookings and tickets, the need for special welding gasses and materials, breathing equipment, testing and welding gear, permits for safe work and the export of equipment to wherever they might be, that he had left behind. It was all still whirring along busily without him.

He smiled, thinking about how that had been his life for so many years, and of the money he had been paid, back in the days when that was all there was to his life. That, and the pride he took in his work. He did not miss it, but it had taught him an enormous amount.

He didn't plan a complicated trip with lots of travelling and sightseeing, being very conscious of the limitations of travelling with a five-year-old, but he wanted to show his family a few of the famous tourist sites, like those he had showed his late brother and sister-in-law, and he knew he had to sort out the issue with his neighbours and the building work. He wished he could just ask the Sibandze brothers to do the job. They would have quoted, bought the materials and completed it in two days, with nothing on paper at all. As it was, he was forced to wade through pages of complicated drawings, compare quotations, complete application forms and try to visualise what was being described. Worst of all, he had to work out what the attorney's letters meant.

As he began going through some of his old papers connected with his old life, a dog-eared business card fell to the floor. He picked it up and felt a sudden rush of memories flooding into his mind.

Kopec Taxi Service. The number of times Kopec taxis had driven him to the station, or to the airport, or brought him back to his house in the middle of the night after a long trip abroad…

Kopec Taxis. The big grey sedan driving along the motorway as cold rain hammered on the roof and splattered on the windscreen. He thought back to Janislav 'in this case is better for you to call me Joe' and the advice he had given Matt all those years ago, all about matters of the heart and how, if he met a good woman, he should hold onto her. He wondered if he was even still in the taxi game. The card advertised private taxi services from all major centres. He thought it might be a stress-free way of getting from the airport to the North with Khanyi, their daughter and their luggage, after they had all arrived tired, stiff and sore. They could always hire a car from where they were staying.

His idea quickly translated into action and he dialled up the UK number and spoke to a young-sounding girl who introduced herself as Liliana and sounded like she might be Kopec's daughter.

'Just call me Lily,' she said patiently, and he asked her first if they could provide a quote for two adults and one child from Heathrow Airport to Lancashire. When she answered that it would be no problem, they could certainly arrange to meet them at the airport no matter what time the arrival was, he replied without thinking and exclaimed, 'Hau! you can even collect us from the airport!'

There was a long pause. Lily suddenly became very British and professional and her tone changed somewhat, becoming a little sharp and a tad sarcastic. 'How… how?' she replied. 'Well, as I have previously explained, Mr Barton, we are a taxi service, that is what we do, we do run a taxi service. We'll send a car for you, Mr Barton, but in your case, we might run an estate car on account of the luggage.'

The way she pronounced luggage made him smile, remembering the accent of his birthplace. He tried to explain that he didn't mean '*how*', but was merely exclaiming, 'Hau!' but it was too nuanced and involved and Lily went on, untrammelled.

'I don't doubt, but you'll be needing a child seat fitted then, Mr Barton?'

He took a moment to work out what she meant, then he answered, 'Yes, we will, thank you. Luckily, she's used to travelling in one'.

'Right then, Mr Barton, if y'cud joost let us know the age of the yoong child, only we've to mek sure we fit the right one,' she replied. The accent sounded familiar to him, and he found himself soaking it up and slipping easily back into North Country English himself.

She said us '*uzz*', not us, and pronounced young '*yoong*', with a distinctly audible 'g' ending the word. He wondered briefly to himself how much Khanyisile would understand of the strong accents up North. After giving her PJ's age he asked Liliana, 'Is Mr Kopec still driving?'

'Oh, Hell, aye,' came the reply. 'That's me dad. He owns the business and still drives most days. We can't get him out of the cars. He won't stop; he loves it too much. I'll let him know you called.'

He requested, if possible, for Janislav himself to meet them, and explained that he was an old friend and customer. He had travelled with him many, many times about six years back, and he might remember Matt Barton. Liliana warmed to Matt and assured him that she would pass on the message. She sounded friendly and helpful, eager to help and quite excited to be 'tekking a call from so far awa'.

Matt loved the thought of introducing Joe to Khanyi and PJ. It made him feel warm inside, as though somehow a huge circle had been closed around the globe. It was that fateful last conversation he'd had with Joe Kopec that had reassured him more than any other, after those dreadful few months following his brother's death, a conversation that instilled in him the strong conviction that he was right to fly out, with a one way ticket, and would one day marry Khanyisile and set up a new life in Eswatini.

He still would often stop and look at the pictures of Melanie and the children, and of his elder brother Patrick in his graduation gown and mortar board. He had never stopped loving them. He was suddenly excited at the thought of Joe Kopec, with his pointed beard and little Russian cap, meeting Khanyisile and PJ, and wondered how they would get on.

His mind began to wander happily as he thought about taking them to meet Brian Pearson, and his pretty PA Emma, and showing Khanyisile where he used to work. It all seemed so far away now, as though underneath the great canopy of sky spanning the huge continent between them, a mighty canyon had developed, effectively cutting off his memories.

His experiences here had been so different to everything he'd known before. Their wedding, the dancing, the feast, befriending Joao and Teresinha Dos Santos, the warmth he always felt from Gabriel, the hospitality of Padraic O'Connor, all the family's dogs and the big farmhouse he'd inherited, the difference in the light, each so very hard to explain. He wondered if Salikh would be there when they visited.

Chapter 21

A visit to England

IT WAS ALREADY LATE OCTOBER when they flew. They had arranged for Musa to drive them to the airport in Eswatini and, as they packed together, they had to both dissuade PJ from filling her suitcase entirely with her dolls, four different bears, an ostrich, several dolls' blankets, favourite books and two miniature tea sets. She had a seat of her own on the aircraft, and they made doubly sure that they would be seated together. The bear population had to be limited.

Khanyi held Matt's hand very tightly as they took off the first time, and watched her homeland slowly disappearing underneath the wings. The small aircraft turned, banking gently, and immediately headed west. Her last view of the Kingdom was the Lebombo mountain range, gradually turning blue and receding into the distance, with Mozambique and the coastline on the distant horizon.

She did not relax on the small plane, and throughout the take-off, as their speed increased and the engines grew louder, she kept her eyes tightly closed. When the pilot began to slow the aircraft, throttling down and extending the spoilers over the wings, the sound altered, and the aircraft began to shudder as the nose dropped. There was that peculiar moment of feeling momentarily weightless as it began to descend.

She asked Matt with a worried look, 'Is it crashing, Matt? Has it broken?'

He did his best to reassure her, but she remained deeply distrustful of the whole process, and held onto Pumi very tightly. In fact, their precious young traveller was quite relaxed, the new sights and experiences nudging aside some of her painful memories. She had already met and charmed a middle-aged, elegantly dressed Japanese businessman while they were waiting to board, walking up to him in the lounge and introducing herself, and solemnly informing him of her age, and pointing out her two young parents. Mr Shimizu happened to be in an adjacent seat, and after the air crew had taken and hung up his jacket, he amused himself and PJ by drawing little pictures for her of cats, rabbits playing violins, dancing pigs in dinner jackets and bow ties, and haughty-looking peacocks, using a very expensive gold pen, and ruthlessly tearing gilt edged pages from his leather bound journal, handing them over to her like love notes in class.

She thought he was the nicest man ever, and in her clear little child's voice kept saying, "Look, Daddy, look, that man has drawn another picture!" So enraptured was she by this that the short journey passed quickly by, and she barely took in the fact that they had completed the flight and were about to land.

Oliver Tambo International Airport is one of the biggest airports in Africa, with all the urgency, hustle, complexity and accoutrements of modern air travel. Everyone seems to be in a hurry to be somewhere else. Once the plane had stopped moving, Matt helped them unclasp their safety belts, and the three of them carefully descended the steep stairs, with PJ coming down slowly, step by step as small children do, carefully counting each one.

Business travellers are by nature an impatient breed and Matt had to lift her up to allow a busy, self-important young man in a great rush to barge arrogantly past them, already talking loudly on his phone and eagerly making his way down the steps and across the tarmac, desperate to be the first passenger to board the bus. To his chagrin, he soon discovered that the bus would wait for passengers of all ages, both the fast and the slow to climb in anyway, before it departed for the terminal. There were a few elderly people, all slow to board. Then it was further delayed because Pumi Jacqueline, because she was short, found it difficult to climb up the big step from the runway into the bus while wearing her pink backpack. This process took a few moments and then she insisted on finding and thanking the stewardess for the juice she had given her during the flight. The young man flicked his highlighted hair back in exasperation, sighed with annoyance very audibly, and glared at the little girl as though she had delayed him on purpose.

Khanyisile, like a watchful mother will, had become aware of this hostility developing and was doing her best to hurry PJ safely onto the bus with her coat, colouring book, accompanying doll and hand luggage, as Matt wrestled with their other carry-on bags and heavy winter coats. She instantly became very protective and intensely angry and promptly fixed the yuppie with a withering look, her furious eyes flashing coldly, as hard as glass.

Unable to meet the challenge or intensity of her dark eyes, the young man flounced, pulled his sunglasses off his head and then quickly turned away and began frantically tapping away at his cellphone.

As is often the case in any public place, when a man appears to have upset a pretty young woman with a beautiful child, he seldom finds allies, and Matt had to contain a secret smile, seeing the exchanged glances and eyes rolling heavenwards shooting around the bus. The man felt embarrassed, suddenly becoming very aware of the other travellers' support for PJ, coupled to Matt and Khanyi's presence and their evident closeness to their daughter.

Eventually, the sets of doors closed with a hiss, and the long airport bus moved off with a jerk. PJ had never been on a bus before, wasn't expecting the sudden start and would have fallen over. Luckily, her new Japanese friend Yoshi Shimizu was there to save her. Yoshi had noticed her wobbling, smiled down at her and grabbed her backpack just before she overbalanced. Matt nodded his thanks. Mr. Shimizu bowed deeply in a courteous response.

The long queue snaked through immigration but moved along quite fast, and they soon found themselves in the airport building, in transit and awaiting the next, much longer flight. Their luggage had been booked right through to their destination. PJ was still wide awake, and asked Matt if this was England. He tried to explain where they were, and that there was a much bigger plane that was going to carry them to England. He no longer had all his accrued air miles, but still had credit on various airline cards, and they were able to walk proudly into a business lounge, relaxing there for a few hours before the long flight. Matt was used to it, but Khanyi was impressed.

PJ was not particularly excited by the huge variety of interesting things to eat but did like watching the jets through the big windows, and having so many tables to sit at and do her colouring in. She eventually grew tired and slept, leaning against her mum. Khanyi dozed off too, and Matt watched the rolling news and nibbled on snacks until it was time to make their way to the boarding gate.

When the jet finally took off, PJ had already fallen asleep, but when they served dinner later that evening she awoke again, fascinated and excited by her first big flight and finding so many new things to interest her. She was delighted by the miniature little containers of butter, sugar and salt, and the tiny boxes and containers and servings of food. And she loved the idea that they were all going somewhere together. She especially loved the sticker book that a cabin attendant gave to her, entertained by it for a while. The air crew looked after her very well.

There is not much to enjoy during a long-haul flight in economy class. It is mostly a case of surviving the cramped duration and mitigating the misery, but sometimes one can be lucky with cabin crew and on the long leg from Johannesburg to London, two of the flight staff serving on their side of the aircraft took a great shine to miss Nompumelelo Jacqueline Barton. She was showered with children's puzzles and toys, some even sneaked back from business class, and they showed her how to play games on the TV in the seat back above her tray. She was unusually polite, and tried to do as she was told, making her behaviour something of a revelation to the crew. Several times during the flight one of them would lean over and whisper to Khanyi, 'Oh, she's too adorable! Can we keep her!'

Khanyisile shook her head violently and answered NO.

Khanyi was soon too tired to watch any films and fell asleep with her head on her husband's shoulder. She had removed several outer layers of her clothing as she grew warmer after dinner. The couple snuggled under their blankets and the crew turned up the cabin heating, creating an environment more likely to put their passengers to sleep. He felt immensely close to her and protective over them both.

As the cabin lights dimmed and passengers began drowsing, Matt felt again that strange sense of detachment, of floating far above the earth, so remote from the lives of people beneath him. He estimated that they were somewhere above central Africa, nearing the immense emptiness of North Africa. As the big passenger plane commenced a long gentle turn, to begin flying over the Sahara, he looked out of the window at the bright stars above and freezing darkness below.

There were hardly any lights to be seen anywhere below them, but he could see one other aircraft on a parallel but opposite flightpath, its navigation lights visible against the empty cold night. Their huge jet cruised on majestically. To anyone beneath, they were just a tiny outline with two bright winking lights, followed after a time by the very faint sound of distant jet engines rumbling and echoing through the dark sky, driving it relentlessly northwards. They flew over Niger, then the big jet turned away slightly on a more westerly heading, keeping away from the airspace over Libya.

Matt and Khanyi slept fitfully, waking often, and easing their bodies from time to time as cramp set in, feeling the grimy discomfort of sleeping in the same clothes you have been travelling in all day. Pumi, on the other hand, had found a comfortable position mostly resting on her mother's lap, and could stretch out her short legs and sleep soundly.

At some ungodly hour, long before the dawn, the cabin lights came on brightly, window blinds were lifted, sending bright shafts of sunlight across the seats, and a delicious smell of coffee and bacon wafted through the fuselage as the crew began efficiently serving a hot breakfast and coffee to their sleepy passengers. People freshened up, and Matt began to sense the end of the flight looming and thinking through the day ahead.

Khanyi reappeared from her trip down the aisle with her daughter, both looking beautiful and refreshed. PJ wore a new outfit for landing. As they began their descent, the pilot's voice came over the PA system, his laconic announcement casually advising the aircraft passengers that the ground temperature at Heathrow was going to be two degrees on landing. Khanyisile looked horrified, and Matt began explaining to PJ that when they opened the aeroplane doors, cold air was going to come in, colder than she had ever felt before. She looked excited but a bit scared. After being held in a holding pattern over Heathrow for twenty-five minutes, the green patchwork of English fields came into view beneath them and then slowly grew into finer detail, with tiny buses and cars driving quietly along tiny roads. PJ was glued to the window, taking it all in. The landing was smooth and uneventful, a virtually unnoticeable conversion from flying to taxiing.

Collecting all their bits and pieces took some time. PJ had lost a shoe and a vitally important yellow crayon, and locating these items required an extensive search, so they let most of the passengers leave before they began exiting the aircraft. This time there was no bus, but the sudden fresh, wet, leafy smell of England greeted them at the door, briefly, before they walked into the stuffy warm air tunnel that led to the terminal buildings.

Both Matt and Khanyi held onto their daughter's hands very tightly as they plunged into the main flow of international travellers, all rushing in one direction or another. It was a lengthy walk, interspersed with rolling rubber travelators. Immigration was slow but not unpleasant, although Khanyi was shocked to find that the man behind the counter, a stern looking Sikh with a bushy beard and big turban, did not greet them. He just nodded sternly, looking at them through thick glasses. She was surprised to see so many people with tattoos on their arms, calves and necks, and to see Europeans and Indian people cleaning floors and emptying out bins. This was something quite new to her.

'Have all these people been in prison, Matt? So many of them!' she asked, bending his head down to her mouth so he could hear her. On the few occasions she had seen tattoos, it was usually a sign of convicts decorating themselves in prison, and she had not realised it had become so commonplace in Europe. Matt explained that it had become the fashion, and many people did it, even people older than themselves. She was very surprised by this and looked out of the side of her eyes at all the different patterns, trying not to stare.

They emerged eventually from immigration and quickly recovered their luggage. Then, with PJ sitting triumphantly on top of the suitcases, they carefully made their way outside and into the arrivals zone, officially new entries to the United Kingdom.

The cold air hit them like a wall, but it had a pleasant, earthy fragrance to it, decades of layered wet leaves and rainfall. Khanyi tightened PJ's coat and zipped up her own winter coat even more firmly. PJ didn't like the feeling of not being able to move her arms freely and was grizzling at her lack of freedom.

As they walked along the long line of taxi drivers holding up cards, Matt kept his eyes open for Janislav – and there he was. A bit older, a bit greyer, but the same familiar face, with his old cap. He had not been sure if he would be able to recognise him but found that he easily could. Joe was holding up a card that read BARTON FAMILY ESWATINI.

Matt was quite overwhelmed seeing him again and gave him a big hug. Janislav smiled back broadly. 'It's so long time, Matt, so very long time I ghaff not seen you. This your wife and daughter now?'

He introduced himself, starting with Khanyi. After they had lifted her off the luggage, he bent down to speak to PJ, face to face, removing his ancient cap. He said something under his breath in Polish, gazing at the child.

'My name Janislav Kopec but is more simple easy for you to call me by Joe. I was taxi for Matt many times before, now he ghaff come back with beautiful family in this case. This makes me very ghappy to see. How was flight? How is weather that side? Here is little bit cold now, but not rain too much today.'

They made their way towards the big car he had brought, and Joe chatted to them, pushing the luggage trolley along with accustomed skill. Up and down lifts, across roads, out of one building and into another, through sliding doors, he knew the way.

"Mr Matt and Mrs Barton, is real beautiful child you ghaff got, is real a gift from God, so lovely daughter, you sure very ghappy to ghaff her.'

They smiled bashfully as proud parents do. As they reached the car he announced, 'I ghaff brought small present for her. I ghaff to give now, excuse please'.

While Matt strapped her into the car seat, Joe presented PJ with a small bar of chocolate wrapped in a Union Jack, and a tiny brown furry rabbit. She showed them to Khanyi in triumph.

'Little girl, your name Pumi, my name Joe, this is present for you from Joe to say welcome to Britain. Ghaff a nice stay in this case.'

With everyone safely buckled in, Joe used the car phone and let the office know that they had met up and he was on his way, and concentrated on driving them out of the intensely heavy traffic around the vast airport and navigating around London and onto the northbound motorway. Aircraft kept flying over them, sounding so low that they wanted to duck. It was sunny and cold outside, but warm in the car and, as the traffic eased, Matt relaxed and dozed, and Khanyi, seated in the front and feeling more at home, enjoyed being able to stretch her legs. She began peppering their driver with questions.

The countryside seemed to be very tidy, green and lush to her. The tall, graceful banks of trees next to the motorway were so big, and there was so much traffic. Everything seemed to be going faster than at home, even the trucks. There were no scrap cars driving on the road, and no cattle. She wanted to know which direction London was, and which way they were heading, and why the cars were all so dark in colour. She wanted to understand the digital displays across the motorway, and why they kept telling everyone to slow down, even when the road ahead was clear. They chatted comfortably. She found it easy to understand him, and he had no difficulty following her slight accent. Glancing across at her seated next to him he could see she was very pretty woman – in this case, like princess, this wife of Matt's.

Janislav's accent reminded Khanyi in some ways of Joao, and she slowly relaxed sitting beside him, knowing that he was an old friend of Matt's. She felt safe with him.

The big Mercedes estate car drove swiftly out of London, heading towards Birmingham and the North. Khanyisile had never seen road signs saying 'The North' before, and it interested her. After Birmingham, the traffic seemed to thin out a bit, and they pulled off the motorway and took a comfort break. Neither of the adults were hungry, but PJ wanted something, and Joe needed coffee.

They went into the huge motorway services, and Khanyi immediately noticed that no one looked at them as though they were an unusual family. She saw many other families like them, also eating and standing in the shops. They stood in a queue and she bought something with English money for the first time, slow with the notes, and misunderstanding the woman at the till at first. She was surprised at the variety of foodstuffs on sale, and the amount of rubbish left on the tables. They seemed to clear the tables very slowly; there was just one old woman doing it by herself.

After the break, they went back to the car and changed places, Matt climbing into the front and Khanyi in the back with PJ. Soon, both mother and daughter fell asleep, tired from the journey, and Matt chatted to Joe about the things that had happened while he had been away. His business had grown, and he now ran three cars. His daughter was working for him now, and a son-in-law.

'How is your life there, Matt? Is going good?'

Matt answered that he was very happy. He loved being married, and was enjoying being a father.

'I see in this case you ghaff found good woman. Is better for you, Matt. You are more relaxed now. I can see you are all ghappy together. Is very good to see this. My family also, all are good, no big problems. Childs growing up fast, wife also well.'

They headed on into the North and as the landscape changed slightly and became less built up, it seemed to grow more rural and distinctly colder. There was some intermittent rain with low glowering clouds building up. The car was quiet, warm and comfortable and after a time everyone but the driver drowsed or slept. He switched on his car radio and let it burble away in the background, thinking of the thousands of times he had made this journey. He knew exactly when they would arrive, to the minute. The heavy car cruised along fast and ate up the miles effortlessly.

It was already getting dark by the time they reached their hotel, and PJ had been awake for some time, energised now and interested in everything new. They offloaded their luggage and Joe saw them into reception, then shook all their hands, giving PJ a tender hug, his bristles rubbing against her soft cheek. He gave her a small kiss goodbye.

‘Ghaff a good holiday please, little Pumi Jacqueline girl, and enjoy everything and Joe will see you again when you come to the end. This was for me a great pleasure.’

He left them and drove off into the night.

Matt and a porter carried their luggage off the pavement into the small hotel, where they were warmly welcomed at reception.

The following day, Matt arranged to collect his hire car, and then the family went off to see his old house. Everything looked familiar, but some buildings on the route had changed slightly, and he took a few wrong turns. When they reached his house, he parked in the driveway, turned to PJ and explained to her, ‘This is where Daddy used to live before he met Mummy.’

She did not look impressed but looked around. He explained to Khanyi that he needed to go and meet the neighbours, the ones who had asked to dig a ditch across his short driveway. He did not know them. She was shocked to find that he had lived in the house for several years but still never even knew his next-door neighbours. It was unthinkable to her. He tried telling her that he knew what they looked like, and thought he knew what the man did, but that they had never actually met. This distinction was hard for her to understand.

‘Hau, Matt, but you were here all this time and never knew them! But why they never invited you to eat something with them, or have a drink, even after so long? Who are they, where are they from, where are their parents?’

Matt admitted a bit bashfully that he did not know any of these things. He thought the man was called Geoff, because once some letters for him had been put in his letterbox and he thought that he worked for an insurance company. The woman, he seemed to remember, used to have short dark hair, and sometimes used to go jogging. They didn’t have children, but he thought they had a cat.

That was the sum total of all he could tell his wife, and she was distinctly unimpressed. Looking at him, she smiled from under the furry lining of her parka. After living in Africa it also seemed strange to him now, faintly ridiculous that he really didn't know them at all, other than by sight, but in those days he would often be leaving when they arrived, frequently working overseas and travelling or away over weekends, and he sometimes kept odd hours. They had seen each other, had politely nodded heads, and said hello, smiled occasionally or commented on the weather, but the years had gone by without either party breaching the great cultural divide of the low wall and neatly trimmed hedge that divided their gardens, or ever taking the step of introducing themselves to each other.

'Hau, Matt, their house is joined to yours! It's like a mirror of your house. How can you stay next to them for so long but never go to see them properly and know their names? We must go and greet them now so they can know us. We have come from far. We are going to talk to them nicely and then we will know them.'

They knocked on the door and, as they had arranged, the couple were both at home and expecting the visit. A gentle looking man, somewhere in his forties, wearing glasses, a pale blue pullover, a clean pair of cream-coloured chinos and loafers, opened the door, smiled at Matt from the porch and stretched out his hand. 'I guess you must be Matt. I'm Geoff Aldridge. We were neighbours, but I believe you've moved overseas? How do you do?'

He peered out into the front garden and suddenly realised that Matt had company. 'Oh, sorry, I didn't realise, please do come in. I think Sash has just put the kettle on.'

Khanyi and Pumi Jacqueline got out of the car and followed Matt inside, the little family all wiping their feet carefully on the doormat. They stepped respectfully into a warm, sunlit lounge that was immaculately tidy and spotlessly clean. There was a low glass coffee table, some artistically placed hanging chrome light fittings and a deep, cream-coloured carpet. In the fireplace was a faux gas fire, with imitation coals. It gave off almost no heat but looked warm.

Khanyi prayed that PJ wouldn't spill anything and looked shyly around. There was a neat pile of one particular title of house decor magazines on a side table, a few pieces of modern furniture, a huge, wide screen TV, but no bookshelves or pictures on the wall, apart from one, a stylish and moody black and white study, obviously taken professionally at their wedding. A big, comfortable-looking four-piece white leather lounge suite dominated the room. It was like a photograph of the way a designer sitting room should look. Everything was so clean it almost felt sterile.

The door opened and a younger, trim-looking woman in her mid-thirties walked in, light on her feet with short, dark, close cropped hair, wearing cream tracksuit pants and a matching top. Gold bracelets around her wrist jangled as she shook hands. 'Hello, I'm Sasha. It's so nice to finally meet you. It's been a good few years, hasn't it!'

She looked rather surprised to see Khanyi and Pumi Jacqueline in the room, but recovered quickly and welcomed them to her home, offering to take their coats.

'No thank you, Mrs Aldridge, I think we are still a bit cold. We will keep them on for now,' replied Khanyi, chilled from their brief exposure to the morning air. They were both feeling the cold, just from the short drive from the hotel. Matt kept telling them that it wasn't really cold, but she disagreed.

Sasha bent down to say hello to PJ, face to face, and asked her, with her head tilted slightly to one side if she would like a biscuit or some juice. She was trying to be friendly and Khanyi noticed it, warming to her.

'Two coffees, two teas and one juice. Be back in a jiffy!' she said cheerfully, and went out.

She came back with a tray of delicate looking tea things and an ornate plate of biscuits, and some juice for Pumi. They sat down to chat. Geoff explained that the first time he'd realised Matt had gone was when he'd received some of Matt's mail by mistake and the postman had mentioned that he had gone overseas. Matt had asked the new tenants to forward mail. The Aldridges had not met them yet, they had only been in there for a few years, but he believed it was a couple who both worked in banking. He saw the girlfriend coming in and out from time to time. They were ever so quiet and kept to themselves. They had been no trouble at all, and both drove expensive cars.

Khanyisile listened to all this. After a while, her daughter pulled her head down to her level to whisper hotly in her ear that she needed the toilet. Sasha picked up on the request and explained where it was, and Khanyi took her upstairs. The fittings were all high quality, shiny and new, and everything was just as clean as the lounge.

While they were away, Geoff explained the situation with his drainage problem, how water was building up along the garden wall, and asked if he could take Matt outside and show it to him. Once the visitors returned from upstairs, Sasha suggested to Khanyisile the idea of taking them both to a nearby park, as there were swings and lots of things for Pumi to play on. She explained that it was not very far away, just a few minutes' walk, and PJ loved the idea, as long as Khanyi was coming too. So, they decided to go on a ladies' outing, leaving the men to discuss the building work.

The Aldridges noticed with surprise that the Bartons kissed each other, hugging tightly and Matt knelt and kissed his daughter twice and gave her a big hug before they separated. He would never stop doing it for the remainder of his life.

The playground at the park was a short walk away from their house and, although Khanyi had been enjoying the warmth indoors, it was nice to get out and breathe some fresh air and let Pumi run around a bit, although she kept a close eye on her at all times. The two women began tentatively to chat, and she explained a bit to Sasha about how she had met Matt, when he had come out to sort out his late brother's affairs, how she used to work for his brother Patrick and Melanie, and where they lived in the old farmhouse in Eswatini.

Sasha had heard about the terrorist bombing of the passenger jet – it had been major news in the country – and she had known that their neighbour had lost family, but hadn't realised the closeness of the relationship. It saddened her deeply to think that he had gone through that tragedy on his own and they had never gone round to see him at the time, to pay their condolences, or just to say hello. She was kicking herself for being such a cold neighbour.

It was her first time to have such an intimate conversation with an elegant African woman like Khanyisile, especially someone visiting from overseas, and she thoroughly enjoyed it, asking lots of questions and listening intently, rather enjoying Khanyi's softly accented English and the novelty of having her seated beside her on a park bench, with the other young mums all noticing. She felt that she would have liked to become friends with Khanyisile.

Watching her enjoying playing with PJ, Khanyi enquired if she was planning to have children, but Sasha replied rather sadly that they had decided not to have any, although she loved them. They travelled a lot together as a couple and felt that it would make it too difficult for the kind of holidays they took. Khanyi was deeply puzzled by this. She could not understand how any holidays could be more important than children, but she politely dropped the topic and moved onto safer ground. She asked what work Sasha did.

'I'm working in insurance, Khanyisile. I do financial admin for a big insurance company. Geoff was one of our regional managers and he asked me out, and we started seeing each other after that. It is a bit boring sometimes, but the benefits are good, and it's handy that we can go in together most days. He's ever so clever. He does risk assessments and loss adjusting.'

Khanyi didn't know what those things were, but explained that Matt was a kind of specialist welder. He repaired things, and she helped with the invoicing and ordering materials for the workshops, and that they had a small business together, which they ran from the workshops by the farmhouse. This seemed to impress Sasha.

She was very taken with PJ, and pushed her on the swing, spun her on the roundabout and helped her up to the top of a slide. Pumi thought she was a nice lady, and she smelt nice, and began telling her, wide eyed and breathless, all about her friend Charmayne, about all their seven dogs, what things Ndepethe the gardener used to grow and show her, how she had twice seen a snake, how strong Knox was, about Musa the driver, her Nomsa who would scrub her in the bath *with a brush!* and all the important aspects of her life. She assumed that Sasha, as a grown-up, would obviously know all about these people. It was a description of a life that sounded very grand and Sasha found herself constantly reassessing how these people must be living. She was entranced by the child, flashing her lovely smile often, pushing her hair behind her ear on one side, and bending down to hear every word. And she kept hugging her, saying to Khanyi, 'She speaks so well, doesn't she? Ever so clearly! She's got a big vocabulary! She's just a sweetie pie!'

Sasha thought she was gorgeous, simply adorable, the sweetest little girl she had ever met. Khanyisile sat back on the bench, her parka zipped up tightly against the cold, hands stuffed deep into her pockets for warmth, and thought to herself about the strange life Matt used to lead, never even knowing his neighbours. She wondered why he had never met someone like Sasha when he was working here, although she was pleased that he hadn't. She thought she was a friendly and warm somebody, and someone who clearly wanted to have her own children. She thought of their lounge, so clean and tidy, and wondered if all the rest of the house was the same. She had grown to like Sasha in their short time together. In some ways she reminded her of Tarryn Bezuidenhout back home, especially how elegant she was when they first met.

'Well, we'd best be getting back. I expect the boys have sorted it all out now,' Sasha announced, and they lifted a reluctant PJ off the top of the jungle gym.

It was the nicest park she had ever seen, where everything worked and was brightly painted. It had become the highlight of their trip, although she wished there had been other children there to play with.

As they walked back holding hands, she fixed Sasha with a solemn gaze and asked her, 'Have you got another little girl my age as well, Aunty Sasha? Can I play with her next time?'

The young woman's eyes suddenly glistened with tears and she blew her nose and dabbed away carefully at her eyes without messing her eye liner, but answered quietly that no, she didn't, she was sorry.

Khanyi felt that if she had known her a bit better, she would have given her a big hug. They made their way back to the house and found that the men were back inside, in the warm, with fresh coffee brewed, and Matt was busy signing various forms and documents. It was all going to be sorted out, and Geoff had promised he would see to it that the builders did a proper job on the driveway. They said their farewells, but on the way out to the car PJ spotted a garden gnome near the pavement and wanted to go and visit him, never having seen one before. He was wearing a blue pointy hat, with big shoes and a red coat. He had a white beard, and he was standing fishing without a chance in a shallow little pond, at the end of a short gravel path.

She walked up to the gnome and looked at him for a long time, then walked back and asked Khanyi, 'Mummy, what does that short man do over there?' She could not understand why all the adults laughed.

Over the next few days, Matt took them on a few sight-seeing drives. They went into the lake district, then up onto the Yorkshire moors one windy, sunny day, walking briefly on the Pennines, and he showed them a few tourist spots and shops around the town. They visited York Minster, the huge ancient Cathedral together and marvelled at the echoing height inside. But, although they loved the new sights, they would often get back to where they were staying tired of travelling and sightseeing and having to pay for everything that was free at home. Khanyisile liked the fact that no one seemed bothered that she was a black lady with a white husband, and she'd been surprised to see so many other non-white people of different races around in the shops and on the streets, but they were not Swazis. She missed hearing her own language.

Matt visited his solicitor and spent several boring hours in an extremely dull meeting with them, finally seeing his tenants and signing even more documents. The tenants were very respectful, but business-like and not very friendly towards him, and he didn't take his family to see them. Khanyi said she was not interested in seeing where he used to live, because it had been a lonely place which was sad for him, and it would also make her feel sad.

Nearing the end of their brief trip and short vacation, Matt had arranged to visit his old workplace and had set up a meeting with Brian Pearson, his old boss.

It was particularly chilly that day, with intermittent rain, and Khanyi and Pumi Jacqueline were completely wrapped up. Winter vests, layers of clothing, tights under jeans for Khanyi, and leggings for PJ, with gloves, jerseys. Of course, PJ was well coated in both Vicks and Vaseline to protect her against attack from British germs, which Khanyi believed to be virulent, plentiful, and dangerous.

Their child was so well wrapped up that she could barely move, and looked like a short, rather stout person with her arms sticking out. Khanyi still managed to look elegant, in her boots and jeans, despite her heavy winter coat, but she was determined to protect her daughter from the cold and British flu. She felt a bit nervous about meeting Matt's old boss, and had not realised that Brian Pearson, as charming a man as he was, also felt a tiny bit nervous about meeting her.

One thing he knew of Khanyisile was that she was the lady who'd stolen Matt's heart, and had done so very quickly. Basically, over one short visit. A young, single Swazi woman who had taken away from his business, in three short weeks, the best field operator he had ever employed, an internationally qualified, fully accredited, double-coded welder of unusual talent, immensely hard working and able to operate anywhere in the world and travel at short notice. A loyal, conscientious worker who seldom, if ever, required follow up visits to rectify faults or errors.

Of all the men and women he had taken on, gradually building up his business, he probably missed Matt the most, and he'd had big plans for him that had to be abandoned when he resigned. The young man worked with an extraordinary attention to detail, and when he had completed his preparations and was ready to weld, his repairs were usually faultless, even under exceptionally difficult, hot, cramped, humid or generally unpleasant conditions.

He also believed in his heart (but had never expressed except once, privately, to his wife) that in some odd way he thought that Matt probably had some mysterious kind of Gaelic second sight. He seemed to have the ability to perceive what was happening inside the metal, underneath the weld, looking beneath the surface in a way that even the best technicians could not normally match. In some strange way, he could relate to the unusual metals that he had to work with on some sort of metallurgical, granular level that was difficult to explain and even harder to understand. When they X-rayed Matt's welds, he always seemed to know what the results would be before they came back. He could describe what other people could not even see.

Pearson was a professional person himself, a highly qualified metallurgist with a good knowledge of modern welding techniques, and he would often think back to some fascinating, complex and highly technical conversations he had enjoyed with Matt over the years.

One repair Matt had explained to him years ago had always stuck in his mind. He had been casually describing a particularly difficult job, lying on his back inside a Pratt and Whitney JT8D turbofan, a jet engine hanging off the wing of an old McDonnel Douglas DC9 cargo jet, carrying out mirror welds because he could not see the work directly, working back to front, welding on austenitic nickel chromium alloy exhaust struts, while a gale was blowing. The wind kept rocking the stranded aircraft on its undercarriage, howling through the underslung engine, and swaying the section he was repairing. Matt had to allow for each gust and adjust his welding continuously. That was the kind of thing he could do.

He had once told Brian about welding aluminium alloys at some refinery abroad. Repairing leaks in distillation header couplings, working in a confined space almost at the limit of his reach, having to achieve a gas proof X-rayed weld, and having to swap over mid-weld to use his other, less practised hand in order to complete the repairs. Really technical and challenging work, sometimes only seeing the stainless-steel tank and weld area through a small peep hole, while his gas torch was fed through a different, slightly larger access hole cut into the tank's side. Trying anything to overcome exceptionally limited access and vision. He had simply made the welds, achieved those repairs and taken them in his stride.

He never told these 'war stories' by way of complaint, or to be boastful, just informing his boss about some new and interesting problems he had encountered, as though they were routine challenges, perhaps mentioning them over a quick snack lunch, or in a brief car park conversation, both men headed in opposite directions.

Matt had been extremely well paid, because he was highly qualified, gifted and at the top of his game, but he had also earned a great deal for the firm, and Brian knew he'd earned every penny when he was out in the field, and had usually sent him to the most difficult jobs. He only found out some time after he had left that, if he knew he would be working on extremely rare materials, Matt would take the time to contact the suppliers, and research and study the problem in great detail before attempting the welds.

For months after he left, Brian used to get messages and phone calls from production managers and engineering directors in places like Iraq, Russia, Japan, Nigeria, Poland, Sri Lanka, Saudi Arabia, and Chile, busy people taking the time to call him personally, wanting to convey their thanks for the way in which Matt had attended to their fractured pipe, or broken structures, fixed plant and machinery or refinery stoppages. They had realised that his repair work was completed to a different level to most other welders, and often could not quite believe how well it had turned out. Brian missed him and was looking forward to seeing him again.

Emma knocked on the office door and announced that his visitors had arrived. She showed them in, and tried to relieve Khanyi of her winter coat, but she preferred to keep wearing it until she had gauged the temperature in the room. Emma looked as pretty as ever, perhaps a little older, and had given Matt a long, fragrant, bosomy hug, before greeting Mrs Barton more formally. She was enchanted by Pumi Jacqueline, and even persuaded her to take off one of her outer layers. Relishing the feeling of some freedom to move, PJ shyly said a brief hello to Brian Pearson, then ran to the window to look at the view from his office.

Emma stayed to chat for a while, enjoying the spectacle of Matt and his new family, and taking in the tall, regal-looking African beauty who had become his wife. Khanyi had loosened, but not removed her heavy coat, and was shaking hands with Brian, telling him a little about the flight and the journey. Emma thought she was lovely but felt that she didn't really know how to begin a conversation with her. She was wearing boots with heels, making her look quite imposing. Emma thought she looked like someone out of a magazine.

Brian slipped into his business-like shorthand, a form of speech that Matt had grown accustomed to. He was trying his absolute best to make the little family welcome, but had not met someone like Khanyi before, and very seldom ever had young children in his office.

'Aah, good Matt, welcome back, lad. This is your good lady, is it? I'm Brian, Brian Pearson, good to finally meet you!'

He went on, 'First class, excellent, do sit down, uhm it's er, Kalicine? Khasanile? Khaanayise? I'm terribly sorry, my dear, don't seem to be able to grasp it, you will have to tell me it again, always hopeless with foreign languages, so you're the famous Mrs Barton, Matt's wife, lovely, great, most welcome.'

He continued, thinking aloud, 'And, of course, this little one must be your first, that is, she would be your daughter, lovely, super, have heard of her of course, wonderful. Now, what can we get for you all? What would the little girl like, hmm? A drink? A snack? Perhaps a biscuit? What about a sandwich? Something from the canteen? What about a sausage roll? A fizzy drink? Emma will sort you out, won't you Emm?'

Khanyi said her name again slowly, syllable by syllable, and embarrassed him slightly by doing a miniature curtsey as she shook his hand, briefly bending at the knees, taking his hand in both of hers.

'Hello, Sir, I'm KHA.. NYI.. SI.. LE. I'm very happy to finally meet you,' enunciating each part slowly. 'And this is our first born, Pumi Jacqueline, but you can call her Pumi or PJ.'

'Right, good, great, got it, Pumi Jacqueline, fine with that one, right, good Kha.nyi.sile, got it. Do call me Brian, no standing on formalities, eh! Super, so good to finally meet you in person. Matt hasn't told me what brings you to these parts. Bit of a holiday, eh?'

Emma bent down next to Pumi and tenderly asked her a question, receiving the full gaze of her extraordinary green eyes in return, enquiring if she would like to have some juice, or some biscuits, and offering to bring her some paper to draw on, and some coloured pens. This idea went down well. Pumi nodded and Matt glanced across to his old work colleague, silently thanking her with his eyes. He could see that Emma was thoroughly enjoying their visit – they were being treated like royalty – and to his surprise Brian and Khanyi were already getting along famously.

She took a seat in one of the big chairs before his desk, crossed her legs and sat back, and he began asking her how they'd met, what it was like in Eswatini, how things were going there with the economy and so on. He had a host of detailed, complex questions to ask but was adept at setting younger people at ease and getting them to relax. Khanyi even unzipped her coat and finally stood up and took it off, for it to be whisked away and hung up by Emma.

Fairly early on, he made her laugh, saying, 'So this is the lovely lady who stole my best welder away from me. Well, it's easy to see why, eh Matt? hmm?' She felt more relaxed after that. In her gentle Swazi-accented English, intriguing and novel for Brian and Emma to hear, she tackled his questions one at a time, fully, and in some depth, answering them as best she could.

'Mr Brian, I am a Swazi. I used to work for Matt's brother Patrick and his wife Melanie. I cared for their children and kept the house. When they became late, Matt visited to sort out all the business and the problems, that's when we met. He is a kind man, like his brother; also very clever. Once he started repairing things, many people started bringing them for repairs. Now we have a small business together and I am helping him.'

'Right, Khanyisile, terrible business that, dreadful shock to us all here, especially for young Matt. So, you two sort of got together after that awful business, eh! I remember him phoning me, of course, yes, jolly good, excellent, every happiness, tremendous.'

'Yes, we were married almost six years back. We still remember your present. It was very kind, Mr Pearson.'

'Oh, please don't mention it. My pleasure, super, well done the pair of you. Good to see young Matt looking so relaxed, I always wondered when he might meet a good woman, excellent, and you are comfortable over there now, I take it? No plans on coming back, eh Matt? I can't tempt you back here again? My offer still stands…'

'No, Brian, it's kind of you, but I think we won't be moving now. It sort of grows on you after a while. We are well settled there now; we've made a life together.'

'They still have that king chappie there, don't they? A youngish fellow, I recall. How is that all going?'

They spoke about Royalty and Eswatini for some time, then Matt asked Brian if he could take a walk around and say hello to the ladies in the canteen, and people he knew. Brian accompanied him for part of the way, eager to show him some of the changes and proud of the many improvements they had made to the business in the last few years. He escorted him as far as the stores, then had to return to his office to take an important call from Germany.

Khanyisile stayed behind, chatting to Emma, but she and her daughter relocated into the warmth of the reception area. Pumi continued drawing pictures for her captive audience, making a blue cat for Emma, two red chickens for Brian Pearson and a picture of the aeroplane for Daddy. The financial admin staff passing by were fascinated by her ability to switch to SiSwati whenever she spoke to her mum, the sharp clicks of her mother tongue resounding around the office, and then back into English when she spoke to them, and after a while she wasn't so shy, and began telling Emma about Nomsa, who looked after her while Mummy was working, and all her dogs. Emma, who had children of her own, proved to be an avid listener.

Matt had discovered his old friend, the storeman Salikh, talking furiously on the phone, embroiled in a heated argument about the overdue delivery of some welding equipment to Singapore. He had grown a few grey wisps in his beard, and had picked up some weight around his face, something he blamed entirely on his new wife's cooking skills. The two friends caught up easily, gossiped and laughed, reminiscing about funny events for almost half an hour. Then they both returned upstairs, back to Mr Pearson's office. Salikh took four calls while Matt was with him.

Salikh was at first rather overawed by Khanyi. He was bashful and went a bit quiet, but he welcomed them both warmly and stayed and talked for a while. He was unsure how to relate to this well-spoken and elegant woman, or their child. He hadn't really come across anyone quite like her before, and thought she was stunning. But then she charmed him, and joked with him about Matt's love for cornflakes, and he gradually relaxed, became his normal, boisterous self again, and asked them a little about their lives at home. At a certain moment he turned aside to Matt and silently mouthed the word 'Wow!' to him, at the same time making that universal sign of burning his finger, meaning she was hot. Matt smiled at him, knowing it meant solid approval. He was glad that Salikh liked her, and was quietly proud of his 'hot' young wife, doing so well meeting all these new people at once.

Brian emerged from his office again, the overseas call over. Fresh coffee appeared and he, the storeman and Matt swapped old work stories for a while. Then, as the MD began glancing at his watch, Matt sensed it was time to leave. It had been a visit he had both dreaded and looked forward to, but he could still feel the warmth from his old workmates, and his special relationship with Brian was intact. Emma felt she knew them all well enough to give them all warm hugs, and kissed Pumi Jacqueline goodbye, asking her to look after Matt and her mummy for her and pat all the seven dogs.

They walked back to the car and Khanyi was noticeably quiet, thinking of the years Matt had worked there, and how they had all been welcomed. There were also proper somebodies here, good people, truly kind to them, genuinely welcoming, and they all knew Matt from before, when he was younger. She had begun to realise better what it meant to them when he'd left the firm. She thanked him for bringing them there to see them; it helped to fill some gaps in her knowledge of his previous life.

Chapter 22

Found

In the Usutu, Ginindza was on the move, walking along with his steady pace, far from the forest road, seeking out an old beehive, looking for an old familiar colony of bees. He knew them from old. Bees that were not so aggressive, that used to gather regularly and swarm into a deep crevasse between two rock faces. It was well-hidden, near the edge of the forest by a grove of tall gum trees and was difficult to find, but not too high off the ground, with only a little climbing required. The problem was that his own tracking signs had been covered up and altered over time, as the young trees had grown in height, and he had to remember clearly the place where to leave the path and cut away to the north and west.

He had been speaking to his friend Lindiwe after they had both received unexpected financial rewards from the Barton family, and their discussion had reminded him of the time he saw the running men and little girl. He had never possessed a bank account, but trusted Lindiwe enough to request that the money was paid into her account, and then he would ask her for some cash from time to time. He had bought paraffin, radio batteries, a pair of fine new boots, good tobacco, a blanket and a coat so far, and the money left was still plenty. Sis Lindiwe had wanted to know his age, and he was trying to work it out, but he knew he was poor with numbers. He did remember hearing news that the previous king, Sobhuza the second, had been crowned by the queen in England, and ascended to the throne as king of Swaziland, and believed this was in 1967. He was a grown teenager at that time, so believed himself to be seventy something years. He had already left primary school and was working when the king was enthroned.

His mind was wandering freely as he walked, listening for the honey bird, and he thought again of that little girl child, the beautiful one, wondering how she was growing now, and if she had been able to recover in her mind after her experience. She had been left fearful. He had been very surprised by the reward – it meant about a year's good income to him – but he had little to give back in return, and had decided to make a gift of some wild honey to her family, once he managed to find it, and intended asking Lindiwe to somehow get it to them. She would know how.

It was a warm morning above the foliage, clear but not too hot, and the sun was visible in shafts of bright light, streaming down between the trees at an angle onto the forest floor. The light was creating an odd striped effect on the ground, almost like the sides of a dusty brown zebra, the straight black shadows cast by the tree trunks contrasting with the deep bed of pine needles, light brown in the afternoon sun. The pine sap was running, and the air around him was fragrant.

The fallen needles were everywhere, scattered lightly across the little used old footpath he was following, and he could hear them crunching under his feet. It was also unusually quiet, an almost windless day, with the treetops and high forest canopy barely moving. A good day, he hoped, for stealing honey, as the bees should not be ill tempered if he found them, but drowsy. They disliked rain, great heat or wind, and such weather made them more dangerous and irritable.

He was watching carefully for two saplings he had bent down and tied with bark about six months before, as that marked the place where he should turn and leave the path. He was on the same path he had shown to that policeman, and walking along it reminded him of how he had heard the men's voices, disturbed by the sounds of them running that time before, and how he had hidden out of sight to watch them. He did not want to get too close to the dark stream and white rocks where they had taken the child, fearful of the evil spirits lurking there by the water, and memories of deeds that had happened there in the past.

In the distance, slightly to one side of the trail, he discerned something light coloured. He thought it looked like some edible mushrooms, close by the foot of a tree and a little way off the path. As he drew closer, he could make out that it was a colour unlike everything around it, but the thing was partly hidden, just as the mushrooms usually are when they grow on the forest floor, usually partially covered in pine needles. He wondered what he was seeing. Then, as he crouched to look more carefully, a strange prickling started moving over his scalp, reminding him of the feeling he sometimes got when there was a dangerous snake or a snare nearby. Something he could not see had reached towards him from the forest and was disturbing him.

He drew closer, but as he did so, felt a sudden coldness growing around him, as though his skin were crawling, and then the air about him seemed to grow thick and harder to breathe. His nerves were set on edge. There was strong muti hereabouts, and he was immediately cautious and afraid.

He slowed his pace, intensely wary of the unknown, and sure now that the tiny glimpse of colour he had seen was not natural but something off balance that did not fit easily into its natural surroundings. He prayed it was not an item of clothing, as such things were invariably a bad omen. There were many bodies hidden in secret parts of the forest. The rain would wash away the tears, and the elements would eventually wash the drying eyes from their sockets, but the bones always remained and were seldom buried. He had occasionally stumbled across such things and, fearful and chilled, had never returned to those places.

He stopped some distance away and stared intensely at the object, moving his head suspiciously to one side for a better view and angle.

It was neither cream, nor yellow, nor white or light brown like the mushrooms, and was even unlike the poisonous ones. It was that strange colour he did not know, almost like the inside of an animal or a deep wound. The little part of it that he could see looked pink.

He walked slowly up to it, still unsure, knelt beside the path, and then gently swept away the covering of needles and dirt. What he had seen that confused him was the heel part of a child's shoe. He touched it tenderly, feeling at it with tentative fingers, and eased it out from under its covering, flicking off the spiky dry needles. It was still bright and clean, with flowers lining a stalk on each side, and a big white flower on the top, and all the remainder of the shoe pink. He had seen part of the sole sticking out of the forest floor covering, and suddenly the image came back to him of that little girl's legs and her feet, one with a shoe and one without.

This was her shoe. He must return it to her, it must somehow be given back, it could go together with his wild eucalyptus honey. It needed to be re-joined to her. The air around him seemed to be humming, but no longer with a sense of foreboding. He felt as though a weight had been lifted from him. Something that was unresolved in the back of his mind had been settled, fulfilled and completed, and the atmosphere returned to the peaceful day before him, and his simple mission.

He was in no great rush. He sat back on the deep crunchy bed of pine needles, thinking of that day, of the frighteningly fast ride in the car, of meeting the big Zulu man Mkhize, *UKnox*, and of that coloured policeman who moved so fast, light and nimble on his feet like a buck. He remembered hearing the loud crack of three gunshots, Kwa! Kwa!....Kwa! sharply echoing through the trees. The smell of blood on the forest floor, and the damaged face of the one who was shot.

He saw that little ntombi with golden hair, her body shaking and crying, held tightly in Knox's massive arms, fearful of those around her, and the sudden noise when emapoyisa arrived in numbers in their dark uniform. How they were happy and excited because the child was still alive and intact.

Watching them arresting the injured one, that one making a noise like an animal being choked, handcuffing that short one and then roughly dragging the body of the other dead one up from the river. The tall man, that Satan who had been carrying her, clamping her mouth was shot dead. There were big holes in his corpse. He never went to look over the bank onto those killing rocks to see the place, or the blood that was shed. It was nothing he wanted to carry in his mind and the rain was going to clean it. Then Rennie asked him if he recognised the two men, and he saw them well, he remembered the ugly drawn face and hollow cheeks, and he knew they were the ones he had seen running with her before.

He loosened his small khaki cloth knapsack and laid it carefully on the ground in front of him, dusted off the little shoe and closely examined it. Very faintly, washed by many rains, he could just see the outline of a small foot sunk into the soft pink sole. He held it in his hand, slowly tracing the outline of her tiny toes with one finger, seeming to read something from it, then remained there, sitting down on the forest floor and looking at it for several minutes more.

Then, as though decided, nodding his greying head, he carefully wrapped it in a red cloth he always carried and stashed it in his bag, safely underneath his old bee smoker, the herbs, his packets, knives, spoons and other possessions he carried to make fire and smoke out bees.

He took out his ancient packet of *Gwaai*, and rolled himself a loosely packed brown paper cigarette, his senses calmed by everything falling into place. He lit his smoke and leant back against the very same tree next to where the shoe had been lying. The fragrant smoke drifted upwards and spread around him, and he inhaled deeply, feeling the sense of peace that tobacco can bring to a smoker coursing through his blood stream. It was made even more pleasurable knowing that what he was doing was not permitted. He sat there quietly and smoked in the dappled sunlight, took a sip of cold, sweet tea from his bottle, spat out the odd wisp of tobacco and felt his body gradually relax.

Something that had been left unfinished was almost ended now. It would become complete when the shoe was returned to that first born child, and he, Ginindza, was the one supposed to find it, because the forest was his home and it could not hold secrets from him. His ancestors had brought him to this place to make it easy for him to finish everything that must be finished. He knew they had guided him there.

He eased his back against the tree and drew on the hand-rolled cigarette deeply. As he smoked, his thinking cleared, like when the soft, creamy grey clouds shrouding the moon slide silently away, revealing its shining face. In that moment, like that magical instant when pure, clear moonlight suddenly spreads its grace and light across the land, bathing all creation in silver, the emotional burden of his memories lifted from him. His mind was peaceful, and like clear water now. Crystal clear and still. Suddenly, he could see everything acutely. He knew he would be led to easily find the bees today, knew that on this day of all days he would be able to harvest their sweet honey without angering them, and would not be stung too often.

The bees would know his smell and forgive him his theft, because a certain reparation had still to be made to that child. A debt remained to be paid for what happened to her in the forest, and this thing belonging to her must still be returned so that she could once again be complete and happy, there in the lowveld where she stayed with her family. These things all became clear to him, sitting, resting against the bark of the tree.

He himself had touched that child once, had felt her soft child's skin and felt her golden hair, and knew from the feeling echoing all about him in the natural universe, from the trees standing like silent sentinels around him, that this thing was hers and must somehow be returned to her. Such a thing should be given to her soon, he decided, and that strong woman Lindiwe would know how to transport such a thing and restore it to the girl child again. She was used to such matters.

The shoe, given together with a gift of honey that he would yet find. That was his task today, and his heart was lifted by realising it, knowing so clearly his course of action. He would be released from that harrowing memory at last.

Chapter 23

Another homecoming

MATT, KHANYISILE AND PUMI JACQUELINE returned from their visit to England a bit more relaxed, all three of them still healthy, and they had somehow managed to leave some of the worst moments of her abduction behind them, left scattered randomly in their wake, displaced by the new memories and images from their holiday.

Sometimes, God slowly erodes the unbearable, leaving only the shadows of the worst days and hours, a pale memory of what had passed. The adults felt renewed and refreshed.

Khanyisile had not found Britain as wet as she was expecting, although it still felt unbearably cold to her on most days. She had been shown some very pretty views, golden autumn trees, lovely landscapes, and many old buildings and huge old churches, and found that most of the places they had been into were comfortably warm, unlike houses at home were in the winter.

She had also experienced for the first time the wonders of heated towel rails. They had overnighted in several places where the bathrooms were equipped with them. Gleaming chrome racks, with warm, clean, deep, fragrant towels waiting for them. The first time she had helped PJ out of her bath and wrapped the little girl in a warm soft towel, it had been a revelation to them both. PJ now actually enjoyed getting out of her bath, because she didn't have to feel cold and had a warm towel to look forward to. Khanyisile felt shy to say so to Matt, but privately thought it was perhaps the best thing she had discovered in all the time they were there.

Her second abiding experience, and one that had surprised her, was that their family unit, still quite unusual at home and in South Africa, had already become commonplace in Britain. She had seen many other couples like them, and in many other combinations. Black men with white women, Indian girls with white men, white men with what she would have thought to be coloured ladies, but who were considered black in Europe, and she had become keenly aware of these couples, and noticed many other mixed families with children, and many young mothers. It was nice not to be the novelty. She enjoyed especially that when they went into a restaurant as a small family unit, no one stared at them or made snide remarks. When they visited shops, there were no nasty comments hissed behind hiding hands. In all the time they were there, travelling around, she never experienced anything like what she had experienced many times at home. They were welcomed everywhere and this had surprised her.

Many English people seemed to admire her daughter, but she watched them all very carefully and when they travelled, little girls seemed to be drawn to PJ, always wanting to say hello to her, or play with her, or talk to her on buses and trains. Whenever these children were sniffing or coughing, she would watch them carefully, and warn PJ in rapid SiSwati about catching a cold. She considered that the English had generally been friendly people, even though they usually failed to greet. Matt explained to her that they didn't mean anything by it; they just didn't know her yet. Whenever she would thank a server after breakfast or greet an attendant in a shop, they always seemed to be surprised and looked at her blankly, as though such behaviour was quite unusual. To Khanyi, it was natural. Only Joe from the taxi, that nice lady Emma and Sasha liked it when she thanked them, and they seemed comfortable with it. These things she had noticed.

They always misunderstood her when she said Hau! and she always had to explain what she meant. But how can you explain Hau! to one who does not know?

She had also noticed that Matt's way of speaking had changed a bit while they were there. He had begun to sound more like he used to talk when they first met. His English accent had changed in some way, as though it was coming back onto his tongue. He had been very careful with them both, always making time to listen to PJ, no matter what they were doing, bending over to listen when she was worried about their sleeping arrangements or wanting to know what was happening next.

They had never once let her out of their sight during the whole holiday, and Khanyi, especially, watched any men around her like a hawk. Once or twice she had sensed something not quite right, and whispered to Matt, who immediately picked her up and carried her away, no matter how much she was enjoying whatever she was busy with. Sometimes, the way some Indian men had looked at her child had felt wrong and she had quickly noticed their stares. Both parents' sensitivity around adult strangers was heightened, though they had not told anyone they met what had happened. It was too difficult to explain, and much too painful to remember. They were hoping that PJ could slowly forget it too.

They were met at the airport by Musa, having safely recovered their luggage in Johannesburg and transferred onto the Eswatini flight. She loved being back in the Kingdom again, being greeted warmly at immigration, and greeting the officials back in her own language. They told her that her child had grown. After the rich loamy smell of England, the distinctive scent of the wind and old trees, and the centuries of wet vegetation, layer upon layer, the completely different smell of sugar cane in flower and the lowveld was strong, and it smelt of home. Khanyisile took in the distinct smell of the Swazi dust, of distant wood fires and kraals, and let the feeling of the intense November heat soak into her. The sight of a family of warthogs comically scampering across the road in front of them, and the cheerful, ribald, outrageously flirtatious jokes made by the airport workers, were somehow all warming her heart. She felt flooded with love, overwhelmed with love for her own family, for her relatives, her home and country. It had been interesting to travel, to see where Matt used to stay and where he had worked, but she could never live in such a cold place.

When they reached home, they carried the cases inside, and PJ ran around hugging all the dogs. Then she said she was tired now and wanted to sleep. She washed, changed, brushed her teeth and fell into bed, surrounded by a host of her favourite soft toys. She fell asleep almost immediately.

Khanyi had other ideas. During their trip, they had often slept with PJ in the same room, as she was too scared to be alone, and they had often both been so tired when they did go to bed during their trip that they just went to sleep. The rooms had been small, and their chances for lovemaking were few. They had missed the uninhibited time and space for making love that they always enjoyed in their own home. She had a certain gleam in her eyes that Matt knew well, and with the suitcases standing around like voyeurs, still closed and unpacked, she shut and locked the front door, then kissed him deeply, slowly walking backwards, pulling him relentlessly towards their bedroom.

Khanyi almost fell over, tripping over PJ's backpack lying outside her room and they giggled like teenagers, stifling the noise, her eyes shining with supressed laughter. They began undressing each other as they staggered backwards, excitement growing. Their bedroom and big double bed loomed, light coloured, firm and welcoming in the dark, and he felt as though everything but her scent, her soft breasts pressing against his chest and her body against him was falling away from him. Nothing else mattered. His senses swirled around, and he felt dizzy. Her slim waist and the swell of her hips aroused a wanting in him that he no longer had to resist. She felt herself slowly melting, losing herself and sinking into the delicious sense of intimacy they had missed and been unable to find in the places they had stayed in.

They both knew each other's needs, and through touching and feeling, gave what the other needed most. He was there with her, hungry for her and wanting her as much as she wanted him, and with eager anticipation they fell into bed together, using their young bodies to wring everything out of each other until they could erase the memories of those two dark days when they thought they had lost their daughter. The familiarity of the room, the windows, the sounds of their world, closed around them and everything else drifted away. Eventually, much later, satiated, and tired out, they slept entwined, one of her legs between his.

Chapter 24

Closure

THE PHONE CALL CAME DURING a normal morning. Khanyi was between chasing up three debtors, arranging a payment for materials, and keeping an eye on the time so that Musa could collect PJ from the school lift. She had restarted attending school after returning from their holiday, when she had wanted to see her friends and tell them about what she had seen in England and on the aeroplane.

Khanyisile was working in the study, their small office. She answered and immediately recognised the polite, rather formal tone of Detective Inspector Rennie's voice, his soft coloured accent and slightly rolling 'r's instantly identifying him.

'Hello, good morning, is that Mrs Barton? This is Richard speaking, DI Richard Rennie.'

'Hello, Inspector. It's Khanyisile here. How are you sir?'

'I'm very well, Khanyi, thank you. How is the family? How are y'all doing, there in the lowveld?'

'No, we are all fine now, we are all fine, even Pumi, she is okay now. We were away, we went on a trip to overseas, but now we have returned. How can I help you, Mr Richard?' She still wasn't quite comfortable calling him Richard.

'Well, uhm, Khanyisile, I need to deliver something to you. There are some things that Lindiwe Mavimbela and the old Mkhulu Ginindza have given me, which they asked me to bring to you. I actually have to come to Mlawula tomorrow. I wanted to know if I could pass by your place and drop them off?'

'Aah, no problem, Mr Richard. We will be here. You can come at any time. We will be happy to see you again. I know Matt would be very happy to see you. Also Knox, if he is here when you come.'

She paused, unsure how to word what she wanted to say. 'What about some food, Mr Richard. Can we prepare you some food for when you come, because you will be coming from far?'

He was very touched by this offer but declined. His wife liked to have her husband eat with the children at night, and he knew better than to come home and not be hungry.

Detective Inspector Rennie drove down the following day. He needed to question a Mozambican *impimpi* they had placed at the sugar terminal, a man who was reporting on some large scale sugar theft involving trucks and railway wagons, and he planned to go on and see the Bartons, after meeting his informer and getting that matter out of the way.

The Shangaan man had now given the Police enough information for them to act, and his evidence would split the case wide open, but it was getting close to the time when he would suddenly have to seemingly abscond, automatically get dismissed for absenteeism and no longer work there. Then they would swoop and make the arrests. The meeting had gone well, conducted in absolute secrecy far away from the sugar terminal, near the ruins of Brown's garage, far off the road and out of sight. The embedded impimpi had passed on a lot of detailed information with key names, times, amounts and places.

As he arrived at the gate, he remembered the last time he had been there, arriving late at night with Lionel, Knox and the child, and how exhausted he had been. The dogs calmed when he extended his hand to them, realising as dogs will that he was not scared of them and was no threat. Ndepethe, in his khaki overcoat, came shuffling out from a small stand of banana trees and opened the gate for him, and he drove slowly up the drive, the bakkie wheels crunching on the gravel, his mind flooding with memories of that long day and night. He noticed storm clouds beginning to gather in the distance, deep in the southern skies.

Khanyi came out of the house, closely followed by Matt. She looked a bit thinner than he remembered, and was perhaps a little paler, but she greeted him warmly, giving him a tight squeeze. Matt followed, embracing him in a man's shoulder hug, and patting him on the back like a long-lost friend.

'Inspector Rennie! Richard, man it's good to see you! It's been too long. How are you keeping?'

He explained that he had been busy and had not been in that part of the country for some time. They went indoors and offered him coffee and something to eat. They sat down together, and he looked across at them both and began.

'Mr and Mrs Barton, I need to inform you of a certain development. You will most likely recall that Ndzinisa's accomplice, the one who was known as Boy, was sentenced to forty years imprisonment, but I need to advise you he will not be serving his sentence.'

This caught both of their attention, and they looked at him in amazement. Khanyi's eyes were already blazing angrily.

'No no, Mr and Mrs Barton, it's not what you think. Don't worry. There was an incident at Balekane prison last week, I understand from the warders there that a certain argument developed over the ownership of some cartons of cigarettes. You know they are used like a currency in prison? Well there was apparently some sort of dispute between the prisoners, involving Boy, and two Somalis. Apparently, it rapidly became heated and violent, and then a fight broke out in the yard. It all happened very quickly, so the warders are suspecting it might have been a planned thing. You know they don't like having muti murd…'

He stopped and hesitated, thinking he needed to soften his words and be more careful.

'The normal prisoners who are incarcerated don't like having inmates who hurt children around. It seems that this guy that we detained, this Boy, got stabbed repeatedly by certain prisoners using weapons that cannot be found, in such a way that no one saw what really happened. It usually *is* like that in prison. They might use a sharpened toothbrush someone has hidden on his person, or a sharpened spoke, a piece of bed spring or even a spoon, ground to a sharp point. We don't know. They make weapons out of anything they can, make a handle for it and hide them in funny places.

'It seems they found him with multiple stab wounds, so it looks like several of the guys joined in. The warders think it involves some Zimbabweans, a gang who smuggle cigarettes. He may have cheated them or clashed with the Somalis, or short paid someone or something. We will probably never know. There was a dispute of some kind and someone expecting money never got paid what he was expecting, or what was agreed. That's what they tell me, but none of the witnesses will talk. Anyway, after they began attacking him, the prisoner, Boy, couldn't shout for help because he has no voice. No one heard anything'.

Matt nodded; Knox had told him a little bit about it.

'He died before the warders could get to him. He bled out at the scene. They stabbed his heart several times, and the artery in his neck. The prisoners were all standing around him, hiding the fact that he was down, fallen on the ground beneath them. They normally tend to do this when someone is being punished. When the warders moved in, they searched them but couldn't find the murder weapons. All the knives and weapons had somehow disappeared. The other prisoners, those standing nearby, all claim they never saw or heard anything, and, of course, there are no witnesses from within the gang. Probably none are willing to come forward. But this stabbing, Matt and Khanyi, this stabbing means as far as the two men goes, those who abducted your daughter, the case is now closed. Both are now deceased.'

He paused, as though deciding whether to tell them more.

'But this Boy was heavily questioned in hospital and eventually gave up the name of the Sangoma who ordered… the one who told them what to do, and she has now been arrested in South Africa in connection with abduction, and two previous children who also disappeared here. You will not have to come to court, nor will your daughter, Mrs Barton. The case on your side is now closed. I'm going to be giving evidence in that trial.'

He sat back, watching their expressions as they took this in. Khanyi's eyes had filled with tears and she blew her nose, still upset. He wanted to cheer her up. A chill wind had come up quickly, and swept through the house carrying on it the faint smell of rain, new rain on hot tarmac, parched soil and dusty trees. An open window was banging somewhere in one of the bedrooms.

'But I have another reason for coming. MaLindiwe and the old man Ginindza asked me to give you something. He says he got them both from the forest.'

He reached down beside his chair and presented them with a blue plastic bag, wrapped and tied up with the fibrous stem of a plant. Inside this, there were several large, sticky honeycombs, packed with rich, strong blue gum honey, the clear plastic bag closed tightly at the neck with brown string. The honey had seeped out during the journey and was lying deep and brown in the bottom of the bag. But beneath this was another package, something wrapped in newspaper, and Khanyi gently lifted it out and unwrapped it. Inside was Pumi Jacqueline's missing sandal, freshly washed, scrubbed hard with Sunlight soap and spotlessly clean. The tiny rows of flowers on it shone brightly in the afternoon light. She gasped out loud, amazed.

'Hau, Richard! Where does this come from? This is PJ's lost shoe!'

'Ginindza said it belongs to your daughter. He wanted to return it to her. He says he knew it was lost from that time, and he happened to find it. The honey is a gift from him. He wanted me to thank you for the reward. He said he found the shoe in the forest, close to where he saw her being carried.'

Matt and Khanyi put the little pink shoe onto the coffee table. Neither of them wanted to touch it at first. Khanyisile had discretely hidden the other shoe, and it had been kept out of sight since PJ was returned to them, but that was now several months ago. They had bought her other pairs of shoes, new sandals, but none were quite as beloved or pretty as her pink pair. The couple looked at each other, unsure if they were going to 'find' the other one and return them to her, or not. They would first check with the special doctor she had been seeing. They thanked the detective warmly for the gifts.

DI Rennie took his leave, and the Bartons asked him to thank Ginindza and Lindiwe, and thanked him for visiting them. Matt escorted him out to the turning area at the end of the driveway. Rennie climbed into his double cab, leant his head forward and picked at a speck of dirt on the driver's side mirror. He seemed to pause, then sighed heavily and spoke quietly to Matt, who was standing by the driver's window. The rain was getting closer and big heavy raindrops began to hit them, the random droplets becoming increasingly frequent, sounding out an early warning ahead of the real storm. The rain splattered against the roofing sheets and driveway, smacking loudly against the body and windscreen of Rennie's bakkie.

'Matt, you know that Boy's voice was damaged when he was arrested. Knox told me he might have accidentally crushed it when he captured him. Knox is a big man; his hands are like – well you know how Knox felt about those men.'

Matt knew very well what Knox was capable of. He had saved his and Khanyi's life once before, and was devoted to the family, and was willing to risk his life protecting them.

'After Knox grabbed him and threw him, after he landed, this Boy individual had no voice, he could not shout at all, couldn't make any noise, so my contacts there at the prison tell me they think he died because he couldn't shout for help when he was attacked.' He paused and sighed heavily. 'Just like the young children they used to take from their parents'.

His coloured accent strengthened as his emotions grew within him, and his eyes grew tearful, outraged at what they had done before they stole PJ.

'Matt, little PJ, your daughter… she was not the first child they took, there were at least two others we know about...and there are some bodies we have never found.'

He paused, suddenly looking serious, and then looked ahead, gazing into the distance, pressing his lips together. He rubbed his eyes.

'Matt, I don't want you or Khanyisile to think too much about this abduction anymore. You know, it's, it's really finished now. They will never do their business again; they are both dead'. He paused, 'but you must run inside man, you're going to get wet! And anyway I must get going.'

He looked briefly into Matt's eyes with his own light hazel brown eyes, and they understood each other. Matt nodded. Rennie touched the horn and drove slowly away. He did not look back.

It started raining properly and by the time Matt was back indoors he was soaked and already needed to change his shirt. He thought that PJ would probably be too big for those pink sandals now, and they had both noticed that she'd only ever mentioned them once, suddenly telling Khanyi about them one evening out of the blue, and weeping to her that she was sorry she had lost one. That was before they even went to England. She had not been asking about them the way she used to if one went missing.

They decided to keep them together as a pair but would keep them out of sight and hidden for a few more weeks, and then pretend to find the missing one. She seemed to have almost forgotten about them for now. Perhaps, one day, when she was much older, if she asked, they would maybe tell her the story of how an old man she barely knew had cleverly found her missing shoe, without mentioning the forest. Or perhaps not. She was a clever child, and it might lead her to ask more questions. Nothing had been taken from her but her innocence and trust, and now even her shoe was returned. Most of all they had her safe; nothing else mattered. They had time to decide. That event was over, and she had other shoes she loved almost as much.

Matt would tell Knox what happened to Boy, he was a man with a secret past who never forgave those who started a blood feud, and Matt knew he would be happy to know that Boy had been killed. The news would make him quietly sing his old war songs again to himself as he patrolled the property.

The rain fell over their homestead like a blessing, initially coming down hard, then settling down to a refreshing steady shower that they knew would not last long, bequeathing to them in its passing the legacy of a cool, delightfully fresh afternoon of scented air, an evening view of scenery washed clean, and a clear sunset without dust.

Khanyisile began preparing lunch for PJ's return from school. She thought they could all have bread and honey but had to think of how she could strain out all the bee's wings, the little fragments of honeycomb and tiny plugs of wax. She knew wild honey like this, so sweet, dark and strong that it gave you a headache if you ate too much. It was straight from the wild bees and smelt faintly of woodsmoke. They would eat it together with soft white bread, and she would give half to Knox. There was plenty.

Honey from the forest.

Glossary of non- English words and expressions used in The Reckoning

THE WORDS BELOW ARE COMMONLY used in Eswatini and Southern Africa. These informal definitions are to assist readers unfamiliar with their meaning or the use of them in speech. In many cases there is no exact English equivalent to the word, which may have other hidden meanings. The explanations given are from colloquial usage in everyday speech and should not be regarded as formal translations.

A querida meu amore – my sweetheart, my love (Portuguese)

Babelomncane – small father, a lesser uncle-like figure, or one who is an uncle

Bakkie – a pick-up truck, often referred to as a van. A real van with an enclosed body would be referred to as a panel or delivery van.

Bobabelomkhulu – the plural term for all the big fathers

Bomake – collective term for women who are mothers

Bomake – also the women, women's groups or organisations

Boxer – an old well-known brand of strong hand rolling tobacco 'imbhoza'

Coloured – in Southern Africa, the expression 'coloured' has a different history and meaning to many other countries. It is only used to refer to people having mixed-race parentage or origins. This is entirely different to the way the term is used in certain other countries to refer to any people of colour with any ethnic origins, or any of their descendants (i.e. as a synonym for 'black' that some find offensive). In South Africa, it remains a legal classification under the Population Registration Act and in Southern Africa the term is not generally considered offensive or derogatory. In this context, it merely means a person of mixed race.

Dagga – marijuana/cannabis

Dimon – a demon

Doek – a head covering made of fabric (Afrikaans)

Double cab – a four-door pick-up truck

Emahiya – Swazi traditional fabric and clothing, where a bolt of cloth is wrapped around the wearer.

Engelsman – Englishman (Afrikaans)

Enkhosi – as in 'I thank you' or' I praise you' said in a respectful manner

Goggos – or goggas /hohhos, any type of insects

Gogo – a grandmother, an old lady

Gwaai – home grown tobacco.

Haiybo – definitely not

Hayikona – no its not or no don't, or no I disagree, don't continue.

Hau – a common exclamation used in modern Siswati speech for a multitude of reasons; surprise, astonishment, shock, horror, disbelief, admiration, sympathy, all varying according to the tone used.

Impimpi – an informer, or a spy, placed to provide information on criminal activities, usually for authorities or police.

Imbhoza – Boxer tobacco

Kerrie – short for knobkerrie, a fighting stick with a club end used for hitting skulls

Ketane -chain, emaketane – chains

Laaitie – a youth, younger person, teenager or child (from Afrikaans) spelling varies

Lalela – listen to me, or be at peace, similar to 'calm down'

Lobola – bride price traditionally paid to parents of a bride, historically usually paid using cattle

Magwinya – like vetkoek (Afrikaans), a type of plain doughnut, smaller than vetkoek

Make – respectful, affectionate term for an older woman who may fill a mother figure, used before the surname.

Makewami – my mother, or an affectionate greeting sometimes extended to one who is not your mother

Malume – uncle, Umalume, the uncles

Mlungu – a European person

Mnumzane – head of a household, historically a lesser chief, local headman, or honourable gentleman. A term of respect, like Nkosi or Mister, but for one who is not a chief.

Muti – traditional medicine, usually containing herbs, roots or animal parts, very occasionally human.

Muti murderer – a ritual killer involved in the removal of human parts for muti purposes, involved with witchcraft, still punishable by the death penalty in several African countries.

Nompumelelo – the full Christian name given to Nompumelelo Jacqueline Barton, also referred to as Pumi, Mpumelelo and PJ.

Nyaope – a dangerous habit-forming hard drug smoked like crack

Obrigado – Thank you (Portuguese)

Phuma – get out, leave

Sawubona Bhuti – I see you brother, but a polite greeting to a man of similar age, who may not be a real brother

Shesha – be quick, hurry, something urgent

Sis, Siswami – sister, my sister, fond term used for a woman close in age to your own who may be an actual sister or a close friend, Sis Lindiwe Mavimbela is not Ginindza's sister, but his friend.

Siyakhulile ekhaya – approximately like asking 'may we come in?' whilst greeting at the same time

Sjambok – a shorter whip used as a weapon or a long cattle whip

Skelem, skellems, schellum, skelm – a rogue, scoundrel, thief, a petty criminal, also sly, wickedness, evil, villains, sometimes used to describe behaviour as well as people. Originally Dutch, now in widespread use.

Stompie – a cigarette butt

Takkie or takkies – in UK, trainers, soft-soled running shoes, plimsols (Afrikaans).

Thuthuka – to improve, lift up, used here as a name

Umfana – boy

Umkhulu – grandparent, often grandfather
Unkafa – you die
Vuka lapho – wake up there
Yini umkhulu? Yini inkinga? – approximately 'What is it Grandfather, what is the problem?'

Printed in Great Britain
by Amazon

78614632R00141